A SENSIBLE
ARRANGEMENT

Books by Tracie Peterson

www.traciepeterson.com

House of Secrets • A Slender
Thread • Where My Heart Belongs

LONE STAR BRIDES
A Sensible Arrangement

LAND OF SHINING WATER
The Icecutter's Daughter •
The Quarryman's Bride •
The Miner's Lady

LAND OF THE LONE STAR
Chasing the Sun •
Touching the Sky •
Taming the Wind

SONG OF ALASKA
Dawn's Prelude •
Morning's Refrain •
Twilight's Serenade

STRIKING A MATCH
Embers of Love •
Hearts Aglow • *Hope Rekindled*

ALASKAN QUEST
Summer of the Midnight Sun •
Under the Northern Lights •
Whispers of Winter
Alaskan Quest (3 in 1)

BRIDES OF GALLATIN COUNTY
A Promise to Believe In •
A Love to Last Forever •
A Dream to Call My Own

DESERT ROSES
Shadows of the Canyon •
Across the Years •
Beneath a Harvest Sky

HEIRS OF MONTANA
Land of My Heart •
The Coming Storm •
To Dream Anew •
The Hope Within

LADIES OF LIBERTY
A Lady of High Regard •
A Lady of Hidden Intent •
A Lady of Secret Devotion

WESTWARD CHRONICLES
A Shelter of Hope •
Hidden in a Whisper •
A Veiled Reflection

YUKON QUEST
Treasures of the North •
Ashes and Ice •
Rivers of Gold

LONE STAR BRIDES

BOOK ✦ ONE

A SENSIBLE
ARRANGEMENT

TRACIE
PETERSON

BETHANYHOUSE

a division of Baker Publishing Group
Minneapolis, Minnesota

Published by Bethany House Publishers
11400 Hampshire Avenue South
Bloomington, Minnesota 55438

Bethany House Publishers is a division of
Baker Publishing Group, Grand Rapids, Michigan

Printed in the United States of America

ISBN 978-1-61129-258-9

Scripture quotations are from the King James Version of the Bible.

Cover design by Gearbox

Photography by Steve Gardner, PixelWorks Studios

Dear Reader,

Please join me in celebrating this, my one hundredth book. Over the course of twenty some years, I have enjoyed being published in Christian fiction. My writing has always been a ministry for me, and my heart has been blessed by the letters I've received from you that have shown how God has used the books to change lives. I'm very blessed to do what I love and to see God use it for His glory.

God bless all of you
in His love.
Tracie Peterson

Chapter 1

Marty Dandridge Olson looked over the letters once again. There were three, and each contained a variety of information meant to assist her in making a decision. A life-changing decision.

"Hannah would call me mad," Marty mused aloud. She picked up one of the letters—the latest—and noted the first line: *I have enclosed funds enough to cover your travels to Denver.*

Marty shook her head. *Am I mad? Crazy to seriously consider this matter?*

Putting the letter down, Marty got to her feet and paced the small kitchen. She put a few pieces of wood into the cookstove and stoked the fire. The chill of the day wasn't that great, but she was restless and it gave her something to do—something other than contemplate those letters . . . and what had happened four years earlier.

Now nearly thirty-five, Marty was a childless widow who was known for her spunk and ingenuity. She was the kind of woman who seemed destined to a life in Texas. Surrounded by family and friends, Marty had known a life of love and relatively little want. Why, then, was she so desperate to leave it all behind?

She had lived her entire life in Texas, or very nearly. Her birth in Mississippi had taken the life of her mother, leaving her to be raised by a deeply saddened father and loving older sister. Hannah had been more mother than sister to Marty, and at nearly twenty years Marty's senior, Hannah's guidance and wisdom had seen Marty through many difficulties.

If only her wisdom could have saved the life of Marty's husband.

"Thomas." She whispered the name and smiled. "You were always so very stubborn. I doubt anything could have saved your life once you determined to die."

Her beloved husband had died four years ago to the day. Gored by a longhorn bull, Thomas had suffered massive internal injuries but had remained conscious until the very end. Even now, Marty could recall his final words to her.

"I reckon I've made a mess of Christmas, Marty, but never you mind. It ain't worth troublin' yourself over, so don't you go mournin' me for long." The pain had been clearly written on his face, but he'd held fast to her hand, although his voice had grown weaker. *"I've loved you . . . a long time . . . Martha Dandridge . . . Olson. Don't reckon . . . there's a . . . better wife to any man."*

"*So don't leave me,*" she had begged, kissing his fingers.

He had given her a weak smile and then closed his eyes one last time. *"I gotta go, gal."* And with that, his hand went limp in hers and he exhaled his last breath.

Marty remembered it as if it had been yesterday. How

she had mourned him—the loss unlike anything she'd ever known. Folks told her time would ease the pain, and in truth it had . . . a little. But time had done nothing to fill the emptiness. There were days when she feared the loneliness would swallow her whole.

She looked back to the table where the letters lay. Could this be the answer she sought? Could her decision fill the emptiness once and for all? The clock chimed the hour, and Marty knew it wouldn't be long before the Barnett carriage showed up to take her to her sister's for the Christmas celebration.

Marty took up the letters and tucked them in the pocket of her apron. There had been a time when she might have prayed about her decision, but not now. After God had refused her prayers to save Thomas's life, Marty had hardened her heart. God was now only a bitter reminder of a trust that had been broken.

"I'm going to do it," Marty announced to the empty room. "I'm going to marry a man I've never met and do not love. I'm going to marry him and leave this place forever."

★

That evening as she settled in to exchange gifts with her sister's family, Marty looked for the right moment to break the news. She had already determined she wouldn't tell them about the classified advertisement that had started her plans. The Dallas *Daily Times-Herald* had run the request for a full week.

> Texas-born man now living in Colorado, working as a banker, wishes to correspond with a Lone Star lady. Seeking potential wife who would display the virtues, sensibilities, and wisdom

of a strong Texas woman. Must be willing to leave Texas for Colorado.

Marty was more than willing. She didn't desire to remarry and still wasn't sure why she'd responded to that ad, but after the man's first reply, she had known it was fate that had brought them together. Jacob Wythe wasn't looking for romance or love—just a woman who would bear his name and act as his companion.

"You aren't payin' attention, Aunt Marty."

She looked up to find the entire family staring at her, her nephew Robert standing to her left with a gift extended. Marty flushed. "I am sorry. I was just thinking on . . . well . . ." She smiled and let the words trail off. "Let's see what we have here." She took the gift box.

Hannah seated herself beside her husband, William. "I hope you like it."

Marty pulled a bright red ribbon from the box. "I'm sure I will. You always have a way of figuring out just what I need most."

She opened the box to reveal a set of four small leather-bound books. Lifting one, she spied the author. "Jane Austen. Thank you."

"We knew you'd taken to reading more," William Barnett offered. "Hannah said these were some of your favorites years ago."

Marty nodded as she perused the titles. "Hannah used to read them to me. Andy thought himself above it all, but he always managed to sit close enough to listen in."

Hannah laughed. "Our brother was not half so sly as he thought himself."

"Speaking of Andy," Marty said, looking up from the box, "have you had word?"

William nodded. Marty had to admit she held her brother-in-law in great affection; his marriage to Hannah had been the best thing that had ever happened to the Dandridge family. After the death of their father, William had stepped in as protector and provider.

"We had a letter just a day ago. Hannah wanted me to save it for tonight—kind of like havin' Andy and his bunch with us."

"Now's just as good a time as any," Hannah declared. She pushed back a graying blond curl. At fifty-three and despite years of hard work, she was still a beautiful woman.

I envy her. I envy her peace of mind and happiness. Marty shook her head and looked away. Envy was a sin . . . but so too was lying.

William pulled the letter from his pocket and opened it while Robert took a seat. "Andy and the family send Christmas greetings from snowy Wyoming."

Marty shook her head. "I think he was ten kinds of fool to move his family up there. He never liked the colder weather."

"Yes, but since Ellen's family is from that part of the country, it seems only right," Hannah reminded. "And they did live here for the first five years of their marriage. Long enough that we got to know little John. I'd love to visit them and get to know Benny, as well. He must be six years old by now."

"Do you want me to read the letter, or would you rather talk about the family?" William asked with a grin.

Hannah elbowed him. "Read the letter."

William nodded.

"We are doing well. The longhorn seem to take the weather in stride. The herd increased again this year, and Ellen's pa is pleased with the way things are going. John and Benjamin send their love. They both ride like they were born to a saddle. John can rope and help with branding as well as any of the hands. Benjamin isn't far behind in abilities, as he is in constant competition with John."

Marty chuckled. "Imagine that."

Hannah laughed, as well. "Given the way you two always tried to outdo the other, it's no surprise."

"Yes, but I was a girl, and it shamed him if I could do something better than he could," Marty said. "I wonder if he'll teach them steer-sliding."

"I still remember when they taught me," Robert said, joining in. "Seems like a mighty dirty trick to play on a fella."

Marty smiled fondly at the memory of her brother teaching his nephew to steer-slide. It was a joke they played on all the new greenhorns, telling them that they had to learn to slide under a steer just in case they found themselves in a perilous situation. To everyone's amazement, it had actually saved the life of one young fellow long ago, but Marty couldn't remember his name.

"It was just a matter of initiating you to ranch work," Hannah said, excusing the matter. "I've noticed it's not a prank you've given up. Weren't you showing young Micky how to slide under the fence just the other day?"

"I didn't attempt it myself," Robert replied. "I just told him it was something he needed to learn if he was gonna be one of our ranch hands." He gave them a mischievous grin. "I figure if it was good enough for me . . ."

"Do you want me to continue reading?" William asked.

"Sure, Pa. Go ahead." Robert settled back in his chair and folded his arms with a sly smile. "Didn't mean to stop you." William looked down to the letter.

"Ellen sends her love, as well as good news. You'll remember our sadness three years ago when we lost our little girl just after birth. Then last year Ellen miscarried, and we feared we might not have another child. Well, the doctor just confirmed that she's expecting and due to deliver sometime in the spring. We are of course quite hopeful that all will go well."

"That is good news," Hannah said. "I know Andy wanted a big family, and Ellen was so sick after that miscarriage. It's an answer to prayer."

Marty bristled at the mention of prayer, but said nothing. William finished the letter with Andy sharing plans they had for celebrating Christmas, as well as his intentions for the ranch. Marty tried to appear interested.

"I'd say Uncle Andy has a good life in Wyoming," Robert declared. "He sounds happy with his little family."

"You should be thinking of getting a wife and family of your own," Hannah told him. "You are twenty-six after all, and you have proven able to take on a great deal of responsibility. Your father and I are quite pleased with your work here." She paused and gave him a knowing smile. "I believe Jessica Atherton would be even more pleased if you gave her a formal proposal."

"Jessica's still a child. Although I will say folks have been trying to pair us off since we were young'uns."

"That's hardly true, Robert. I have never wanted any of my

children to feel that we were choosing their spouses. I never did abide arranged, loveless marriages. And I know Carrisa and Tyler don't feel that way."

"Then why are you trying to marry me off?" Robert asked with a smile. "I figured with my sisters gone from home, you would want to keep me around."

Hannah shrugged and scooted in closer to William. "It's not your company I mind, but I would like to see you happily settled."

"She wants more grandbabies," William declared.

"Well, we do only have the one. Of course, I was like a grandmother to Andy's boys, but now they're in Wyoming and so far away. Not to mention they have her parents there to spoil them."

Marty felt an aching in her heart at the banter between them. The thought of having children always made her sad. She and Thomas had been married for ten years but she had been unable to carry a child to delivery. Marty blamed herself, even though Thomas never did. The sorrow was one she had hoped to bury with her husband, but that hadn't been the case. Her niece Sarah, Hannah and Will's oldest girl, had just given birth in September to her first son. Hannah and Will had returned from Sarah's home in Georgia some three weeks earlier, and the baby was all that Hannah could talk about.

I would have made a good mother, but God apparently thought otherwise. I was a good wife, too. Thomas always said I was the best woman he'd ever known. I never gave him cause to doubt my love or my faithfulness.

"You seem so distant this evening." Hannah's comment brought Marty back to the present.

"I'm just tired." Marty motioned to the gifts she'd brought. "Why don't you open my presents now?"

Hannah nodded, and Robert jumped up to hand out the gifts. Marty had spent a fair amount of time on each of them. For William and Robert she had crafted warm robes, which quickly met with their approval.

"I've needed a new one for ages," William admitted.

"I know. I asked Hannah what I could make for you." Marty smiled.

Robert leaned down to kiss her on the cheek. "Thanks, Aunt Marty."

William nodded. "Yes, thank you very much."

Hannah opened Marty's gift and gasped. The bundle revealed a lacy cream-colored shirtwaist. "Oh, it's beautiful. Oh, Marty, your work is so delicate." She ran her hands over the intricately embroidered neckline. "This must have taken hours."

"I remembered you admiring something similar when we were shopping in Dallas last summer. I've been working on it, as time permitted, ever since."

"Well, this is by far and away grander. I shall cherish it always. Thank you."

The room grew silent, and Marty figured it was as good a time as any to share her news. She'd mulled it over at length and had concluded that the best thing she could do for herself, as well as her sister . . . was lie. Something she had always been quite good at.

"I have a bit of my own news to share," Marty began. All gazes were fixed upon her. "I'm going to be traveling soon."

"Truly?" Hannah looked stunned. "Where are you going?"

Marty drew a deep breath. "Colorado. Perhaps Wyoming to see Andy after that."

"Why Colorado?" William asked.

"I have friends there," Marty said. She had already planned for this part of the lie. "Remember the Stellington sisters? We were in finishing school together, and they were my best friends."

"I remember," Hannah said.

"Well, they've invited me to stay with them for a time in Colorado Springs. I thought it would be nice to get away from the ranch and . . . all the memories." She added the latter to appeal to Hannah's sensitive nature.

For several minutes no one said anything. Marty hoped it might remain that way. Though she didn't want to lie to Hannah, she knew her sister would never approve of Marty running off and marrying a man she hardly knew. In time, Marty would have to let her know the truth, but for now, this was much easier.

"I must say," Hannah finally said, "this is something of a surprise."

"Well, I'd been considering it while you were away, but I didn't want to leave before you'd returned. Now you're back, so it seems a good time."

"But winter will be a difficult time to travel," William said thoughtfully.

"I'll take the train, so it shouldn't be a problem."

Hannah frowned. "How long do you plan to be away?"

"Well, that depends." Marty shrugged. "I hoped that maybe you could run my few head with yours and keep an eye on the place." She didn't want to tell Hannah that she had every intention of selling the ranch. Hannah would know something was up if she made that kind of announcement.

"What's Bert got to say about it?" William asked.

"Well, he's all for returning to work for you." Bert Harris had come to help Marty with the ranch after Thomas's death. He'd worked a great many years prior to that on the Barnett Ranch, and Hannah had insisted Marty allow him to assist. "Bert said with expenses on the increase, it's probably for the best."

William nodded and rubbed his chin. "He's been worried about the low water levels. It isn't near as bad as the drought was in the '80s, but we're still suffering for water. I don't have a problem with this plan, Marty. You tell Bert he's welcome to bunk here again."

"And you'll put him on your payroll?" Marty dared to ask. She hoped the question wouldn't arouse suspicions. "I mean, since I won't be around to oversee him and you can use him to work for you, I just wondered . . ."

"Of course we'll pay his wages," William replied. "He'll do far more for me than he will for you anyhow. You haven't but about fifty head. We'll just run them with ours, and if you aren't back by spring, we'll separate them out and brand the new calves with your mark."

"Or you could just take them in pay," Marty said. "I don't mean for you to be out money on account of my . . . desire to travel."

"Surely you aren't planning to be gone so long as that," Hannah said, leaning forward. She gave Marty an intense look. "Are you?"

Marty shrugged and tried to appear unconcerned. "I might. Especially if I travel to see Andy, as well. I want to make provisions for every possibility. I figure I can close up the house and send the livestock to you. You can keep the animals as pay for checking in on the place from time to time."

"Nonsense. That's what family's for, Aunt Marty." Robert set aside the robe he'd been admiring. "I don't mind going over there to check things out. I'll see to it."

"Thank you, Robert. Thanks to all of you. I know it might seem sudden, but as I said, I've been considering this for some time now."

"I suppose if your mind is made up . . ." Hannah didn't finish her thought, and again the room fell silent.

Finally, William reached out and took up the Bible. "Why don't I read the Christmas story?"

"I'd like that very much," Hannah said.

Marty thought she looked worried. *I hope she won't try to change my mind on this. She always thinks she knows best, and this time . . . well . . . this time she doesn't.* Marty bit her lip and lowered her gaze to avoid giving Hannah any opportunity to question her further. She gave a silent sigh.

Just don't challenge me on this, Hannah. Just let me go without a fuss, and we'll all be a whole lot happier.

Chapter 2

Jacob Wythe couldn't help but pull out the last letter from Martha Olson. "Marty," he reminded himself with a smile. Rereading the beautifully penned script, Jake leaned back in his leather chair and breathed a sigh of relief. She had agreed to marry him, even knowing he wanted a marriage in name only.

"Mr. Wythe, I've brought the ledgers you requested."

Jake looked up to find Arnold Meyers, his secretary, standing in the open doorway. In the younger man's arms were several large record books. "Bring them in and put them on the table over there." Jake stuffed the letter into his pocket. He'd only been made bank manager in September, after the previous manager had died. Having worked for one of the other Morgan Bank branches, Jake was singled out to take the position due to the owner's high regard for his proven abilities. Given Mr. Morgan's faith in him, Jake had taken it upon himself to carefully study the bank's records. The more he familiarized himself with the details, the better he felt about his duties.

The younger man deposited the ledgers, then turned back

to face Jake. "Mr. Wythe, I understand congratulations are in order. Mr. Morgan said that you are to be married."

Had anyone other than the bank's owner spread this information around, Jake would have reprimanded the man. Now, however, he supposed Morgan had made it public knowledge. "I am. My bride-to-be will arrive soon after the New Year, and we will marry immediately."

"Will there be a large wedding?"

Jake shook his head and got to his feet. "No. We've both been married before and are fine to wed without any fuss. Now, if you'll excuse me, I need to get back to work." He crossed to the table.

Arnold took the statement as his dismissal and left the office without offering further comment. Jake was grateful, as he had no desire to explain anything of his past to the young man. His past was, in fact, filled with more sorrow and poor choices than Jake cared to reminisce upon.

Picking up one of the ledgers, Jake returned to his desk and tried to focus on the task at hand. Instead, the past came unbidden and flooded his thoughts. Josephine was the first image that came to mind. She was his last attempt at falling in love. The lovely young woman had been the daughter of his father's good friend in California. She was flirtatious and flighty, but Jake had fallen hard for her. They'd married three years earlier, and Jake had never known greater happiness. At least for the first few weeks. After that Josephine grew bored and began to nag him about travel and finding a bigger and better house. Her expensive tastes were more than he could keep up with; however, it was her constant and loudly voiced disappointment in him that caused Jake to grow bitter.

At one time Jake had thought her very much like another

young woman he'd fancied himself in love with years before. Deborah Vandermark lived with her family in eastern Texas. When ongoing drought caused Jake's father to sell their Dallas ranch and move to California, Jake hadn't wanted to leave Texas. So rather than join his father, Jake had gone looking for work elsewhere. Unfortunately, the ranching life he loved was not afforded him, and he took a job working for the Vandermark Logging Company.

He couldn't help but smile at the memory of Deborah and her family. The Vandermarks were good people—people he would have very much enjoyed remaining near.

"I would have loved to have married Deborah and called them my own family," he mused. But Deborah had married another, leaving Jake feeling more displaced than ever before. It was then that he had decided to join his family in California and return to college to complete his studies. At least that had been a wise choice. Perhaps his only one.

Opening the ledger and turning one dusty page after another, Jake noted the figures for the first quarter of the year. As they headed into 1893, he wanted to assure himself that the bank was completely solid. There had already been rumors of instability to come, and Jake wasn't about to wait until trouble was upon them to learn whether or not his bank could survive. But try as he might, Jake couldn't help but return his thoughts to Deborah and Josephine.

The two women he'd loved were both dark-eyed and dark-haired. Both were beautiful and intelligent, but where Deborah was kind and godly, Josephine had a wild streak that often made her seem cruel. Cruel and unfeeling. Barely six months after they'd married, while Jake struggled to establish himself in his new career, Josephine established herself with another man. Leaving nothing more than a hastily written note, Josephine deserted him for an adventure with this stranger. Less than six months after that, word came that she had died from some disease in a South American hospital. Jake hated himself for feeling more relief than sorrow.

But now I'm slated to wed again. And for what purpose?

As if on cue, Paul Morgan, the bank's owner and a distant relative of the well-known financier J. Pierpont Morgan, bound into the office without Arnold even having a chance to announce him. Josiah Keystone, branch bank president and board member, followed in the owner's footsteps.

"Mr. Morgan. Mr. Keystone," Jake said, getting to his feet. "I've just been going over this year's books."

"You're a good man, Wythe," the owner declared. "I was skeptical at first about promoting a junior officer to head manager, and had it been anyone but you, I would never have considered it. However, seeing your work and believing you capable of more, I'm glad to have taken the chance."

Keystone nodded. "Yes, in just this short time you have done a great deal to reorganize this establishment. It's to your credit that things are running so smoothly."

Jake was relieved to hear their praise. "I'm glad to know that, sirs."

"If I had ten more just like you, my other branches might run in an equally efficient manner," Morgan said. "But that's not why I've come today. With New Year's just two days away, I wanted to invite you to join us Sunday afternoon for tea. Mrs. Morgan hoped you might otherwise be uninvolved, as she wanted to know more about this new bride of yours."

Breathing a sigh of relief that there was nothing more pressing than an invitation on the old man's mind, Jake smiled.

"I would love to join you on New Year's Day, but you will have to remind Mrs. Morgan that I haven't yet acquired my new bride. She is slated to arrive in the middle of January."

"Well, you know how anxious women can be."

"Bank boards, too," Jake murmured under his breath. He'd been badgered to marry since accepting the branch management position. An unmarried man in a position of such responsibility had worried the board members.

Apparently neither Morgan nor Keystone understood his muttering. At least neither acknowledged it, and for that Jake was relieved. He hadn't meant to be so flippant.

Morgan smiled and took a seat opposite Jake. The man's dark hair was graying at the temples, giving him a most distinguished appearance. This, coupled with the expensive cut of his suit and top coat, left little doubt that this was a man of means.

"Have you set the date for your wedding? You know the board is most anxious to see you settled."

Jake nodded. He was already settled, as far as he was concerned. He'd taken up residence in the house allotted him in a rather imposed manner. The board had presented him with loan papers and the keys on the day they'd promoted him to bank manager. He'd had little choice but to accept the offering. Even so, the house was quite lovely and positioned in the best neighborhood in Denver. It wasn't exactly what Jake would have chosen for himself, however. He was far more inclined to live modestly and save his extra money. He'd mentioned this to Morgan, only to receive a strict dressing-down on how a bank manager had a certain reputation to uphold.

"The wedding will take place when my fiancée arrives in Denver. As you know, I am a widower and my bride-to-be is a widow. We don't see any sense in making a fuss. We plan to be very quietly married in the rectory rather than the church as soon as Mrs. Olson arrives."

Morgan nodded. "I'm glad to hear it. It will put everyone's mind at ease once you are settled in as a family man. Married men are much better risks than bachelors." He smiled and cast a quick glance at Keystone. "I think we can all remember our wilder days without good women in our lives to keep us on the straight and narrow." Keystone laughed, but Jake only nodded. He couldn't agree with the men.

Josephine caused me more trouble than good. The straight and narrow wasn't a path she was at all familiar with, nor did she want it for me.

"So I will tell the board that you have arranged to marry by the middle of the month. Sunday you may tell Mrs. Morgan the same. I know she'll want to throw you a party."

"That isn't necessary," Jake protested. "I would never expect someone of your social standing to even give us a second thought."

"Nonsense. I believe you will make something of yourself in no time at all," Morgan stated, getting to his feet. "I have confidence in you, and I'm not one to be ashamed of small beginnings . . . just small endings." He gave Jake a nod. "I believe there are great things ahead for you, my boy. If I thought otherwise, you wouldn't be in my hire."

"Thank you for your confidence in me."

Morgan nodded. "We will see you Sunday, then. Good day." The men exited the room as quickly as they'd entered.

Jake sat back down and considered the bank owner's words. Great things for this man would no doubt be associated with banking, and that wasn't what Jake wanted for his future.

Ranching was in his blood, and it was the same that called out to him on a daily basis. He longed to return to the land—to the hard work. He enjoyed fending for himself, sleeping out under the starry skies. He didn't even mind long hours in the saddle. It was office chairs that made his back ache. He'd only taken on this career in order to set aside enough money to purchase his own ranch. Unfortunately, it was taking a lot longer than he'd planned on.

"Sir?" Arnold peeked in through the open office door. "It's closing time. Will you be staying on this evening?"

Jake glanced at the ledgers and shook his head. "Lock these records up for the holidays. I'll get back to them when we return on the second of January."

"Very good, sir."

Jake paid little attention as Arnold scurried around to do his bidding. The younger man was small and pale and didn't appear to resent the business attire that threatened to strangle the life out of Jake. Neckties and stiff collars were akin to torture devices, as far as Jake was concerned.

How he longed for the days of a well-worn shirt, riveted pants, and a sturdy pair of boots. Jake gazed out the window for a moment and sighed. Would he ever see Texas again?

★

Sunday afternoon, Jake found himself seated in the grand salon of the Morgans' palatial home. Located near Sixteenth Avenue and Grant Street, the large Queen Anne was only one of many gems set in Denver's Capitol Hill crown. Most of Denver's high society held court on "The Hill." The opulent homes were graced by equally fashionable people who seldom left the confines of their wealthy estates except to visit other people of equal means. Jake thought it all rather nonsensical. In Texas, his father had been one of the wealthier ranchers before the drought. That didn't mean isolation, however. If anything, it sent people his way on a daily basis. He had good breeder cows and strong bulls. He grazed some of the finest beeves in the South and had made a small fortune during the postwar years.

"Mr. Wythe, I was just telling Mr. Morgan how happy I was to hear about your upcoming nuptials," Mrs. Morgan said, interjecting herself into Jake's memories.

An immaculately dressed servant offered Jake a cup and saucer. "Would you care for cream or sugar?" the woman asked.

Jake shook his head. He was no great lover of tea to begin with, but adding cream and sugar only seemed to make it worse. "No, thank you."

Mrs. Morgan frowned and cast a sharp glance at the servant. Jake had no idea what the woman had done wrong, but she quickly scurried back to the tea cart looking most dejected.

"As I was saying before my girl interrupted, I was glad to hear that you have the wedding date planned. Mr. Morgan tells me that your fiancée is to arrive around the middle of the month. Is that still correct?"

"That's correct, ma'am." Jake drank from the teacup and forced a smile.

"Why such a delay? Could she not leave her people in Texas?" Mrs. Morgan asked in a demanding tone.

Jake put the cup down. "She is visiting friends in Colorado Springs." He smiled and tried to change the conversation. "I must say, this is a beautiful drawing room. Is that Italian marble?" He nodded toward the fireplace.

"Oh goodness, yes," Mrs. Morgan said, looking down her nose at him. "We had an entire shipload delivered to America when the house was being built."

Just then Paul Morgan and several other men entered the room. Jake had no idea where they had been. Since his arrival, he'd only been in Mrs. Morgan's company and was beginning to feel uneasy.

"Mrs. Morgan, please forgive our delay." Mr. Morgan gave his wife a nod, then turned to Jake. "Mr. Wythe, may I introduce some of my associates. Just so happens they are my friends, as well." Jake got to his feet. "This is Mr. Charles Kountze, a man well known in our banking industry."

"It's nice to make your acquaintance, sir."

"Pleasure is mine. I've heard some great things about you from Paul."

Morgan ignored the reference and continued to make the introductions. "This is John Brown; he's the owner of that monstrous structure at Ninth and Grant. I've heard it said that folks call it 'the schoolhouse,' but I cannot say *I've* heard it said."

Brown laughed and extended his hand to Jake. "It's because I have so many children—nearly a dozen. It's good to meet you, Mr. Wythe."

"Likewise, sir."

"And this is Mr. Moffat." Morgan stepped aside so the two men could exchange pleasantries.

"A name I know well," Jake admitted. Fact was, he knew each of these men by name and reputation, although this was his first encounter with them face-to-face. The two men shook hands.

I'm standing in the presence of royalty.

At least Denver's royalty. Jake retook his seat as the men settled into chairs. He marveled at the collective worth of the gentlemen gathered there. Their fortunes came from banking, mining, railroads, and a vast number of other investments. Each was a savvy businessman whose actions had done much to develop Denver into a thriving metropolis.

"Again, I apologize for the delay in joining you here today," Morgan said, refusing a cup of tea from the servant. He motioned her instead to the liquor cabinet. "I had hoped to conclude our business prior to your arrival. After all, this is a holiday."

"A new year, 1893," Moffat said, shaking his head. "Hard to believe this century is nearly gone from us. This year stands on sandy foundations, but if wiser minds prevail, we will see it soon reinforced."

Jake had heard all manner of rumors concerning the state of finances in America. The government about to take office blamed the Sherman Silver Purchase Act, which had required the government to purchase silver using bank notes based on silver or gold holdings. People had been arguing for and against bimetallism as a major issue of politics since the act had gone into effect two and a half years earlier.

The servant returned with a bottle of amber-colored liquor and five glasses on a silver tray. She started to pour Morgan a glass, but he took the bottle from her and held it up. "Gentlemen, may I interest you in a drink?"

"Oh, Mr. Morgan, must you?" his wife questioned.

"My dear, it is a holiday, and we are celebrating. I promise we will only imbibe in one small sampling." He winked at the men and smiled, adding, "For now." The woman rolled her eyes but said nothing more.

Jake shook his head when Morgan looked his way. He held up his teacup. "I'm perfectly fine." There was no need to explain that hard drink had once been his downfall. He had sworn off the stuff ever since making a fool of himself in front of Deborah Vandermark. Even Josephine's nonsense had not caused him to forgo his promise to leave off all alcohol.

"I had forgotten you were a teetotaler, Wythe," Morgan said, as if he disapproved. The man seemed to just as easily put it aside, however, as he moved on to the next man.

"We have a responsibility to our country," Brown declared, taking a glass from Morgan, "but more so to our own community and state. Silver is king in Colorado. We will see to it that Colorado stands strong. We have the resources here to back our financial institutions and must prevail in keeping order."

"What say you, Mr. Wythe?" Kountze asked. All gazes turned to Jake.

For a moment Jake wasn't sure what to say. He had no idea of his opinion mattering in the least. "I believe," he said in slow, measured thought, "that taking preventive measures is always preferable to reflecting on hindsight and regrets of what should have been done."

"Well said, young man. Well said," Moffat agreed. "I've been laying foundations for success since before I was your age. I went to work as a child in a nearby bank, and by the age of sixteen I was promoted to assistant teller. I have owned properties, created businesses, and now labor to see a railroad completed that will connect Denver to Salt Lake. This can only serve to benefit our fine city."

"Gentlemen, I have no desire to sit and listen to a business discussion," Mrs. Morgan interjected. "Today is a day of rest and a celebration of the New Year. I would ask you to postpone your choice of topics to another day."

Mr. Morgan smiled and nodded, while the other men offered their apologies. Jake felt a sense of relief as the conversation turned first to the weather and then to some of the artistic touches that could be seen in the architecture of the house. Even the liquor seemed to be forgotten.

"Yes, yes, the windows were something I had to have," Mrs. Morgan admitted. "After seeing your beautiful stained glass, Mr. Kountze, I could hardly do without."

Kountze chuckled. "I suppose it wouldn't be fitting to let our ladies' desires go unmet. I have learned in my lifetime that keeping the women of the house happy is almost certainly a guarantee of one's personal contentment."

"And shortly Mr. Wythe is to learn that lesson for himself," Mrs. Morgan said with a knowing smile. "He is to wed soon."

"Congratulations, Wythe," Morgan's associates offered nearly in unison.

Kountze nodded in approval. "This is indeed a day of celebration. And might I inquire after your young lady? Tell us about her."

"She's a widow from Texas . . . my home state," Jake added the latter as if it would matter to these men. "Her name is Mrs. Martha Olson."

"Is she of means?" Mr. Brown asked.

Jake didn't quite know what to say. He'd never really inquired as to Marty's financial circumstances. At first he'd figured if she was answering an ad for a mail-order bride, she couldn't be much to look at. Then she had sent her picture, and Jake knew that wasn't a problem. He figured she wasn't financially secure and needed to find a husband who could take care of her needs.

"Let us refrain from such vulgar talk," Mrs. Morgan said before Jake could reply. "I'm sure we shall enjoy getting to know Mrs. Olson—Mrs. Wythe—for ourselves."

"I hope so," Jake replied. "I believe Marty, uh, Mrs. Olson, will be a pleasant and genteel addition to my home. I've been too long without a wife, as your good husband pointed out."

Chapter 3

Marty shifted uncomfortably as the stage hit yet another rough spot in the road. Why she had ever allowed the Stellington sisters to talk her into taking the stage from Colorado Springs to Denver was beyond her. After several train delays, her friends had assured her that this service, for women only, was one their father had made available for ladies of means traveling unaccompanied from Colorado Springs to Denver and back. The journey, although not as fast as by train, would afford her comfort and amiable companions.

Looking across the enclosure at the three dozing old ladies positioned in the seat opposite, Marty couldn't help but smile. They had been all talk the first twenty or so miles of the trip. But now even the younger matron and daughter who sat beside Marty had stopped their incessant arguing and fallen silent. The only men were the stage driver and his shotgun rider. No doubt they were glad to be riding topside. Marty envied them.

Cradling her carpetbag, Marty considered what was to come. They had changed horses at the Seventeen Mile House; their next goal would be the Four Mile House, but Marty knew that was still more than an hour away. She was thankful that the weather had been so nice—though far colder than what she'd known in Texas, she knew the temperatures had been mild for the area. And though there was no stove on the stage as there had been on the train, Marty was used to taking such matters in stride. Much of her life had consisted of desperately hard work, along with occasional periods of ease and pleasure.

And now I'm to marry a stranger.

The thought left her feeling both nervous and excited. Jacob Wythe had promised her a life of ease in his last letter, a life filled with pleasantries and beauty. Marty wasn't sure what all that might involve, but it had to be better than life in Texas, where death stalked her at every turn.

She rubbed her gloved fingers along the ivory handle of the carpetbag and tried to imagine what her new life would bring. Mr. Wythe had told her of his lovely house and the servants who would see to their needs. She considered pulling out the letter again to read Jacob's descriptions of Denver, then thought better of it. To open her bag would cause her to jostle the matronly woman beside her, and Marty had no desire to stir up a conversation. Besides, she had nearly memorized the lines of each letter.

This decision had not come easily; neither had it come without a price. She could still hear Hannah's insistence that Robert accompany Marty at least as far as Colorado Springs. Marty knew her older sister was concerned for her safety, but Marty also knew it was important to make a stand. She had done her best to assure Hannah that she would be perfectly fine—that traveling by train in the 1890s no longer necessitated a chaperone for a woman in her position.

Hannah had been less than convinced, and Marty thought

this almost comical for a woman who, during the War Between the States, had ridden off alone to help nurse a small band of hostile Comanche who were suffering from smallpox. Throwing out that memory in the face of Hannah's protests quickly quieted her sister, but still didn't win her approval. Nevertheless, Marty had her way.

I'll miss them.

There was no doubt about that, and Marty didn't pretend otherwise. She loved her family. It was Texas she hated. Texas and ranch life. She thought of Thomas again and gazed out across the landscape at the horizon. He would have liked Colorado—especially the snow-covered mountains. He might have even wanted to move there, Marty mused.

One of the old ladies began to snore, causing the matron's daughter to giggle. Marty had thought the silent young woman asleep, but even if she had been, her mother's sharp elbowing now put an end to that. The daughter straightened and gave a howl of protest, which only served to awaken the sleeping old women.

"Oh, do be quiet, Amanda," the matronly woman demanded. "You've disturbed the entire coach."

"It's not my fault! You hurt me. I am most likely bruised the full length of my side." The girl clutched her right side for emphasis. "I don't know why we have to go visit your aunt anyway. She's old and she smells funny."

One of the older women let out a *tsk*ing sound and turned to her traveling companions with a shake of her head.

"Oh, stuff and nonsense. You do go on." Her mother was clearly in no mood for her daughter's whining, and neither was Marty. She was prepared to say as much when the unmistakable sound of a shot rang out.

Before they could say another word, the shotgun sounded from overhead and the stage picked up speed. Marty leaned out the window and hollered up to the driver. "What's happened?"

"Bandits!" the man yelled. "Get down in there!"

Marty pulled back inside and turned to the other women in the coach. They were now all wide awake. "Do any of you have a weapon?"

The women collectively shook their heads. Marty opened her carpetbag and pulled out a Smith and Wesson revolver. "Well, I do." The matron gasped and her daughter pretended to swoon. Marty knew it was pretense, because the girl had given this performance multiple times on their journey.

With precise action, Marty loaded the .32 caliber top break without even doffing her gloves. Thomas had gifted her the gun the summer before his death. It was mostly for warding off rattlers and copperheads, but Marty had no difficulty protecting her welfare from snakes of the two-legged variety.

"You don't really mean to fire that thing, do you?" the matron asked.

Marty aimed the gun out the window as the first glimpse of a rider came into view. "I most certainly do." A bullet ricocheted off one of the hubs of the stagecoach. "You ladies would do well to keep your heads down." The shotgun boomed again, and this time Marty added her own precisely aimed shot.

Her traveling companions offered no further protest. Ducking low in their seats, they murmured prayers aloud instead. Marty could now see there were at least two riders. She hoped there weren't more. Surely between the shotgun rider and her own efforts, they would be able to hold the bandits at bay.

The bandits fired a flurry of shots in rapid order. Marty felt the horses pick up an even faster pace and fought hard to keep her aim straight. The shotgun echoed a reply, as did the little .32 revolver. Marty quickly ejected the spent cartridges and reloaded the gun. One of the riders had gained on them considerably and was nearly to the rear of the stage. Leaning as far out the window as she could manage, Marty aimed and fired again just as the shotgun blasted. The rider fell back, wounded. She had no idea if her bullet had helped to cause the damage, but she felt a sense of satisfaction as the shotgun was fired again and the rider dropped from the saddle.

"We got at least one of them," she declared to the women. Not even one of the formerly talkative old women responded. They were all terror-stricken and looking at Marty with new respect.

Marty smiled to herself and turned her attention back to the task at hand. There was no sign of the other rider. She wondered if he'd crossed to the opposite side of the stage. Unconcerned with the matron's protest, Marty threw herself across the older woman and her daughter to look out the opposite window. The stage was slowing now.

Straightening, Marty called up to the driver, "Are they gone?"

She heard the man calling out to the horses and the stage rolled to a stop. Without thought to her safety, Marty opened the door and jumped out. She wasn't used to the extra forty pounds of heavy traveling clothes and nearly went to her knees. Righting herself, however, she looked up to where the driver and his shotgun messenger sat. Only now the driver was slumped in the seat, clinging to the reins as the other man did his best to keep him upright.

"How can I help?" Marty called up.

"Mac's shot up bad," the man said. "I can't say I'm much better off. My arm's no good. We barely got the team stopped." His voice sounded strained.

Marty lifted her heavy wool skirt and tore a huge strip of petticoat. Casting a quick glance down the road, she felt relieved that no riders were in sight.

The matron and one of the old women had poked their heads out the windows. "What's going on? What is happening?" the matron demanded to know.

"Our driver and the shotgun are badly wounded," Marty replied.

"What are we to do?" the old lady asked fearfully. "Those men will soon return, and we will be . . . oh my . . . we might be . . . ravaged."

Marty would have laughed out loud had it not been for the precariousness of the situation. "I think they meant to rob us. Now, stay put while I help the men with their injuries."

She hiked her skirt again and put her booted foot on the hub of the stagecoach wheel. The wheel was nearly as tall as she was, and with the extra weight of her clothes it wasn't an easy feat. Not only that, but she was still trying to adjust to the higher altitude. She panted a bit as she struggled to place her right foot on top of the wheel rim itself. The nervous team refused to stand still and began to back up. Marty barely managed to grab hold of the rail at the front of the driver's box before she lost her footing. With strength she didn't know she possessed, Marty managed to swing her foot up to catch the edge of the front boot. All the while she vowed to herself that she would never again wear this many layers of clothing.

It seemed to take forever, but in fact only a few seconds passed as she hoisted herself awkwardly into the boot. Straightening, she secured the brake and took the bloodied reins from the wounded man and wrapped them around the rail. The shotgun rider cast her an apologetic glance as he slumped back. The driver was now unconscious.

"Sorry, ma'am. I couldn't hold 'em." Both sleeves were blood-soaked, and the man's face was nearly as white as her shirtwaist.

"It's not a problem. We have them now." Marty handed him the torn material. "Use this to stop the bleeding as best you can. How's the driver?"

"He took a bullet to the back and one grazed his head. I think he's still alive."

Even with the brake set, Marty knew it was dangerous to ignore the team of six, but she had to see to the driver. Doing her best to keep sight of the reins, she leaned across the slumped man and felt his chest. He was still breathing. Her gloved hand came away even wetter with blood, however.

"How far to the next stagehouse?"

"A good six miles," the messenger replied. "But I can't drive—not this way."

"I understand. I didn't mean for you to. I'll drive the team."

"You, ma'am? But you're just a little bitty thing." The man struggled to tie off the material around his wounded arm. "I can't let you do that."

"Nobody else is able to do it," she told him. "I've driven wagon teams before. I can handle this, as well. You just settle in and direct me."

Marty managed to straighten the unconscious driver enough that she could take a seat. Calling down to the passengers, she released the brake. "We're heading out, ladies." It was the only warning Marty gave before she snapped the reins. "Yah!" she bellowed and the team stepped into action.

By the time they reached Four Mile House, Marty's forearms burned and her hands cramped. She had pushed aside her discomfort, knowing that the lives of the driver and shotgun were reliant upon her getting them medical attention. She had pressed the team to their limit and couldn't help but sigh with relief at the sight of the station.

The stagehouse operators appeared for the relay change. They stared up in stunned surprise at the small woman. "We were attacked," Marty called down. "These men need a doctor fast!"

The two men who'd come to change out the team quickly went into action to retrieve the wounded men from atop the stage. Meanwhile, the women passengers spilled out from the coach. The matron and her daughter were sobbing in each other's arms, while the old women were chattering on and on about their brush with molestation and certain death. Marty waited patiently while the injured men were taken inside the house. She was relieved, however, when a young man bounded up the side of the stage and took the reins from her hands.

"I'll see to this now, ma'am." He gave her a grin as big as Texas. "You sure are somethin'. Ain't many women—especially one so purty—that could handle a team like this."

Marty looked at her bloodied clothes and thought of how disarrayed her hair and hat must be. She smiled and shook her head. "Perhaps you can tell me where I might clean up."

"I'll help you, ma'am," an older man called. "Let me get you down from there first."

Marty stepped to the side of the boot and allowed the

man to help her from the stage. She felt her knees very nearly buckle as her feet hit the ground again.

"Easy there, ma'am." The man held fast to her arm as Marty drew in a deep breath and steadied herself.

"Thank you. I'm fine now." She allowed him to escort her into the house, where the other women had gathered. Everyone paused and turned their gaze to Marty. One of the older women came forward and took Marty's arm.

"Come with me, deary. I'll help you get cleaned up. You saved our lives, you know. You're a heroine!"

Marty shook her head. "No, I only helped our men. They are the real heroes."

The old woman kept moving Marty toward a stand with water and fresh towels. A woman Marty didn't know appeared and began to help.

"I'm Sallie," the woman explained. "I'm wife to the station manager here. What's your name?"

"Mrs. Marty Olson." She glanced around the room. "Was there someone nearby to help our driver and his man?"

Sallie smiled and stripped the bloodied gloves from Marty's hands. "Dr. Bryant is just a mile away. I already sent my boy to get him and the sheriff. You did real good in bringing them on in, Mrs. Olson. Probably saved their lives. I'll get these bloody gloves soaking in salt water. Since the blood is still fresh, I'm thinking we can get it out."

Marty's mind flew in a thousand directions. She worried that the men had no one to tend them while these women were fussing over her. She wondered if the boy would get the doctor in time and whether the sheriff would be able to find the culprits who had attacked them. But most of all, Marty worried about what her betrothed might think once he heard about the commotion and how Marty threw propriety aside to shoot at the bandits and then drive the stage. He had wanted a proper lady for his bride—a Lone Star bride, to be exact.

Goodness, what will he think of me now?

★

"That's really all I can tell you," Marty told the sheriff the next morning. "I saw two riders. They were masked, and one had a sorrel mount, but I don't recall the color of the other horse." Marty continued to hold the mug of hot coffee she'd been given. From time to time she sipped the strong concoction and hoped it would give her the strength to complete this ordeal.

"That's quite all right, ma'am. You've done more than enough." The sheriff gave her a broad smile. "There aren't many women who could have done what you did. Thanks to you, both Mac and JR are gonna make it. Doc says they might have bled to death out there on the road if you hadn't gotten them in here. Oh, and JR says your shooting was probably what drove those men off. They most likely knew it was a stage full of women and figured to rob them of their jewelry and doodads. They sure weren't expecting there to be another armed protector inside."

"New driver's ready and the stage is set to head on to Denver," a man called from the door. Marty's traveling companions bustled off toward the stage, their babbling conversations creating quite a cacophony.

"They'll be talking about this all the way to Denver," the sheriff said, grinning Marty's way.

"No doubt." She put down her mug and got to her feet. The bloodstains on her traveling jacket and gloves had been scrubbed out the night before, and for the most part, Marty had been restored to proper order.

"Do you have friends in Denver, Mrs. Olson?" the sheriff asked, escorting her to the stage.

Without thinking she answered, "I'm to meet my fiancé. We were to have married yesterday, but with the train delay and then the attack on the stage . . . well, I suppose we will marry today. If he'll still have me." She had her doubts that a banker would appreciate her antics, even if they were heroic. But it was too late to worry about that now.

"Well, he'd be a fool if he didn't. In fact, I tell you what," the sheriff said, pausing at the stage with Marty. "If he doesn't want to marry you, you just make your way on back here. I know a dozen or more boys who'd snatch you up in a minute."

Marty couldn't help but smile at the man's expression of admiration. "Thank you, Sheriff. I'll keep that in mind."

Chapter 4

"Oh my, such excitement," one of Marty's gray-haired traveling companions declared.

"Why, we might all have been killed but for you," another said as the others agreed.

"I think it's scandalous," the woman who introduced herself as Mrs. Merriweather Stouffer announced. No one was sure if Merriweather was the name of her husband or the woman herself, and sadly no one really cared.

"Our father said that a woman ought to be able to handle a firearm," one of the old women commented, nodding to her companion. "Isn't that so, Ophelia? You remember, don't you? Papa always said that a woman with a keen eye and steady hand could take care of herself."

"Oh yes, sister. I do remember. Papa was always so very wise." The woman nodded with a look of absolute certainty.

Marty fought back a smile. The old women who had babbled most of the way from Colorado Springs were now even more infused with stories and tall tales. Not only that, but they'd made their admiration and gratitude toward Marty abundantly clear. The matron and her daughter still held her in contempt, and with exception to the occasional comment, they said little. Perhaps they feared Marty might turn her gun on them if they were to become too annoying.

The stage came to a stop, and in the time it took the shotgun messenger to climb down and open the door, a crowd swooped in and surrounded the stage. Questions were called out to the driver and his man. Marty could see there were several reporters, and two photographers were already setting up their cameras.

Good grief. That's all I need.

"Folks, if you'll calm down, I'm sure the ladies inside will be happy to speak to you," the driver announced. "Be polite, or otherwise you'll be escorted off the premises."

Marty clutched her carpetbag closer and leaned back further in her seat. The older women hurried from the stage as if all the world were waiting for them. They immediately launched into exaggerated accounts of the peril they had faced to anyone who would listen. The matron and her daughter disembarked and immediately began to wail in loud sobs that drew the attention of the reporters away from the babbling women. The older trio looked quite annoyed at this development.

The entire fuss, however, allowed Marty to slip from the coach and blend into the crowd of people. She searched each face, hoping to find Jacob Wythe and escape before the reporters learned her identity.

"Mrs. Olson?"

She startled and hesitated to answer.

The man smiled. "Mrs. Olson?"

"Yes?" She found herself gazing into the face of one of the handsomest men she'd ever met. His photograph did him no justice. She couldn't help but return the smile.

"Mr. Wythe?"

"The same." He let out a long breath. "We heard about the attack on your stage only this morning." He tugged at his starched collar, looking most uncomfortable.

"But you received my telegram? The sheriff assured me he would send one."

The blond-haired man nodded. "He did, ma'am. But it only said that you'd been delayed overnight. I assure you, Mrs. Olson, had I known what had taken place, I would have driven down to pick you up at Four Mile House."

"Marty," she corrected. "Please don't call me Mrs. Olson."

He grinned. "Marty. I don't think I mentioned in my letters how much I like that name. It suits you, too. Of course, you should call me Jake."

"I'd like that very much. I wasn't at all certain if you were that casual in your daily living."

"Ma'am . . . Marty, I would be nothing but casual if I could get away with it."

She relaxed a bit. "Well, I reckon I would, too."

"'Reckon,'" he repeated. "You speak like a true Texan."

"That's good, because I am," she replied, a bit curious at his comment. "Was I not supposed to?"

A chuckle escaped him, and his own drawl seemed a little more pronounced. "Well, you see, up here . . . in my new position as bank manager, 'reckoning' is reserved for bank ledgers and seldom mentioned in common speech. I've had to work hard to sound . . . well . . . less Texas cowboy and more Colorado banker."

"But I thought Denver to be a very western town. You mentioned mining and cattle as two of the larger industries." Marty glanced around her, noticing the buildings and well-orchestrated streets. "I suppose it is a bit more dressed up than I figured to find. Having grown up on a ranch, I didn't get into town all that often. Certainly not all the way into cities like Dallas."

"Oh, it does me good, ma'am—Marty—to hear you talk about Dallas. I have to say I miss Texas more than my own parents." He paused and gazed behind her. "Oh, it would seem you've caught the attention of the press. No doubt they want to hear from you. They're coming this way now."

"Oh bother." Marty cast a frantic glance in the direction of the reporters and then back to Jake. "I really don't want to talk to them. My family will worry. They . . . well . . . I didn't tell them I'd come to get married. I'm really sorry, but perhaps you could get me out of here without having to speak to them?"

"I can't see that happenin' now." He frowned. "Why don't you just tell them you came to Colorado to visit friends? Don't say anything about marryin' me."

She threw him a grateful smile. "Thank you, Jake. If it got back to my sister before I could write to tell her, she'd be hurt."

"Mrs. Olson! Mrs. Olson!" the men called to her.

The crowd parted, and all faces turned to Marty. She swallowed hard and waited as the gathering closed in on her.

"We understand you fought off the attackers with your own gun," one man said, giving a quick doff of his hat.

By now Jake had moved away from Marty and she stood alone. She glanced around for some sight of him and found him sandwiched between several curious onlookers. Marty looked back to the man who'd just spoken.

"I did."

"Tell us what happened," another reporter urged.

"We were attacked, and I helped to defend the stage," she said as though it were something she did every day.

"How many were there?"

She shrugged. "I only saw two."

"One of your traveling companions mentioned there being at least a dozen," the man said. The crowd seemed to hang on to his words.

Marty smiled and repeated, "I only saw two."

"And did you kill those two?" the reporter asked.

"Who can say? I fired my gun. Like my brother-in-law taught me, any time you draw a weapon, you have to be ready to use it, and you have to be ready to accept the consequences. I may have killed a man."

"May I quote you on that?" the man asked, writing furiously on a pad of paper.

"Of course," Marty said with a shrug.

"And then you nursed the unconscious driver and staunched the flow of blood from his associate's wounds—no doubt saving their lives—before risking your life to handle the fear-struck team and bring the coach and passengers to safety?" the first reporter questioned in rapid fire.

They made it all sound so dramatic, and while it had been a most anxious moment in Marty's life, she hardly saw the need to write it up in such a way. She had no chance to reply, however.

"Mrs. Olson, where are you from and what brought you to Denver?" This question came from a new man, who looked to be acting in some sort of official capacity. He eyed her with marked intent.

"I beg your pardon?" Marty asked in return.

The man touched the brim of his hat. "The name is Haggarty. I'm one of the owners of this stage line."

"I see. To answer your question, I hail from Texas and am here in Colorado visiting friends."

"Will you be staying with your friends here in Denver?" the man asked. "I may have need to speak with you regarding this matter."

Panic struck Marty. What should she say? She didn't want to explain that she planned to be married as soon as she could get away from this interrogation. Realizing that everyone was watching and awaiting her answer, Marty shook her head.

"I . . . my plans are uncertain. Now, if you'll excuse me, I must arrange for my things. Once I'm settled with my . . . friends here, I can send word so that you can get in touch, should you have further questions."

"Mrs. Olson, we'd like a picture." The first and most annoying of the reporters took hold of her arm and moved her through the crowd back to the stage. "I wonder if you would climb back into the driver's seat—and hold your gun like you're firing it?" He looked at her with great anticipation. "Maybe over your shoulder like this." He acted out the pose he wanted.

"I should say not," Marty replied, rather appalled at the thought. "I only wish to get my things. No picture." She pulled away from the man and hurried toward the stage office. Several questions were hurled after her, but Marty kept moving forward, ignoring the clamor.

Mr. Haggarty appeared at her side and ushered her into the office. "You don't seem too excited to play the heroine."

She met the man's questioning expression. "Two men nearly lost their lives—they may still die. I hardly see this as an occasion for celebration and playing the heroine. We could have all been killed. My hope is that you would better spend your time seeing to the safety of your travelers."

"Pardon the interruption . . . Mrs. Olson?"

A large man with skin as black as coal called from the door. "Mrs. Olson, I's your driver. I has your trunks already loaded."

Marty breathed a sigh of relief. "Thank you." She gave Haggarty a nod. "Good day, sir. I'll be in touch."

She hurried from the office and allowed the stranger to lead her toward an enclosed carriage. The tall man slowed his step. "Mr. Wythe sent me. He be already inside."

A sigh escaped her lips. "Thank you. I think I would have risked traveling with the devil himself to get away from that ordeal."

The man laughed. "My mama done whooped the devil right outta me years ago. Name's Samson, ma'am."

Marty threw him a smile. "Glad to meet you, Samson."

———

Jake watched with pride as Marty Olson settled herself across from him in the carriage. Samson closed the door and had the carriage on its way before anything else could delay them.

"You handled yourself well, Marty."

She leaned back against the leather upholstery, looking exhausted. "I never anticipated such a grand welcome to Denver."

"I hope it won't put you off on our plans."

"If you mean do I figure to back out of the wedding, then the answer is no. I'm a woman of my word. I hope you are a man of yours."

Jake chuckled. "I most assuredly am. I wasn't raised to go back on my word."

Marty fidgeted with her carpetbag. "I'm glad to hear it, but I wouldn't blame you if you had changed your mind, given the situation."

"Marty, I think you figure me to be ashamed of what you did, but I'm not. You're exactly what I advertised for. A woman of character and ability. You evaluated the situation that life gave you, and you fought back. You probably saved lives in your actions. I can't be faultin' you for that."

"But a man in your position," she began, "a position that demands respect and . . . well . . . dignity . . ." She fell silent and looked toward the window.

"My dignity isn't hurt by your saving the lives of those people. Society will think what it will, but the way I figure it, we will just work it to our advantage."

Marty looked up, and her expression was one of confusion. Jake smiled. "The people of Denver are adventurers. This isn't that old of a state—nothing like our beloved Texas. Folks out here might put on the pretenses of being high society, but a good many of them started in places rougher than ours. They might make like they're shocked, but I'm bettin' most will hold you in esteem for what you did. I know the men will—if not the women."

"I hope you're right. I came to be a help to you in your social standing. You said you needed a wife to please the bank board. I hope they don't mind a woman who can shoot."

Jake couldn't hold back his laughter. "Marty, once they meet you they'll probably offer you a job at the bank. The first lady guard."

Marty giggled, and he could see that she was relaxing a

bit. She was more beautiful than he'd anticipated. Her blond hair and blue eyes were a sharp contrast from the looks of Josephine and Deborah.

"So, are you . . . uh . . . ready to tie the knot?"

She nodded. "I suppose I am."

"We might as well get to it, then," Jake said. "We can marry on the way to . . . our house."

With those words, the atmosphere changed and the tension increased again. Jake realized that despite the easygoing conversation, they were strangers. Strangers who were to marry and share a home together.

Marty obviously sensed it, too. He saw her look away again, and this time she bit her lower lip. He wanted nothing more than to ease her mind.

"I meant what I said."

She threw him a cautious glance. "I don't understand."

"In the letters. I meant what I said. I intend for this to be a marriage of convenience—a union in name only. I don't want you thinkin' otherwise. I didn't get you out here on false pretenses. I don't intend for you to be a real wife to me."

Marty nodded. "I appreciate that you appear to understand my unease. I'm not generally a woman who does things in such a rash manner. Even so, answering your advertisement and coming here seemed . . . well . . . almost predetermined."

He wasn't at all sure he understood her meaning, but nodded just the same. "I want to reassure you that you'll have full access to a beautiful home, a bank account of your own, and the freedom to do pretty much as you please. There will, of course, be obligations—parties and other gatherings. I do have certain demands placed on my shoulders—demands that

I'd just as soon forgo but find impossible to escape. You'll have demands, too."

"I understand. But I can't say that my wardrobe is exactly worthy of grand social events. I am a modest woman, and while I lived better than many in Texas, I was never one for fancy garb."

"That won't be a problem. I'll see to anything you need. My housekeeper already mentioned it, in fact, and I asked her to arrange for a dressmaker and so forth." The carriage slowed, and they heard Samson halt the team.

Jake looked out the window. "But besides that, Marty, I'd like it if we could be friends. My family's all back in California, and even though I've lived here a bit, I don't make friends easily."

Her sweet expression reassured him of his choice. "Of course we will be friends, Jake. I very much look forward to it, in fact."

———

The carriage halted, and Samson opened the door. "We be at the church."

Marty gazed at the large stone church in surprise. The huge steeple seemed to reach forever into the gray-blue skies. "A church wedding?"

"Actually, a rectory wedding, if you don't mind." Jake sounded hesitant—almost as if he feared her response.

Marty actually breathed a sigh of relief. "I don't mind at all. I was hoping we weren't going to make a circus of this."

He shook his head and offered Marty his arm. "No sense in it. We both have been married before, and we aren't children to be impressed by a lot of tomfoolery. You told me you liked to keep things simple, and I took you at your word."

For reasons she couldn't explain, his statement made her almost sad. They weren't that old and even if they had been married before, Jake made it sound as if they were past their prime. Were they really putting aside all the pleasures of youth?

"Frankly," Jake continued, "I find it kind of refreshing."

"What?" Marty asked as they moved toward the sandstone structure.

"That we don't have any pretenses between us. We both know why we're here. I like that."

For a moment, guilt washed over Marty. She managed to sidestep most of the reprehensible feelings, but one lingered. She had lied a good deal through the course of her life. Well, perhaps *lie* was too harsh a term; she often did nothing more serious than leave out important details—especially if they might get her into trouble. Marty had also been given to making mountains out of molehills, despite Hannah's attempts to wrest it out of her. But now . . . now she felt herself falling right back into her old ways. A lie had brought her here. Her life with this stranger would be a lie. The world would believe one thing, while in truth they would be another. It would be her greatest exaggeration.

"You don't think this is wrong, do you?" she asked without thinking.

Jake stopped. "You havin' second thoughts?"

Marty pushed down her concerns and smiled. "No," she lied, afraid it would be the first of many. "You?"

Jake laughed. "Hardly. I just wanna get this over with and get on with my life."

The door to the rectory opened just then, and a smiling dark-suited man welcomed them. "Ah, the happy couple.

Come, come. I have the witnesses ready and the arrangements have all been made. Soon you will be joined in wedded bliss."

Marty looked away lest he see her roll her eyes. Wedded bliss indeed.

Chapter 5

Marty settled once more into the carriage seat. She was married. She stared down at the ring on her finger. It was a lovely piece of jewelry, a large emerald surrounded by smaller diamonds.

"I hope you aren't disappointed in the ring," Jake said.

She studied him for a moment. There was such a look of hopefulness in his expression that she couldn't have admitted to such an emotion even if she had felt it. Which she didn't. "Not in the least. I'm stunned. I've never had anything so grand. My other wedding ring was a simple gold band."

"I was going to buy you just that, but Mr. Morgan, the owner of the bank, insisted that I purchase something bigger and better," he explained. "He gave me a bonus, in fact, for just such a purpose."

"It's lovely and fits nicely." She pulled her gloves back on and smiled. "Almost as if it were meant for me. I will cherish it—thank you." Discomfort edged her emotions, and Marty quickly changed the subject. "So tell me about the place we are to live."

Jake shrugged. "There again, it wasn't what I would have

picked out, but Mr. Morgan insisted. Fact is, it came with the job."

Apparently this Mr. Morgan had a way of bullying people into doing things they ordinarily wouldn't do. Marty made a mental note to remember that name.

"So is it all that bad?"

"No." He eased back against the seat, causing his hat to slide forward. He straightened again and adjusted the brim. "It's beautiful. It's grand and glorious, and in the words of Mrs. Morgan, 'It maintains the essence of elegance.'" His poor attempt to mimic the woman made Marty smile. Jake shook his head. "Much more so than I would have ever wanted. Mr. Morgan says that a man in my position has to live the part. For myself, I would just as soon live in a less pretentious neighborhood and save the money. That way, one day, I could buy my own idea of the perfect place."

She nodded. "So we're to live in a grand house. Is it very large?"

"I recall the paper work saying something about eight thousand square feet," he replied. "Seems like you could fit five or six families in there."

Marty's eyes widened. Her home in Texas had more than enough room and wasn't anywhere near that size. "Oh my. I suppose it will be a lot of work to keep up."

"That's why we have people to work for us."

"People?" She frowned. "Oh yes, I remember you said you had a staff to keep the house."

"You'll get to meet them soon enough. The house came with servants—again, something Mr. Morgan insisted on and not at all my idea. Look, we're just now arriving."

Marty glanced out the window at the three-story redbrick

and stone house. There was a large porch on the front, some six steps up from the ground. An impressive turret stood to the right of the porch and a roofed balcony was atop the porch itself.

"The house is made of Colorado red sandstone," Jake announced. "The rest is local brick."

"It's quite lovely . . . and big." Marty quickly took in the dry brown grass contrasting with several large green pines. "I had thought there would be snow," she said.

"There was. We had a white Christmas, but a warm southwesterly wind melted it. Don't worry, we'll no doubt see some more."

She smiled. "I've never seen very deep snow. We only had small amounts in Texas. Well, there was one snow that proved worse than most, but even so, it melted quickly."

He nodded. "I think I know the one you mean. Well, around here you can never tell what to expect. The mountains make for interesting weather."

"They are beautiful . . . the mountains," Marty remarked. "I've never seen anything like them. My friends in Colorado Springs hoped I would return and go with them to the top of Pikes Peak. A local carriage company treats sight-seekers to the adventure. It takes all day, and at the top, they say you can hardly breathe. I can hardly breathe at this level."

"Altitude can be kind of hard on a body. We're not that high here, so it should be less troublesome. Even so, after a time you'll adjust." The carriage stopped, and Jake reached for the door before Samson could open it for them. "Come along, Mrs. Wythe. I'm anxious to show you your new home."

Marty allowed Jake to help her from the carriage. His hands held her waist for only as much time as was needed to plant her feet firmly on the ground. His familiarity surprised her, but Marty said nothing as he guided her to the front door.

A distinguished-looking gentleman, probably fifty or more years of age, opened the door and stood waiting. "Welcome home, sir. Madam."

"Marty, this is Brighton, my butler and valet. He sees to most of my needs."

"How do you do, Mr. Brighton."

The man's expression remained sober. "Madam, it is my pleasure to meet you."

"And this is Mrs. Landry," Jake continued.

Marty hadn't even noticed the three women who'd positioned themselves just in front of a grand oak staircase. The oldest of the three stepped forward. "I'm Mrs. Landry." She was an unassuming woman with a neatly coiffed head of gray hair. She wore a dark blue gown with a high collar. "I oversee the staff here, including Mr. Brighton, although he doesn't believe that to be the case." The older man gave a harrumph but said nothing.

"Mrs. Landry," Marty said, nodding. "I'm Martha Ols . . . Wythe, but everyone calls me Marty."

"I shall call you Mrs. Wythe," the woman said, giving the slightest smile. "We all shall call you Mrs. Wythe." She turned to the other two women. "This is Kate." The short redheaded maid bobbed a curtsy while Mrs. Landry continued the introduction. "Kate works with me to keep the house in order. She's fairly new but learning quickly."

"Very nice to meet you, Kate."

"Ma'am." The girl looked to Mrs. Landry as if further explanation were needed.

Mrs. Landry cleared her throat. "Yes, well, Kate will assist you as lady's maid until you can secure your own hire. Mr. Wythe let us know that you would not be bringing a woman with you."

Marty laughed without meaning to. "No, I don't have a maid of my own." Mrs. Landry frowned, as if this announcement lessened her opinion of Marty. "I'm really quite capable," Marty continued.

Jake interrupted. "You'll need a maid. The parties, teas, and other social functions will require you to dress for the occasion. I'm told women often change clothes as many as six times a day. You'll need a woman who can dress your hair and help you with your clothes and bath."

She tried her best not to look surprised by this news. Changing clothes more than twice in one day required a special event back in Texas! Marty supposed she should have figured on such a thing, but since she'd been old enough to dress herself, she'd been doing pretty much just that. The only time she'd had help was when she was first learning to wear a corset, and even then Hannah had taught her how to lace herself in after a time.

"I'll have the employment service send over some women for you to interview," Mrs. Landry continued. "Kate will need to return to her household duties as soon as possible, as I cannot manage this house on my own and Brighton believes a manservant should not have to attend to dusting the high chandeliers and washing the windows, although he is the best candidate for the tasks."

This time Brighton refused to remain silent. "I explained to Mrs. Landry that it is not expected of a proper butler. I trained with the best of instructors as a young man in England. I will not have this hoyden of a housekeeper poison your mind against me."

"Hoyden? You dare call me a *hoyden*, you English-trained ninny? You pride yourself on going all the way to London to learn how to help a gentleman into a jacket or to open a door."

"Yes, and in England it is the butler who runs the household, madam. Not the housekeeper."

"Well, in case you didn't know it, Mr. Brighton, this isn't England. I can fetch a map if you doubt me."

Jake snorted and Marty turned to find him completely amused by the tirade. He shrugged at her questioning gaze. "I don't even bother to go to plays or operas. I can get all the entertainment I need here at home just watching these two."

"Such codswallop," Brighton declared. "Sir, if you need me, I shall be polishing the silver."

"At least he stoops to help me with that," Mrs. Landry spouted at Brighton's back. "I guess the English deem that an acceptable job for men."

Jake didn't bother to hide his grin. "See what I mean?"

Marty could only nod in agreement. In Brighton's absence, Mrs. Landry moved to the other woman. "This is our cook, Mrs. Standish. Up until now she worked alone, but Mr. Wythe has arranged for an assistant. She will arrive in three days—on the twenty-third."

"I would imagine Mrs. Wythe is quite exhausted," Jake declared, helping Marty from her coat. "Why don't we show her to her room."

Mrs. Landry nodded. Jake placed Marty's coat and his own on a nearby chair. He took off his hat and put that atop the coats before offering Marty his arm once again. "I hope you will enjoy living here." Mrs. Landry motioned Kate to see to the discarded wraps.

Marty looked around at the cream and blue colors of the entryway. "If this is an example of things to come, I'm sure I will." Although she was still rather stupefied by the jousting with words between the housekeeper and butler.

They began climbing the grand staircase, with Mrs. Landry leading the way. "As I mentioned in the carriage," Jake stated when they were nearly to the top of the stairs, "I have set up a bank account for you. Mrs. Landry has one as well for the running of the household, so you needn't share your funds."

"That really wasn't necessary," Marty replied. "Thomas and I always shared everything. I'm sure I could just come to you if I need something."

Jake nodded. "I understand, however, you will see the advantage of this soon enough. There's no need for you to check in with me and account for every penny you spend. First you will need an entirely new wardrobe. As I mentioned earlier, I had Mrs. Landry arrange for the dressmaker to arrive next week. Mrs. Landry tells me the woman knows exactly what you will need for your debut into Denver society, since she supplies clothing to many of the wealthiest matrons." Marty noted that his Texas drawl was once again carefully controlled. "Some gowns will have to be ordered from abroad, I'm told, but the dressmaker will see to all of that."

"Am I to have enough gowns to change six times a day?" Marty couldn't keep the teasing from her tone.

Jake grinned. "That and more. Mr. Morgan insisted I could not let you appear less than what your station demands."

"Sounds like Mr. Morgan insists on an awful lot," she muttered.

Jake didn't bother to respond but simply said, "I have also given you enough to do whatever you'd like with the house. If you prefer different rugs or draperies—even furniture—you should feel free to arrange for it. I have no preference. All that you see was in place when I arrived."

"I suppose Mr. Morgan was responsible for that, as well?" She met his amused expression.

"No, actually, Mrs. Morgan sent some of her people here to oversee the decorating. They did a nice job—don't you think?"

Marty glanced around as they made their way down the hall. There were beautiful carpets atop highly polished hardwood floors. Paintings graced the walls, and at the end of the hall a huge window was trimmed in billowing multicolored damask drapes. Why would she even consider changing it? It was all so very beautiful.

"They did, indeed."

"This will be your room," Mrs. Landry announced when they reached a door on the right. She led the way into the massive bedroom and stepped aside for Marty to inspect it.

A large canopied bed graced the space to Marty's left. On either side were beautifully carved side tables with fresh flowers. Marty had to smile. Jake had arranged for fresh flowers in the dead of winter. That was most considerate.

Opposite the bed, a beautifully tiled fireplace offered a welcoming fire to warm the room. The mahogany mantel held several knickknacks, including the statuette of a woman in Grecian fashion, a collection of cherubs surrounded by gold framing, and several other pieces that would require closer inspection.

"As you can see for yourself, you have a comfortable sitting area." Mrs. Landry moved to the side of the hearth. "If you need the fire built up, simply use this and someone will come to tend it." She showed Marty the servant pull.

Noise arose just beyond Mrs. Landry, and she turned to open a door not far from the fireplace. "This is your bathing and dressing room. Samson has just now deposited your trunks, and I have a warm bath waiting for you."

Marty looked at Jake and shook her head. "I had no idea."

He laughed. "I said it was a big house."

She explored the bathing and dressing area, an incredible room of marble and brass. There were large armoires, a chest of drawers, brass rails for hanging clothes, as well as a large tub for bathing and a sink and vanity where Marty could sit and fuss with her appearance for as long as she liked.

"Indoor plumbing, I see."

"Yes, we're thoroughly modern, although I didn't arrange for a telephone to be put in. I wasn't all that keen on people calling me at all hours," Jake admitted.

"I can understand. This is far more than I need," she said, shaking her head again. "I never expected anything so wonderful. We were still using a pump and outhouse in Texas." She smiled at Jake, who gave her a wink.

Mrs. Landry ignored the comment. "I'm afraid the fainting couch did not arrive in time, but is expected next week."

"I shall endeavor not to faint until then," Marty said most seriously before breaking into a giggle. She worried only a moment that Jake would be offended, but when she heard him chuckle, she relaxed.

Mrs. Landry ignored their merriment. "I will have Kate unpack your things and press them. Meanwhile, I will assist you into your bath." She went to the far wall, where another servant pull awaited. She signaled for Kate, then turned to face Marty and Jake. "Mr. Wythe, would you like me to show Mrs. Wythe your quarters, as well?"

Marty flushed and looked away. Perhaps the servants hadn't been informed of the arrangements. Jake seemed unconcerned, however. He moved to where Mrs. Landry stood by yet another door and motioned Marty to join them.

"This small passage adjoins your rooms to mine. There is a lock, as you can see, so that no one can disturb you." He opened the door and moved quickly to the end of the short corridor. Opening the far end exposed light from yet another large room. Marty walked into the expanse and marveled at the space.

It was a decidedly male room, done up in dark greens and heavy wood furniture. A desk stood against the wall at the far end of the room, and Marty could see from the look of it that Jake used it regularly for business. On the wall were oil paintings of Texas-styled cattle scenes as well as a stiff, but obviously much used, coiled rope. How strange to find it nailed to the wall of a bedroom.

For a moment Marty imagined herself back in Texas. She had nearly forgotten that Jake was a Texan. Spying a few books with ranch-related topics, a rather large yellowed map of Texas spread atop a nearby table, and an impressive bronze statue of a horse and rider, Marty knew she wasn't likely to erase Texas from this man's mind anytime soon.

"It seems very nice. Is it my imagination or is it smaller than my room?"

"A little bit," Jake admitted. "But it was the room I wanted when I moved in. The larger room seemed to be much more suited for . . . a . . . couple. I believe this was the nursery before I arranged for it to be redone."

Marty looked away in discomfort and pretended to study the bronze statue. "Very nice."

Kate appeared just then, and Mrs. Landry instructed her regarding Marty's trunks, while Marty could only look on. The two disappeared into the dressing room, leaving Marty and Jake alone. She saw the amusement in Jake's expression and couldn't help but question him.

"You look rather pleased with yourself."

"I'm just enjoying your surprise at everything." A clock chimed and he checked his pocket watch. "But now I will have to leave you in Mrs. Landry's capable hands. I have a meeting to attend. I will return to join you for supper. Enjoy the house, Mrs. Wythe."

Marty watched him leave out another door that she could see led back to the hallway. Mrs. Landry returned just then and directed her back to the bathing room. "I would imagine you are exhausted from your travels. Once you've bathed, I will pack you into bed and you can sleep until supper. Kate will come and help you dress for dinner and arrange your hair. It will be only you and Mr. Wythe dining, and Cook is preparing lamb. I hope that meets with your approval." All the while Mrs. Landry helped Marty from her clothes.

"Lamb is fine."

"In the future you and I will meet to discuss the menus for each meal. You must let me know if there are any particular foods that you abhor, or ones that you love, for that matter." She had stripped Marty down to her shift and corset.

"Now just sit here and rest while I see that the bath is still warm enough, and then we can finish with your clothes."

Marty did as she was told, knowing that the wheels of this massive machine could not be stopped even if she wanted them to be. No doubt Mrs. Landry was used to running this house as an army commander ran a fort. It wouldn't make sense to try and disturb the flow of things. At least not today.

After the bath, which Marty very much enjoyed, Mrs. Landry helped her into bed, then quietly exited the room. Marty marveled at the luxurious softness of the bed and the silky feel of the fine linens that graced it. She had never known such comfort, nor such exhaustion. She closed her eyes and tried to imagine how she would ever explain all of this to Hannah. Whispering aloud, she composed her letter.

"I'm to have my own maid, and a dressmaker will arrive to create a wardrobe fit for a queen. There are servants and eight thousand square feet of opulence to be explored." She yawned and tried not to fight the sleep that was gradually overtaking her.

"And Mrs. Standish will have a new assistant in the kitchen in three days' time," she murmured, smiling to herself. "On the twenty-third."

Speaking the date aloud caused Marty to reopen her eyes for just a moment. That meant today was the twentieth. The twentieth of January—her thirty-fifth birthday.

"Well, happy birthday to me," she murmured and closed her eyes again. "Happy birthday to me, indeed."

Chapter 6

Jake sat at work feeling rather pleased with the way things were progressing. The weekend had gone well, and he and Marty seemed able to share the house quite amicably. Because she had just arrived on Friday, Jake hadn't even approached the idea of them attending church services their first weekend together. He knew from things she'd said that while raised in a Christian home, Marty had very little interest in such matters for herself. There would be time enough to explain to her that proper society would expect them to be seen in services every Sunday.

He refused to worry about it, however. Reviewing the columns of numbers on the ledger, Jake instead thought of how surprised he'd been by Marty's quick wit and good nature. She even managed to take Brighton and Mrs. Landry in stride. No doubt in time she would come to find their mock arguments amusing. Truth be told, Jake suspected that the two held more than a passing fancy for each other.

A knock sounded on his outer door, and Jake looked up to find Arnold entering the room. "Mr. Morgan and several board members are here to see you."

Jake frowned and looked at the clock. They had no agreed-upon meeting today. He stood to receive the men as they filed into the room.

"Wythe," Mr. Morgan said with a nod.

"Mr. Morgan, gentlemen," Jake said, nodding to each man. He looked to Arnold. "Please bring in more chairs, Mr. Meyers."

Arnold hurried to do Jake's bidding and had everyone seated comfortably within a matter of minutes. Jake remained standing, wondering what this gathering was all about.

"So . . . what can I do for you today, Mr. Morgan?"

"Well, we have come, in fact, with congratulations." The older man smiled. "We understand you were married last Friday."

"Yes," Jake said, still guarded. "Mrs. Olson arrived by stage, and we were married immediately."

"We read all about a certain Mrs. Olson driving the stage," board member Mr. Palmer said with a sly grin. "Would that have been *your* Mrs. Olson?"

Jake swallowed hard. "Yes, sir. I must admit it was. Although I will add that the circumstances necessitated it."

"No doubt. We heard that she saved the entire stagecoach from a dozen armed marauders," Josiah Keystone added.

"I heard she single-handedly killed half of them by herself," the remaining man and former governor of Colorado, Mr. Cooper, declared.

"I assure you, gentlemen, it wasn't quite that dramatic. The stage was attacked, that much is true, but Marty . . . Mrs. Wythe tells me that she only saw two men approach. She fired at them, along with the men responsible for the stage. She has no way of knowing that anyone was wounded by her efforts, however. I also assure you that while she did find it necessary to take charge of the stage, she in no way sought publicity for her actions."

"Relax, Mr. Wythe. No one here is taking umbrage with you or Mrs. Wythe," Morgan interjected. "In fact, I find it all rather amusing. I can hardly imagine Imogene being as capable in her velvets and silks."

"You've got yourself a regular Annie Oakley," Keystone added. "Sounds like she's a woman who can hold her own. Did you see the picture they drew of her? I don't know if it's a good likeness or not, but she looked like she could have taken on an entire army."

Jake had indeed seen the drawing. He had purposefully hid the newspaper from Marty, however. He knew she had no desire for public attention, and this might only make her worry that her sister would learn the truth of what had happened before she had a chance to write and explain.

"I did see it. It looks nothing like her," he answered honestly. "And she only had one pistol, not two. I'm afraid the artist took great license with his rendition."

"Well, I enjoyed the article all the same," Mr. Palmer threw in. "I enjoyed it immensely."

Jake wasn't at all sure how to respond. Despite having told Marty otherwise, he had figured once word got out about her unseemly arrival, any desire to see him or his wife in public social settings would be discarded. But now it seemed as if these men were actually admiring Marty's performance. He sat down rather hard and awaited further comment.

"She's a real novelty," Morgan continued. "I can hardly wait to meet her. Imogene said that she must be a woman of divine courage."

That comment caused Jake to let out his breath in relief. If Mrs. Morgan hailed Marty as a conquering heroine, then all would be well. The community would no doubt take a cue from her.

"I believe she is," Jake replied. He rubbed his sweaty palms against his trouser legs. "Thank you."

"Well, that brings us to our other reason for coming by," Morgan continued. "Imogene is planning a party for Valentine's Day, as she does each year. Only this year, she wants to incorporate a celebration to honor you and Mrs. Wythe. There will be a supper and dance, although we will end the festivities by ten since the fourteenth does fall on a Tuesday."

Jake nodded and wrote a note to himself regarding the party. "That is very kind."

"We will expect you by six so that you and Mrs. Wythe might stand in the receiving line and greet our guests. It will be the perfect way to introduce you. It will be a formal affair, so you will be expected to attire yourself accordingly. Do you have white tie and tails?"

"I do. If you'll recall, you helped me arrange a very fine suit of clothing for the Christmas season," Jake replied.

"Of course." Morgan nodded and looked to his friends. "My tailor is the best in town." He looked back to Jake. "That will be exactly right for the Valentine's party. I'm sure that Mrs. Wythe will have something lovely to wear."

"But tell her to leave her six-shooter at home," Cooper teased. "We wouldn't want her rewarding us with a repeat of her arrival into our great city."

The other men laughed, but Jake could only muster a smile. He still felt uneasy with these men and their place in society. He was a fish out of water, and they knew it as well as he did. Truth be told, Jake was almost certain they preferred it that way. It gave them a sort of edge—a pretense of control.

But that was all it was, Jake assured himself. A pretense. Nothing more. These men did not own him, even though he was greatly indebted to them. There wasn't a single thing they had offered him that he couldn't walk away from. And while they didn't know his real purpose in accepting the high-paying job, Jake felt no remorse.

I'm only here as long as it takes to put aside enough money for a ranch. No longer. Texas is my home, and that is where I'm bound to return.

★

Marty smiled at the sour-faced woman. "Well, Mrs. Sales, it would seem your references are in order. I appreciate your taking the time to speak with me today."

"Yes, madam."

Uncertain what else to do, Marty looked to Mrs. Landry for help. "If you'll come this way, Mrs. Sales, I will see you to the door. Mrs. Wythe will notify the agency if she wishes to retain your services." Mrs. Landry led the way and the seemingly unhappy woman followed. She was the fifth woman sent over by the agency, and Marty liked her no better than the first four. Most were quite dour and rigid. All had worked for numerous years as ladies' maids and were well versed in their duties, even if Marty wasn't. They impressed Marty as women who would impose their will upon her rather than take instruction.

Mrs. Landry returned. "There's one final applicant."

Marty sighed and looked beyond the housekeeper to where

a young woman stood with her face turned slightly to the right. She was staring at the floor, as if too shy to meet anyone.

"Miss Alice Chesterfield," Mrs. Landry announced. She turned to the girl. "Give Mrs. Wythe your references."

Alice stepped forward, but her gloved hands were empty. Marty could see that the small woman couldn't be very old.

"I'm pleased to meet you. May I call you Alice?"

The girl nodded, but still refused to lift her head. "I wanted to apply for the job, but . . . well . . . I have no references."

"Why would the agency send her to interview for this position?" Mrs. Landry interjected. "I'll turn her away and send a letter of reprimand to the employment official."

"No," Marty declared, seeing something in the girl that touched her heart. "That won't be necessary. Alice, have a seat."

The girl looked up in surprise. It was then that Marty caught sight of the scar that ran down the right side of her face. The nasty pink scar was evidence that the wound had not healed that long ago.

"Please sit, Alice. I'd very much like to talk to you."

Mrs. Landry was less than pleased, but instead of saying anything, she positioned herself in a chair by the archway and waited for Marty to continue. Alice took the offered chair and licked her lips in a nervous fashion. Her dress was too short for her and rose to reveal tattered boots, but Marty pretended not to notice.

"So tell me about yourself, Alice." Marty smiled, hoping it would relieve the girl's fear.

"I want to say that I know it was wrong of me to come here. The agency . . . they didn't send me. I was there and heard some of the other women getting their instructions to come.

I . . . well . . . I need to work, and I thought I would . . . apply, as well." She straightened her shoulders and fixed Marty with her gaze. "I know that wasn't right, but I need this job."

"Well, Alice, why don't you tell me about yourself." Marty noted her clothes were frayed and far from the latest fashion. They were, in fact, too immature for the young woman, but Marty supposed they were all she had. "I'd like to know about you and why you want to work as a lady's maid."

"I . . . well . . ." She cleared her throat and seemed to carefully consider her words. "I'm seventeen. I know how to work hard, although I don't have experience as a lady's maid. I'm a good learner, and I have an eighth-grade education." The latter she said with some pride, and Marty couldn't help but smile.

"That's wonderful. So you can read and write should I need you to handle correspondence for me."

"Yes, ma'am. My penmanship is quite good."

Marty nodded. "That's definitely a benefit to us both." She could see this bolstered the girl a bit and hoped to encourage her further. "I've always appreciated those who understood the value of education."

"My father saw schooling as very important."

"And who is your father?"

The girl frowned. "Mr. George Chesterfield, deceased."

"I am sorry." Marty could see the pain in Alice's expression. "Has it been long?"

"No. Just about five months ago. He was . . . murdered."

Mrs. Landry let out a gasp that echoed in the room. Marty tried to handle the news in a less stunned fashion, although she was rather shocked to hear the declaration. "Can you speak about what happened?"

Alice nodded. "We were walking home in the evening. My father was carrying some papers for a banker named Mr. Morgan."

Marty immediately recognized the name. Apparently Mr. Morgan was a very busy man. Alice continued to speak.

"Father often carried papers and money for Mr. Morgan— it was his job as a bank manager. I suppose the men who attacked us knew that. The men stopped us and demanded that my father turn over the satchel he was carrying. Father refused and they took hold of me and . . ." Her voice faltered.

Marty thought to stop her, but for reasons she didn't entirely understand, she remained silent and let the girl struggle through her explanation.

"I . . . tried to fight them off." She paused and bit her lower lip. The pink scar seemed to pale a bit as Alice clenched her jaw. "I wasn't strong enough," she finally said. "One of the men held me while another put his knife to my face. She touched her hand to the scar. "He . . . he . . . cut me before I even realized what was happening."

"I'm so sorry, Alice. What a terrible thing to endure."

Alice looked Marty in the eye. "My father screamed at the men to take the satchel and let me go. He rushed them, and the men forgot about me and pushed my father away. He fell to the ground and hit his head. I don't remember anything after that because I fainted. When I woke up again, I was in the hospital. They told me Father had died from striking his head. They weren't even sure I would make it. Honestly, at that point I didn't care if I did."

"I can well imagine," Marty replied. She looked across the room to where Mrs. Landry was dabbing tears from her eyes. "Mrs. Landry, would you arrange some refreshments for us?"

"Of course. Poor wee girl," the housekeeper said, heading from the room.

Marty turned back to the blond-haired girl. "Do you have no other family?"

"No. No one. I'm alone and I need to work in order to support myself. Up until now, some friends from church have helped me get by, but they're moving away and I have no one else. I'm sorry if I've wasted your time." She looked up with an expression that seemed to plead for Marty to assure her that she hadn't done wrong.

"Nonsense. You haven't wasted my time. In fact, I'm very honored that you would share your story with me, Alice. I know it couldn't have been easy for you."

"I'm a quick learner, Mrs. Wythe. Truly I am. I know how to sew and clean. I can fix your hair and maybe even learn some of the new styles. I'm pretty good at figuring things out. If I can see some of the new magazines, I'm sure to be able to copy the fashions."

Marty smiled. "I bet you could. You strike me as a remarkable young woman, and I think you're exactly the kind of employee I could use."

Alice's expression cheered. "I promise. I would do my best. I would give my all."

"You need not convince me," Marty assured her. "I can see that you are very determined."

Alice leaned forward. "I wasn't sure if the job included room and board, but I need a place to live. After the first, my friends will be leaving Denver and I'll be . . . alone."

"We have quarters for you here. A salary, too. Mrs. Landry will see you settled in."

"Of course I will," Mrs. Landry said, bringing a silver tray with refreshments. She placed the tray atop a small table and immediately set to work pouring tea. She handed a cup to the young woman, but Alice shook her head.

"No, if I'm to start right away, I should go get my things." Alice hesitated a moment. "I can start right away, can't I?"

Marty chuckled. "Of course you can. I'll have my driver assist you, but wouldn't you rather have some refreshments first?"

"No, ma'am. I want to get back here as quickly as possible and start learning my job." She stood and touched her hand to her face. "Thank you. Thank you for giving me a chance . . . even though . . ."

"Even though nothing, Alice. You have presented yourself as the better candidate for my needs," Marty said, standing. "I am certain that we will get along famously. Mrs. Landry, would you see that Samson drives—"

"No, that's all right." Alice was already halfway to the door. "I'll walk. It's not all that far." She very nearly flew out the front door, not at all the shy, reserved young woman who'd entered.

Marty exchanged a look with Mrs. Landry. "I know you must think me a fool, but I couldn't stop myself. That poor girl needed our help."

"I don't think you a fool at all, Mrs. Wythe. You have a tender heart, as do I. It will no doubt be the death of us both, but we could hardly send that girl out into the cold with no hope." The housekeeper handed Marty a cup of tea. "We'll need to get her some uniforms. She's smaller than Kate, but perhaps she can borrow one of hers temporarily."

Marty nodded. "And some new shoes. Hers looked rather . . . worn."

"I can take her shopping tomorrow, if that's what you'd like."

Marty thought about it for a moment. "We can both take her."

Mrs. Landry shook her head. "Mrs. Wythe, that wouldn't be acceptable. Mr. Wythe needs you to be . . . well . . . respectable . . . to your position. There are certain rules to your station in life, and I won't have Mr. Wythe shamed because I was remiss in explaining them."

The housekeeper shifted uncomfortably, and Marty couldn't help but feel sorry for her. She barely knew the woman but already liked her no-nonsense style. "Very well, Mrs. Landry. I shall keep to my place. I cannot say I approve of this world of rules, but since I agreed to take it on when I married Mr. Wythe, I suppose I should keep my word." Marty sipped the tea and gave a sigh. "I don't know that I'll ever get used to having servants or rules."

Chapter 7

"I didn't know Mr. Chesterfield," Jake said at breakfast the next morning.

Marty found this surprising. "Apparently you were the replacement for his job after he was murdered."

"I do recall someone saying the former bank manager had died, but little else." He took a drink of his coffee before continuing. "And your maid is his daughter?"

"Yes, and I like her very much. She was injured in the robbery that claimed her father's life. She has a scar that runs the length of her face. When you meet her, try not to be . . . surprised."

Jake smiled. "No worries. I've probably seen worse. And by the way, Mr. and Mrs. Morgan have invited us to their Valentine's ball next month and would like us to arrive by six in order to receive the guests with them."

Marty looked at her husband for a moment. "Is this to be a regular occurrence?"

He seemed confused. "Valentine's parties?"

"No, being summoned by the Morgans," she replied and took a bite of her toast.

Jake shrugged but gave her a grin. "It does seem to be the pattern. You'll get used to it. Mr. Morgan has a way of seeing to it that folks do what he wants. I'm really not sure why he's taken such a likin' to me, but I have to say he's generous to a fault where it's concerned us. Just look at all he's done on our account, and always with the requirement that I not give him credit for his generosity. He's a humble man."

"I can see that you're right about that," Marty said. "I suppose I'm still stunned by my new life here." With Mrs. Landry, Kate, and Alice busy transforming the front sitting room into a fitting area for the expected dressmaker, Marty leaned forward in hopes of not being overheard.

"I know that he believes us to be a love match, but . . . well . . . do the servants know about our . . . situation?"

"You mean do they know our sensible arrangement? This marriage of convenience?"

"Yes."

He shook his head. "No. I think Mrs. Landry might suspect, but I haven't told her outright." He put down his fork. "See, when they promoted me to bank manager and started in on my need for a wife, I lied and told them I had a fiancée in Texas."

"And that's why you placed the advertisement."

"Exactly." This time he leaned in to speak in a hushed tone. "You have no idea what Morgan and his cronies had planned for me. There were entire parties full of eligible young ladies for me to court."

"Sounds like torture," Marty said, smiling.

Jake grinned and relaxed in his chair. "I thought so. Anyhow, I made this big fuss about how I was promised and I couldn't be unfaithful. I told them we planned to marry in another year, but that didn't sit well with them. They started in on insisting I move the wedding date up. They said it worried the board to have a single man in a position of such great responsibility—even a widowed man."

"I suppose there is some merit to that. Married men do present themselves as more stable and respectable in their activities."

"Some married men do," Jake countered. "But certainly not all. There's scandal aplenty in this town, and marriage doesn't seem a sturdy boundary marker for many."

"I'm sure you're right. Just the same, I wanted to know what you'd told folks. I don't want to cause problems by not getting the story straight."

"I appreciate that. I don't want to outright lie if I don't have to—I've already done that in telling them we were engaged. But if you can abide it, I'd appreciate it if we'd say as little as possible."

"It's been my experience, however," Marty said, pushing her eggs around on the plate, "that sometimes details help to keep stories from unraveling. I suggest we agree to certain things, such as when we first met and how. Women are always asking after that kind of thing."

Jake nodded. "Well, we both lived in Texas . . . Dallas area, to be exact. That helps a great deal. We needn't lie about our youth."

Marty considered the story for a moment. "We could say that we grew up not far from each other, implying but not outright stating that we knew each other. I am a bit older than you, but we needn't make too much of that."

"True." He seemed to like her thoughts on the matter. "And we could say that time separated us and we married other people, but we always held fond thoughts of each other." He grinned. "There wasn't a pretty gal in Texas I didn't hold fond thoughts of."

"Exactly." Marty was confident it could work. "We'll say that we corresponded, mentioning we had both lost our mates and after that we got in touch with each other. That's all quite true."

"Seems simple enough."

"Simple details are the best," she assured him. Just then Marty heard a knock at the front door. "I suppose that's for me." She dabbed the napkin to her lips. "I want to thank you for your generosity, Jake. I had no idea I'd be treated to so many fine things. It really isn't necessary."

"Unfortunately, it is," Jake declared. "Mr. Morgan has plans for me—at least that's what he's always telling me. I just go along with things for now."

"What do you mean?" she asked.

"Well, my plans and his don't exactly line up. What I want in the long run—"

"I am sorry to interrupt," Mrs. Landry declared, entering the room, "but Mrs. Davies has arrived, and she is anxious that we should begin your appointment, Mrs. Wythe."

Marty looked to Jake. What did he mean his plans didn't line up with Mr. Morgan's? "I suppose we can resume this conversation tonight at supper."

Jake smiled and got to his feet. He came around the table to help Marty up. "I shouldn't be too late." He surprised her by giving her cheek a light peck.

Her face grew hot at the kiss, and Marty ducked her head like a shy bride. Mrs. Landry only chuckled. "Come along now."

Marty followed the housekeeper through the house and into a sitting room that now looked nothing like it had on Marty's first inspection. Most of the furniture had been moved aside, and several tables were positioned in their place. The women who'd accompanied Mrs. Davies were busy spreading out fabrics, trims, and a large portfolio of dress designs.

"Mrs. Wythe, this is Mrs. Davies," Mrs. Landry introduced. "Mrs. Davies, this is the lady of the house, Mrs. Wythe. She will require a complete social wardrobe, as well as personal items. Mr. Wythe has instructed that one gown in particular is needed for the Morgans' annual Valentine's ball. The gown should be appropriate to the event, of course, and the cost should reveal quality, as this will be Mrs. Wythe's first formal appearance."

The dark-eyed woman nodded and clapped her hands. "Girls, come quickly and meet our client, Mrs. Wythe."

Marty scarcely had time to acknowledge the bevy of women before they were undressing her down to her shift and corset. Mrs. Davies herself took the measurements. She chattered on with her team, making suggestions as she completed her tasks.

"You are so lovely and have a most enviable figure, Mrs. Wythe. Your petite frame will be a delight to clothe."

"Thank you," Marty said, uncertain what else she could say. She'd never thought of her figure being anything special. She was petite, just as her sister, Hannah, but she never considered herself anywhere near as pretty. Where Hannah's features were delicate—like a fine china doll, Marty thought of herself as more earthy and plain.

"Now that we have your measurements," Mrs. Davies continued, "I will show you my book of designs. I have created a great many gowns in my day, so you will be pleased to note that these sketches are quite up-to-date and will reveal the latest in fashion."

She didn't give Marty a chance to reply before pulling her toward the table. "Lynette, bring Mrs. Wythe her dressing gown lest she catch her death of cold."

Marty slipped into the robe, grateful for the extra warmth. The fire had been lit to warm the room, but the temperature outside had dropped considerably since Marty's arrival. She hugged the robe to her neck and took a seat as she waited for Mrs. Davies to lay out her drawings.

"This gown in a silk taffeta would be quite appropriate for the Valentine ball." She placed the drawing on the table in front of Marty. "Note the fur trimming the hem and the sleeves. Ermine will give added warmth, as well as a look of opulence. Accompany it with a velvet cloak, and you'll put all the other women to shame."

Marty studied the gown for a moment. She'd never known anything so elegant. Life in Texas had never been this grand— at least not for her and Thomas. She'd generally avoided events that required formal garments.

"It's beautiful," she finally said, seeing that Mrs. Davies was anticipating a comment.

"The low neckline is perfect for showing off your lovely shoulders."

"I wouldn't want the neckline to be too low," Marty replied. "I'm not comfortable with that."

Mrs. Davies nodded. "But of course. We can trim the bodice with ermine, as well. I believe the gown is well suited for a dusty rose color. It will work perfectly with your complexion and hair." Only then did Marty notice that a young woman stood directly to Mrs. Davies's left, writing down most every word the woman said. "We will set out to create this gown immediately. I will return for a preliminary fitting this time next week.

"Now, here is another gown that I think will be perfect for you," Mrs. Davies said, turning several pages. "Note the full sleeves and high neckline. The bodice is sewn with permanent pleating."

Marty nodded and Mrs. Davies hurried to turn the page. "And here is a gown very similar to one created by the designer Charles Worth. Of course you have heard of him." Marty had no time to reply as the woman continued. "You will note the cascading bustle. This gown is done in two pieces, and I believe it would show off your tiny waist to perfection."

"All right." Marty then found herself studying numerous other sketches and designs. Mrs. Davies kept her so busy and focused on the order of the new wardrobe that Marty lost track of time.

"I believe a dozen shirtwaists in varying styles will suffice for now," Mrs. Davies stated to her assistant. "And a half dozen woolen skirts. Three heavy and three of lighter weight. We can arrange for other skirts in the months to come." She touched her finger to the table. "Oh, we will also need to create undergarments. Please note that," she told her assistant.

Marty tried to protest the number of pieces, but Mrs. Davies waved her off.

"I believe you'll find these color swatches to your liking, Mrs. Wythe." She picked up a board that revealed a vast number of colors. "These will be serviceable skirts that should work well for your informal times. Might I suggest the burgundy, brown, gray, black, and of course the dark navy. I would have two in the black and brown, as they will go well with many of the jackets we will make for you and would be appropriate for walking out."

"All right," Marty simply replied, not feeling capable of demanding her own way. It was a strange position for her to be in, for she'd often stood up to Hannah and Will, and even Thomas to a certain degree. Folks around the ranch knew she wasn't one to argue with, so they generally gave in to her desires—but here, that wasn't even a consideration.

The appointment continued with orders for nightgowns, robes, cloaks, and coats. By the time the clock chimed noon, Mrs. Davies and her merry employees were once again packing their wares and hurrying to return to their sewing house.

"I will see you in one week for the first fitting," Mrs. Davies declared at the threshold, and Mrs. Landry closed the door behind her while Marty sank into the nearest chair.

"Goodness, but that was an ordeal. I can't imagine going through that again."

"It won't be quite as bad next time." Mrs. Landry offered Marty a gentle smile. "Come now. Luncheon is ready, and you must eat before the milliner and cobbler arrive."

Marty had hoped that the departure of Mrs. Davies would signal her freedom for the rest of the day, but it wasn't to be. "I suppose I must choose hats and shoes next?"

"And gloves, stockings, and any other needed accessories. Mr. Wythe said we were to spare no expense."

"Yes, but I'm sure he didn't mean for me to have so much. A dozen shirtwaists! Who needs a dozen? Goodness, but where will I even put a dozen?"

Mrs. Landry gave a tolerant nod. "That is our duty, Mrs. Wythe, and we will arrange for everything to have a proper place. Now come along. Cook has your meal prepared. We mustn't let it grow cold."

The rest of the day passed much as the first part. People were in and out of the house, measuring, marking, fussing over Marty until she wanted to scream. Finally by four in the afternoon, she was allowed to retire to her room for a rest. She fell into the bed without even caring that she was fully clothed.

"What have I gotten myself into?"

"Ma'am?" It was Alice. She stood by the door to the dressing room and bath. "Did you call for me?"

Marty sat up. "No, I didn't call. I suppose, however, if I'm to have a proper rest, I should undress."

Alice smiled and came to help Marty with her buttons. "You will have such a lovely wardrobe when Mrs. Davies finishes. I doubt any other woman in Denver will look half so fine."

"I can't understand all the fuss. I'm not a grand lady, and while I've lived in a house with help, I certainly never needed servants to take charge of everything."

"So you are unhappy?" Alice asked and immediately apologized. "Sorry, ma'am. Mrs. Landry said a lady's maid was not to ask personal questions."

Marty laughed. "Please, you needn't worry about my taking offense. Frankly, I'd like very much for us to be friends."

"But that isn't proper. Mrs. Landry made it very clear that while I am to assist you and be a companion to you if needed, I'm supposed to mostly stay in the shadows and anticipate your needs."

"I'm sure Mrs. Landry did state that. I'm sure it's written up in the rules somewhere, but that isn't how I prefer it. Frankly,

trying to keep up with all the rules is giving me a headache."
Marty allowed Alice to help her from the modest gown she'd
worn that day. Thinking about this dress compared to the
other things that had been ordered, Marty felt rather shoddy.

Slipping beneath the covers to ward off the chill of the
room, Marty gave a sigh. "I've never been one for napping,
but it seems this life is quite tiring."

"It's the mountains, too, ma'am. If you don't mind my
saying so."

Marty closed her eyes. "Yes, Jake mentioned that. I should
think now that I've been in Colorado for a few days, I should
be adjusting. However, I'm beginning to wonder if I'll ever
adjust."

———————————— ★ ————————————

Jake sat across the beautifully set dining table in moody
silence. Marty hadn't yet seen this side of him. He was obviously troubled about something, and she didn't know if it
would be deemed appropriate to ask or whether she should
remain silent. It seemed only natural that she would question him about his day. . . . Didn't all wives do that? She and
Thomas always had.

After being served the soup, Marty picked up her spoon
and dared a question. "You seem tired. Did you have a difficult day?"

"It's not important." Jake attacked a piece of bread. "There
are problems that I have to resolve, and you don't need to
worry about it."

"I wasn't worried," she countered. "I simply noticed that
you looked tired. I presumed the day had given you some
problems. I'm happy to listen if you'd like to talk."

He looked at her for a moment, his brow knit together as his frown deepened. "No. There's no reason to involve you."

"But I want to be involved."

Jake slammed his hand down, causing all of the dishes to rattle. "I said no!"

Marty straightened in defense. She wasn't used to being treated in a harsh manner. Up until now, this man she'd so quickly married had seemed quite lighthearted and easygoing.

With a sigh, Jake put down the bread and shook his head. "I'm sorry, Marty. I had no right to act that way. You're just showing concern for me and I shouldn't have snapped at you. Sometimes I open my mouth just wide enough to stick my boot in."

She could see he was truly sorry. The expression on his face and his tone of voice made it clear that his reaction had been a surprise even to Jake. "I shouldn't have pried. My Thomas and I used to talk out our problems over supper. I learned that from my sister and her husband. I suppose it's an old habit."

"My folks did much the same," Jake admitted. "Supper was about the only time they saw each other for any length of time. Breakfast always seemed rushed so that we could get to work, and lunch was often elsewhere on the range."

Marty nodded. "And while everyone was tired from a day of arduous tasks and difficult trials, supper gave us a time to sit back and review the good and bad of the choices we'd made."

Jake smiled for the first time that evening. "Supper was always my favorite time." He picked up his soup spoon. "I can remember my mother having the table set in beautiful china with a fine tablecloth. Father would admonish her, saying that such things should be used for special occasions.

But Mother said every time we came together as a family was a special occasion."

"I never knew my mother and barely remember my father," Marty told him. "However, my sister always tried to make us a comfortable home. She was more mother to me than sister. . . . Hannah gave up a great deal to care for my brother and me."

"That's what family should do."

"Do you have any brothers or sisters?" Marty asked.

"No, it was just me."

Marty hoped that might be the start of a new conversation, but it wasn't. Before long, Jake was lost in his thoughts again, and Marty had no luck in drawing him back into a conversation.

"The dressmaker said she would come next week for my first fitting." She waited until the new kitchen assistant, Willa, served the main course of roasted game hen before continuing. "The gown she suggested for the Valentine's ball is quite lovely. I'm sure I've never had anything so grand."

"Hmm," Jake murmured without even looking up. He cut into the meat and continued to eat in silence.

"It's going to be a lovely color—a sort of rose. A dark, pinkish rose. There will be white fur trimming the gown." She knew he wasn't listening, so she reverted to a childhood habit that she'd used on Hannah when she wouldn't give Marty her full attention.

"Then Mrs. Davies suggested we turn snakes loose in the music room."

"Whatever you decide is fine," Jake said.

"I suppose they are smaller than bears and won't make as much mess."

Jake looked at her for a moment, and Marty was certain he would call her comment into question. But instead he gave a sigh and got to his feet. "I'm sorry to be such poor company. I think I'll make an early night of it."

Marty watched him leave the room. His meal was barely touched. Whatever troubled him had robbed him of his appetite as well as his personable mood. Perhaps he'd be more willing to explain in the morning.

"But what if he isn't?" She frowned. She really knew nothing about this man. Anyone could put up a pretense for a few days—but what if this was the way Jacob Wythe generally acted? What if she'd married a man of unpredictable moods?

It was only then that the full impact of her decision to leave Texas and marry a stranger hit her. He had seemed nice enough in his letters and even the time they'd shared here thus far had been pleasant. Still, what if he were unstable? That kind of thought had never come to mind until now.

"Perhaps I've been most foolish."

Chapter 8

As the days slipped into February, Marty saw less and less of Jake. When she did see him, he was quite resigned but not harsh. His duties at the bank often kept him there late into the evening, and Marty found it necessary to find ways to busy herself. She read through the Jane Austen volumes her sister had given her at Christmas, then ventured into the library to see what other tomes might hold her attention. If this was to be her life, at least it was peaceful.

Mrs. Davies had come and gone many times since her first appointment. She had arrived for fittings and to get Marty's approval on materials, but otherwise had not delivered a single item. She promised, however, that the rose and ermine gown would be ready in time for the Morgans' party, and that was truly all Marty cared about. But not as most women might. Marty wasn't concerned with looking beautiful or being held in high regard for her taste in fashion. She just wanted to please Jake and not cause him any problems with this elite circle of friends. Thankfully, Alice had been true to her word and had learned her duties quickly.

Marty patted her artfully styled hair and smiled. Hiring

Alice had proven to be one of the wisest choices Marty had ever made. It made Marty happy, too, just knowing that they could somehow extend assistance to the daughter of George Chesterfield. Although neither she nor Jake had ever known the man, they were in a way benefiting from his demise. It seemed appropriate that they should help Alice in return.

Truly, Marty's only complaint was the boredom. The days here in Denver seemed longer than any Marty had ever known in Texas. At the ranch there had always been something to work at—cooking, cleaning, caring for the animals, gardening. Here, there was always someone else to do the work.

Mrs. Landry suggested she get started in remaking the house into her own style, but Marty thought it suited her well enough. For reasons she couldn't explain, there was a feeling of the temporary in this place. Perhaps it was Jake's admission that he didn't care for the place and that he would prefer to live a simpler life. Perhaps now that they were married, Mr. Morgan would understand if they decided to sell this house in lieu of another.

Mrs. Landry suggested various outings, but Marty found the cold difficult to get used to. There'd been no more snow, so the town looked all gray and brown—with little to entice her outdoors. There was also no occasion to entertain or receive guests—she didn't know anyone. The fact that no one had come to present themselves made her feel like an outcast. Mrs. Landry, however, was quick to explain that most people were waiting to be introduced to her at the party or in church. She'd managed to avoid the latter for a second time the previous Sunday, but that would unfortunately not be a luxury she could oft repeat.

"You're expected to show yourself as a respectful, godly woman," Mrs. Landry had told her. "Whether you agree with the sentiments of the pastor or not, you need to be present in the pew."

"I have no interest in church," she'd replied. "God and I have an agreement. I stay out of His way, and He stays out of mine."

She could still see the look of surprise on Mrs. Landry's face. She hadn't argued with Marty, but her disapproval had been evident.

Since it was Saturday, Marty presumed that Jake would be free of bank business, but she hadn't seen or heard from him so far. Not that she really expected to, given his recent moodiness. She hadn't bothered to go down for breakfast, telling Alice that she wanted to just linger in bed for a time. Much to her chagrin, Alice took this to mean she wanted breakfast in bed. The young girl showed up with a tray shortly thereafter, and Marty didn't have the heart to refuse her efforts.

"If you're finished with breakfast, I will take your tray," Alice said, entering the room.

Marty smiled at the young woman. "Thank you. I truly hadn't meant for you to do this, but it proved to be rather enjoyable."

"Mrs. Landry said it's quite routine for a married woman to take her breakfast in bed. I'm happy to bring it up for you every day."

"Goodness, no," Marty declared, pushing back her covers after Alice took the tray. "Eating in bed is for invalids and the sick, neither of which applies to me. I was just being a bit lazy today. It seemed colder and since I had no plans, I thought this to be as good a place as any to remain."

Alice headed for the door. "I'll be right back to help you dress and arrange your hair."

She was gone before Marty could say another word. Walking to the window, Marty could see that it was snowing. In fact, it had apparently been snowing for some time because the grounds were covered in a blanket of white. The snow cheered her, somehow, and she couldn't help but touch her hand to the frosty glass and smile. What a difference from her home in Texas.

Alice returned in short order and went into the dressing room. Marty followed after a moment and found the seventeen-year-old busy arranging hairpins on the vanity. She looked up and pointed to the brass rail, where Marty noted her dark blue gown was ready to be donned.

"I'll be glad when Mrs. Davies gets me some additional petticoats. I have a feeling I won't be very warm in this today."

"I'll keep the fire built up in your room, if you'd like," Alice said, helping Marty to disrobe.

"That's probably a good idea. I have no plans to leave the house. It doesn't even look safe to do so."

"The roads do get very slick at times. Sometimes there are accidents with the carriages."

Marty slipped into a shift and allowed Alice to help her with the corset. "I'm sure people take a great many falls, as well. I remember once in Texas when I lost my footing on an icy path."

"I've never been to Texas," Alice commented. "Is it pretty there?"

"Not to my way of thinking. I was glad to leave it. It's mostly range and farmland, with some of the hottest temperatures you could ever want. The summer days feel damp, even when a drought has split the dusty earth."

"How can that be?"

"The air blows in from the Gulf. It combines with the heat, making you feel as though you're being steamed alive."

Alice continued to dress Marty. "Denver can get very hot in the summer, but it doesn't feel like that. It's hot and dry here. Sometimes the sun just feels like it's sitting right over your shoulder. My skin burns if I'm not careful."

She did up the back of the gown and moved to the vanity. "Shall I do your hair now, or would you rather attend to your stockings and shoes?"

"Let's do the hair," Marty said, pulling the ribbon from her long blond braid.

Alice picked up the brush as Marty took a seat at the vanity. Once settled, Marty gave herself over to Alice's gentle care. For someone who'd never trained as a lady's maid, she certainly managed Marty's needs well.

"Alice, when I interviewed you for this position, you said you were alone in the world. Might I ask about your mother?"

"She died a few years ago—my younger brother, too."

"How did it happen?"

"My father said they died in an epidemic."

"Your father said?" Marty questioned. "Were they not with you when they passed?"

"No."

Marty saw Alice's reflection in the vanity mirror. She looked sad, and yet there was something else. For a moment neither woman said a word.

I've overstepped my bounds. I should never have brought up the subject. Marty immediately tried to think of a way to change the topic of conversation.

"My mother died when I was born," Marty offered, not

really knowing why. "My sister, Hannah, helped my father raise me and my brother, Andy. He's a little older than me. Hannah's the only mother I ever knew. Then our father died when I was just five. I never mentioned this before, but like your father—mine was murdered."

Alice stopped in her preparations and met Marty's eyes in the mirror's reflection. "Truly?"

Marty nodded. "Yes, he had a business partner who was a very bad man. That man arranged to have my father killed. Though I was young, I keenly felt his loss."

"My father was my whole world." Alice began arranging Marty's hair once again. "I didn't really have any other people in my life. Your sister must be so special."

"She is, but why do you say that?"

Alice shrugged. "She could have abandoned you and your brother—put you in an orphanage or given you over to strangers."

The thought of Hannah's sacrifice caused Marty a moment of shame. She had lied to the only person in the world who had gone beyond duty to see Marty cared for and safe. Hannah probably wondered even now how Marty was doing, and Marty had been remiss in her communications.

"That reminds me that I need to write to her. I'm going to need some paper and ink. I can go out and purchase some in the future, but would you mind seeing if Mrs. Landry has some she can spare? After we finish here, of course."

"Certainly." Alice twisted Marty's thick hair atop her head and began pinning it in place. Once she'd finished, she stepped back to assess her work. "It's very simple. Would you prefer I do something more?"

"It's fine. As I said, I don't intend to go out today. Besides,

I seldom wore it much different in Texas. I often just braided it down the back and pinned it on my head. That usually kept all the wild strands in place."

"You won't be allowed to be so simple once Mrs. Morgan gets ahold of you. At least that's what Mrs. Landry says." Alice put her hand to her mouth. It was clear she hadn't meant to speak that information aloud.

"It's all right, Alice. As I've said before, I want you to feel free to say what you think needs saying. I want us to be friends."

Alice relaxed. "I know, but I need this job. Mrs. Landry says that familiarity breeds contempt."

"Well, she's not the first one to say that, nor will she be the last. Familiarity can also encourage love and trust. So I am going to keep my sights on those types of things."

Alice smiled, and Marty glanced again at the scar on her face. The poor girl had suffered so much. The loss of her mother, her father's murder, her own injury . . . they were terrible burdens to carry. Still, the young woman maintained a sweet and gentle spirit.

"Thank you for being honest with me, Alice. Honesty doesn't come easy—I know."

★

By late afternoon Marty had still seen nothing of Jake. Brighton had told her that Jake had gone out early that morning and hadn't left word as to when he'd return. Mrs. Landry berated the man for not having more information to give and the two launched into one of their debates on Brighton's responsibilities as he knew them versus what Mrs. Landry presumed them to be. Marty took that moment to escape and explore the house a bit more.

Finding herself at the kitchen, Marty looked around for some sign of Mrs. Standish or Willa. Neither seemed in residence, but then Marty caught the sound of voices coming from just off the far right of the room. Investigation proved that this was the pantry, and Mrs. Standish and Willa were busily taking inventory.

"Oh, Mrs. Wythe, ma'am. Did you need something?" Mrs. Standish questioned.

"No, I'm sorry for the interruption. I was just doing a bit of looking around. I hope you don't mind."

"Not at all, ma'am." Mrs. Standish looked most uncomfortable.

Marty gave her a smile. "I know sometimes women tend to be very possessive of their kitchens."

This caused the older woman to smile in return. "I am at that, but I don't imagine you'll take up a skillet and start in."

"You might be surprised. I did all my own cooking in Texas."

"Well, you aren't in Texas anymore," Mrs. Standish replied. "We'll have none of that here. You're a fine lady with an important husband. Folks will be looking to you for an example."

Marty frowned and nodded. Why was it that this luxury and opulence was starting to feel more like a ball and chain? She'd never wanted to be seen as a standard for others, and the thought made her feel most uncomfortable.

She made her way to the back door, and only then did she notice how deep the snow had gotten. She'd had no idea it could accumulate so fast. They certainly had never seen snow like this in Texas—at least not in her part of Texas.

Fascination drew Marty from the safety and warmth of the house into the outdoor celebration of winter. Without proper boots on her feet or a coat to ward off the cold, Marty immediately felt the chilled dampness. Even so, this didn't stop her moving out into the yard. She marveled like a child at the snow coming down around her. Never in her life had she seen such a wondrous thing. Reaching up, Marty caught multiple flakes. She laughed and kicked one foot at the white blanket. The snow felt wet and heavy.

Whirling around and around, Marty couldn't help but cast her worries to the wind and enjoy the simplicity of the moment. For the first time since coming to Colorado, she felt carefree and happy—truly happy. She closed her eyes and lifted her face to the sky. The wet snowflakes fell against her skin. Without warning, a large amount of snow hit her arm.

Marty's eyes snapped open, and she found a grinning Jake reaching down to scoop up a handful of snow. Without taking much time at all, he formed it in a ball and lightly tossed it at her shoulder. She ducked and by the time she rose up, he was already forming another.

"I don't imagine you've ever had a snowball fight, have you?" he said in a teasing tone.

"I haven't. But I must say it does get one's blood up." She reached down and pulled a handful of snow into her fist. She flung it at Jake as his third snowball met the target of her hip.

He easily sidestepped her attempt and laughed. "You need practice, Mrs. Wythe, and a lot of it if you're going to hit your mark."

"If you'll recall," Marty said, hurrying to form another snowball, "I'm a pretty fair shot. At least enough of one to scare off bandits."

He laughed again. "But you weren't throwing snowballs at them."

"I'm sure to get the hang of this, as well." She tossed the missile and this time hit his leg. "See, what did I tell you?"

Jake reached down with both hands and formed a massive ball. Then to Marty's surprise, he lifted it and came running in her direction. Uncertain what to do, she froze in place until he was nearly upon her. Only then did her senses return and she began to run, slipping and sliding on the snow-covered ground.

Jake's chuckles filled the air. It was a magical moment, and Marty found herself laughing with delight. This was the Jake she enjoyed, the man she was glad to have married.

"You can't outrun me," he called, gaining on her.

"Oh, you think not? I have an older brother, and you should probably compare notes with him. Dress or no dress, I can move pretty fast when I need to." Just then, however, the wet snow seemed to take hold of her and Marty lost her footing. She fell face-first into the cold white depths.

"Marty!"

Jake sounded terrified, while Marty laughed so hard it must have sounded for all the world as if she were sobbing. He came to her and lifted her in his arms. "I'm so sorry. Are you hurt?"

She tried to sober and answer his question, but the moment got the best of her and laughter spilled from her like water over a falls. Seeing that she was all right, Jake joined in her delight and carried her back to the house.

"You're soaked to the skin and will be half dead by night if you don't get into a hot bath." Jake hurried up the back stairs and into the house, much to Mrs. Standish and Willa's surprise.

"Mr. Wythe! Mrs. Wythe! Whatever happened?"

This only caused Marty to laugh all the harder. Jake carefully lowered her feet to the floor, but the water-soaked skirt acted against her and, combined with her shaky legs, Marty's knees buckled. Jake caught hold of her and hoisted her into his arms again.

"Willa, have Mrs. Landry see to it that Alice gets a hot bath arranged for Mrs. Wythe. Mrs. Standish, we'll need something warm to drink. I believe Mrs. Wythe is quite overcome by her introduction to Colorado winter weather." He gave Marty a wink. "I shall play the hero and carry her to safety."

Marty felt her heart skip a beat at the gleam in Jake's eyes. She was beginning to wonder if safety around this handsome man would continue to be possible. Apparently bandits robbing stagecoaches weren't the only perils of which she should be aware.

Chapter 9

Jake's mood lightened considerably after their snowy encounter, and Marty stopped worrying about whether she'd made a mistake in coming to Denver. What was done, after all, was done.

There remained a great deal they didn't know about each other, a lot that they would need to learn, but she hoped in time they could at least be good friends. She liked to imagine them growing old together in an amicable friendship. Perhaps they would travel, as Jake had mentioned in one of his letters. Marty found the idea intriguing.

Jake proved an honorable man. He never suggested their marriage be anything more than they had agreed to, his character proven daily in his kindness and generosity to her—and without expecting anything in return. Well, anything other than keeping up appearances. With this in mind, Marty agreed to attend church at Trinity Methodist Church when Jake asked her to do so the Sunday before Valentine's Day.

Truth be told, Marty had no desire to pretend her heart was in it. She had told Jake very frankly that she remained at odds with a God who listened to one person's prayers and seemingly ignored another's, answering in whimsical fashion at His leisure. Jake listened and nodded, not disagreeing. When Marty had concluded her comments, he simply told her to do what she felt best. She was touched that he wouldn't impose church services on his wife—the wife demanded by the bank board, the wife required to meet society's expectations.

It was with this latter thought in mind that Marty finally acquiesced. Part of their marriage agreement was for Marty to fill exactly this role. She had given her word, and if that meant she had to sit through stuffy, meaningless church services to prove to society that she was a proper and fitting wife to Jacob Wythe, then that was what she would do.

Attired in one of her new gowns, a powder-blue worsted-wool suit, and white velvet cloak, Marty felt rather like a princess. The enclosed carriage had been readied with blankets and warming pans so they could ride to the church in complete comfort despite the rather blustery day.

"They certainly do not have weather like this in Texas," Marty marveled. "I've known some cold days, but nothing like this."

"Mr. Morgan tells me it can get much worse," Jake replied. "Last winter was my first here, and it wasn't all that bad. Sure wasn't as cold as this."

"You came here from California, didn't you say?"

He raised his eyes to meet hers. "I did. That's where my folks moved after they sold off our ranch. But my heart's in Texas and always will be—much as I appreciate the beauty of Colorado."

Marty frowned. "What do you mean?"

He seemed to lose himself in thought for a moment. "Well, it's like I've said before—ranching is in my blood. I grew up on a ranch my grandfather started, and I plan to one day return and buy it back or at least buy something nearby. I have my heart set on it. Ya'll can take the boy outta Texas, but ya can't take Texas outta the boy."

His drawl reminded her of his origin. She bristled and tried to stay calm. "You've never mentioned that before."

"I haven't? I thought I wrote to you about that first thing. That was one of the reasons I wanted a Texas bride. I knew she would understand my love for Texas and want to return there one day. It was a particular bonus to me that you'd been a rancher's wife. You already know how to do the job." He grinned.

"But not all women love Texas," Marty dared to say. Jake didn't seem to notice, however.

"It's like I told you a while back, my plans and Mr. Morgan's take two different directions. Mr. Morgan would see me continue to seek social status and civic popularity. At least that's what he says. I'm not sure why he's taken such an interest in me, but I suppose it had something to do with my father's influence and that of his California business cronies. Anyway, he sees me continuing in the business of banking."

"There's nothing wrong with becoming successful in the banking industry."

"No, of course not. Not if that's your calling."

"I see. But it's not your calling?" She got a sickening feeling in the pit of her stomach.

"No. My calling is to return to Texas. I've always known I would. I'm a cattleman. As soon as I have enough money to buy a ranch, that's what I plan to do. I figured I'd made that clear—and I apologize if I didn't." He smiled. "But you're a

Texan, very nearly born and bred. You've known ranching all of your life. You know how it gets in your blood."

"I do, and that's just the problem."

The carriage stopped and Jake appeared completely oblivious to her comment. "Ah, we're here. Now you can see the inside of the church. It's quite amazing."

Marty wanted to stop him—to demand he listen to her and understand that she had no desire to return to Texas. If this was his plan, then they would need to revisit his dream and their marriage of convenience. But instead, she allowed him to help her from the carriage.

Stepping onto the cleared sidewalk, Marty noted what seemed like a hundred carriages lining the street around the church. Gazing upward, she was again taken in by the tall steeple.

"They say it's nearly two hundred feet in height," Jake whispered, as if reading her thoughts. "Can't really see why it needs to be that high. I suppose it's their little tower of Babel," he mused aloud.

"It's beautiful. I've always liked church steeples," Marty said, remembering her childhood. "It always made me think of us somehow reaching up to God."

Other well-dressed people made their way into the church, barely pausing to offer nods. The wind was growing stronger, and no one desired to endure its chill for long. Inside, Marty allowed Jake to lead her into the massive sanctuary. He stopped at a pew about halfway up on the right-hand side and stepped back to allow her admission. The other occupants nodded in greeting and scooted down to make room.

Marty had barely had time to take her place when music

started booming out from the organ. Glorious music filled the air, unlike anything she'd ever known. The entire congregation rose to its feet for song.

Without any prompting, the people began to sing the doxology in perfect pace with the music. Marty knew the words, but had no desire to partake.

"'Praise God from whom all blessings flow.'"

She didn't feel much like offering praise. For all the blessings that God gave, He also took away. Didn't Job even speak to that? She recalled the verse. *The Lord gave, and the Lord hath taken away; blessed be the name of the Lord.*

"'Praise Him all creatures here below.'"

Discomfort crept up her spine. Marty would have exited the row had Jake not blocked her. Coming here was a mistake. She'd not been in a formal service since Thomas died. That was when her anger at God had reached the boiling point. Until now, she'd been fairly good at keeping that rage under control.

"'Praise Him above ye heavenly host.'"

She tried to calm her breathing and silently wished she'd thought to include a fan in her new white velvet purse. *I can do this. I can do this.* She focused on breathing in and out. *Just a little longer.*

"'Praise Father, Son, and Holy Ghost. Amen.'"

The music and singing ended, and from the front of the cathedral a prayer began. Marty bowed her head, not to pray or even out of respect, but mostly because it helped to calm her nerves. Why was this happening? Why had Jake talked about moving back to Texas—to own a ranch, no less?

I own a ranch—a Texas ranch.

It was one of the little facts she'd not shared with her

husband. No doubt if he knew, Jake would insist on throwing off his banking duties to move her back to Texas that very day.

I won't go back.

Jake tugged on her arm, and Marty could see that everyone was now taking their seat. The pastor welcomed the congregants and spoke of how the blessings of God were upon them that day. She ignored his words and tried instead to figure out what she might do to persuade Jake that remaining in Colorado was the better part of wisdom.

Hadn't he mentioned something about the country struggling with certain financial problems? She tried to recall the conversation they'd shared a few nights back. Jake had spoken of several concerns the bank had regarding railroads that were facing receivership. It was the main reason he'd been under so much pressure. She hadn't completely understood the implications of such actions, but it was obviously not good. If the entire country was having trouble related to money, then Texas would be suffering right along with the rest of the states. Not only that, but there were still problems with the lack of predictable water. Her brother-in-law had been concerned about that even when discussing running her cattle with his.

The congregation rose to listen to the Word being read and then the organ boomed out again with a rousing arrangement of "Onward, Christian Soldiers." Everything seemed to vibrate, as if a part of the music itself. Marty glanced around at the vast sanctuary. Jake had told her the church held over a thousand people. The beautiful and intricate woodwork of the interior was unmatched by anything Marty had ever seen. Someone had taken great pains to make this an incredibly beautiful place of worship.

Seated once again, Marty's mind remained on what she should do regarding Jake's desire to own a ranch. She didn't hear anything of the sermon, and when the service was over, Marty was no closer to figuring out what actions she should take.

When at last they were dismissed, several of societies' finer attendees commented in passing that they would be eager to spend time with Marty at the Valentine's ball, but they didn't linger to talk. With the weather colder than ever, most folks were happy to move on. For this, Marty was truly thankful.

Jake helped her into the carriage, then settled down beside her. "We might as well try to stay warm together," he said, throwing a blanket over their legs. "Sure don't get this cold in Texas."

"I heard talk that the water shortages in Texas are worsening," she blurted without thinking.

"It'll never be as bad as when my father up and sold our ranch. It took me a long while before I could forgive him for that."

"I suppose it would be hard to lose your home."

Jake shifted his weight. "It wasn't just my home. That ranch had been owned by my grandfather and father. It was my birthright—and my father sold it. If he'd just held on a little longer, we . . . Well . . . he didn't hold on, and now I'm here."

"But you seem well suited to banking."

"The ranch was always what I loved most. It was the reason I went off to college in the first place. I wanted to learn more about the business side of things and about any new methods to make the ranch more profitable. Banking was never in my plans." He sounded almost disgusted. "I just happen to be really good with numbers."

"That's a very valuable skill," Marty pressed. She hadn't meant to get him dwelling on the past and all that he'd lost— she'd only wanted to remind him of how difficult things were in that ghastly place.

"Might be, but it doesn't hold my interest like ranching does."

"My brother-in-law owns a ranch, and they aren't doing all that well," she lied. "The drought ruined a lot of water sources, and they are still struggling to get enough water for the cattle. And I don't need to tell you that the price for cattle has gone down considerably. It's a hard time for everyone, but especially folks in ranching. That's one of the reasons I was anxious to answer your advertisement for a wife."

"Agriculture is suffering, too," Jake agreed. "I was just reading that the price is bottoming out for cotton. But these things do tend to cycle around."

"I know you've voiced concerns for the economy and the railroads folding. I think you should count yourself fortunate to have a solid position at the bank." *Please let him see the truth in what I'm saying.* Marty wasn't at all sure to whom she was speaking, but she wished with all her heart it might be so.

Jake looked away and nodded. "I suppose I am. What was it that the pastor said this morning in his sermon . . . about wisdom?" He shook his head. "Something about God giving it if you ask."

Marty hadn't heard the sermon, but she had been well schooled in the Scriptures. "It's from James. It tells us that if we lack wisdom, we should ask for it from God because He gives it liberally."

Jake smiled. "Yes. Yes, that was it. I suppose I should just ask for wisdom about my situation and seek God's direction. I haven't done a whole lot of that, though I know it's what's right."

Marty couldn't hide her frown fast enough, and Jake's brow rose in question. "You seem to be angry at God. Why? I know you said you weren't much for church or religion, yet you know the Scriptures."

"I suppose I'm angry at God because I believe Him unjust and unfair. The Word talks about how He sends the rain where He will. He loves whom He will. He saves one life and lets another die—and very often the innocent suffer."

"But that's not all there is to God. Why would you focus only on that? I mean, I'm not a deeply spiritual man, but I do revere the Lord."

Marty didn't wish to get into a discussion of religion. "My first husband was a God-fearing man. He read the Bible and worshiped God in his heart and in the church. But God didn't save him from being gored to death by a riled-up longhorn. I'm sure you could offer something similar about your first wife. Do you not ever wonder why such a loss was visited upon you at such a young age? The Bible says that God is love, but I see nothing loving in allowing such sorrow and pain."

Jake frowned, and Marty feared that she'd touched a nerve. She'd never discussed his first wife with him prior to this. He'd shared very little regarding the first Mrs. Wythe in his letters. And, because he was new to Denver, she couldn't even question the household staff about the woman. None of them had ever met her.

After several minutes of silence, Marty apologized. "I'm sorry. I often speak my mind without thinking of where it will take me. I shouldn't have expressed my feelings in such a bold way."

"Of course you should have," Jake replied. "I want there to be honesty between us. I've been deceived in the past, and I don't like it. I'd prefer we always be truthful with each other. Don't you think that's best?"

Marty swallowed her guilt. "I do," she lied again. "I think honesty is always best."

"Well then, let me just say that my marriage was not a happy one. Not like yours. My wife was only interested in the next sparkly thing. I guess that's why I'm pleased with your reserve. That's why I wanted a Lone Star bride," he said, seeming to forget she was even there. "Josephine didn't love me. She loved what she thought I could give her. I was ten kinds of fool. Even her folks were embarrassed by her attitude . . . and actions."

"I'm sorry." Marty looked at him, but he continued staring at the carriage top.

"She found someone else and ran off not long after we married. I didn't know where she'd gone, but a part of me was glad to have her gone. She made me so miserable with her nagging about wanting a bigger house in a better neighborhood." He gave a harsh laugh. "She would have given her buttons and bows to be in your place."

Jake finally seemed to realize he was rambling. "I didn't mean to go on like that."

"It's all right. I want to know about you," Marty admitted.

"Well, now you do."

"Where did she go? Did she come back?"

He shook his head. "She ran off with another fella, and then got herself sick in South America. South America of all places! Who even wants to go there?" He shrugged. "She caught some disease, and it killed her. A priest sent us a letter and her things. Her mother cried for weeks on end and very nearly ended up dead herself. Me, I was . . ." He let the words fade. "Never mind. We're home, I see, and Mrs. Standish promised us a wonderful Sunday dinner."

Marty said nothing, but nodded. She couldn't help but wonder what Jake might have said. Perhaps one day he would tell her.

★

Later that evening as Alice helped her ready for bed, Marty remembered her words to Jake and stuffed down an overwhelming urge to seek him out and confess.

It won't do any good to tell him that I own a ranch. I'm not willing to move back to it, and it would only be a source of argument between us.

"Better to leave it be," she murmured.

"What did you say, ma'am?" Alice asked.

Marty suppressed a yawn. "Oh, nothing of importance." Alice finished braiding Marty's hair and secured it with a ribbon. Rising, Marty gave the girl a smile. "Thank you. You've proven yourself quite capable these last few days, and I couldn't be more pleased."

"Thank you," Alice replied. "I know you took a big chance in hiring me."

"We all need a big chance now and then. I don't understand why the bank didn't compensate you somehow for your loss—especially since your father was in their employ and it was their goods that attracted the attention of thieves. But in a way, they are providing now, since Mr. Wythe also works for

Mr. Morgan doing your father's old job. It's Morgan money that pays your salary."

Alice nodded. "I thought of that after I learned about Mr. Wythe's position. God knew exactly where to bring me."

Marty found the girl's comment strange. "Why do you say that?"

"I was in need, and the future looked grim. I didn't see a way out or a hope for making things work. I was broken in spirit, and I wasn't in very good shape—even physically—for several months. Though friends were helping, I knew that soon I'd have to take care of myself. And frankly, as I told God one morning, I wasn't at all prepared to do the job." She smiled. "God knew I was speaking the truth, so He put you in my life. Now you and Mrs. Landry take care of me, and so I am safe once again."

Marty didn't want to discredit the girl's faith, so she only nodded and started for her bed. Alice's next words, however, caused her a great deal of discomfort. "God always knows best. He knows just what we need—even before we know it. He's always making provision for us."

Like He did when Thomas got killed? Like He did when your father and mine were attacked and murdered?

"And don't forget to write to your sister, ma'am. Mrs. Landry put some fine stationery on your desk, and there are several choices of pens and ink. She wasn't sure what you preferred."

Marty glanced across the room to her sitting area. "Thank you. I suppose I should write that letter first thing tomorrow."

Alice nodded and made her way from the room. Marty settled into bed, wondering if she'd be able to find any peace for her soul. The lies she had told and the truth she had concealed rose up to accuse her. Jake wanted honesty between them, but Marty couldn't give that.

She glanced in the darkness toward the connecting door to her dressing room. She could easily cross through to knock on Jake's door. The thought of trying to explain left her without courage, however.

"I can't tell him the truth," she whispered in the dark. "I can never tell him the truth."

Chapter 10

The Valentine's party at the Morgans' residence was unlike anything Marty had ever attended. Even during her time in Georgia while attending finishing school, she had never seen such evidence of wealth. There were at least twenty servants moving in a carefully choreographed dance as they went about their duties. Most were men dressed in smart black suits and white gloves, while a few were women in fashionable black dresses and white aprons. It seemed that the women, however, disappeared with the announcement of the first guests, while the men remained to take outer garments, direct guests to the receiving line, and offer any other needed assistance.

Overhead, massive crystal chandeliers spilled light upon the visitors. Marty thought the crystals sparkled like diamonds and even wondered if, given the Morgan wealth, they weren't exactly that.

Mrs. Morgan greeted Marty with practiced charm, expressing her utter delight to introduce Martha Wythe to society. "I seldom invest my time in these matters," Mrs. Morgan told her in confidence, "but my husband expressed his desire for young Wythe to be well received." She smiled in a knowing manner. "And that, of course, demands that his wife be." She assessed Marty from head to toe. "I can tell we shall be good company for each other."

Uncertain how to respond, Marty simply offered her thanks. Mrs. Morgan didn't seem at all concerned with her silence. Perhaps this was expected. Marty allowed the older woman to position her in the receiving line and make suggestions for how to greet the arriving public.

"What . . . what should I do?" Marty asked in a hushed whisper.

"It's best to keep your comments to a minimum," Mrs. Morgan advised. "I shall conduct the introductions, and you follow my lead."

Marty wanted to laugh. No doubt she feared that Marty and Jake would make unforgivable social mistakes. However, Marty was happy to limit her replies. Most of the people, particularly the women, seemed far more interested in Mrs. Morgan and what she thought of their expensive new gowns.

"Mrs. Keystone, this is Mrs. Jacob Wythe. She and Mr. Wythe were recently married, as I'm sure you will remember."

The pinch-faced woman eyed Marty carefully. "Mrs. Wythe, I've heard . . . about you."

Marty wasn't at all sure if that was a good or a bad thing. "Mrs. Keystone, I've looked forward to meeting you."

The woman nodded and turned her attention back to Imogene Morgan. "Mr. Keystone is unforgivably late, but plans to join us for dinner. He was delayed with some sort of business matter."

"Our men must attend to duty," Mrs. Morgan replied. She dismissed Mrs. Keystone by looking to the next couple in line. "Governor and Mrs. Cooper, this is Mrs. Jacob Wythe."

"Oh, Mrs. Morgan, you should remember I'm no longer the governor," Mr. Cooper responded, giving Marty a half bow. Mrs. Cooper smiled rather uncomfortably and bobbed her head in acknowledgment. Marty did likewise and remained silent, since no one had really spoken to her.

"I want to thank you for joining us tonight." Mrs. Morgan reached out to touch Mrs. Cooper's arm. "I know that you've had a very busy schedule."

"Oh, but I wouldn't miss your Valentine's ball for all of the world. I simply couldn't. I so look forward to this event, and just look at your beautiful gown."

Mrs. Morgan touched the edge of the flowing gold-toned fabric that fell from either shoulder to the ground. "Isn't it marvelous? Mr. Worth's creation."

"But of course," Mrs. Cooper replied, touching the bodice of her own lavender gown.

Mrs. Morgan smiled knowingly. "I recognized his work immediately. I must say that color goes well with your complexion."

Marty tried not to appear bored at the banter. She thought back to times when Hannah and Will had entertained some of the area's wealthier ranchers and their wives. There had been social circles in Texas, but life had a way of being less pretentious. Maybe it was because folks there knew they often depended on one another for their very lives.

The receiving line went on and on until Marty thought she might very well scream in exasperation of the façade of pleasantries. When dinner was finally served, Marty found herself sandwiched between Mr. Cooper and a Mr. Sheedy. And while both were amicable enough, she longed for Jake's company. The men offered pleasantries, asking how she liked

Denver and her new home. Sheedy spoke about some of the houses being built nearby, and Cooper added his thoughts on the growing city. It wasn't until Mr. Cooper leaned close to comment on her unusual arrival to the city, however, that Marty grew uncomfortable.

"I must say, I thought you would be a much fiercer-looking woman." He smiled. "When I read of your heroics in the paper, they made you sound larger than life."

Marty paled. "They wrote about me in the paper?"

"Oh, surely Mr. Wythe showed you the article. He said, of course, that the drawing looked nothing like you. I can see that for myself now. You are a delicate and beautiful woman, and I don't say that lightly. Sweet talk has never been my style."

She glanced around the table to where Mr. Cooper's wife sat laughing at something the man to her left had said. Marty swallowed hard and met Mr. Cooper's gaze. "Thank you, I think."

He chuckled. "I merely stated the obvious. You hardly seem capable of handling a two-team carriage, much less six large stage horses."

Marty smiled finally. "I grew up on a ranch in Texas. I know very well how to handle horses—cattle too. Does that also shock you?"

Cooper shook his head. "No, Mrs. Wythe, I'm beginning to think you could say most anything, and it wouldn't surprise me in the least. You are quite a woman."

"What was that, Cooper?" This came from a man opposite the table. Marty struggled to remember who the man was, but she couldn't place a name with the face.

"I was merely commenting on our heroine, Mrs. Wythe. Many of you may not realize it, but this elegant young woman is the one and same Mrs. Olson who saved the stagecoach a few weeks ago."

There were several gasps from the women; obviously they found Marty's exploits to be unacceptable table conversation. Some women looked away, as if Marty's actions were vile and unmentionable, while others merely frowned. It was apparent that everyone knew only too well about the incident. Most of the men seemed quite supportive, however—most were nodding their heads and offering her a smile.

"Is it true that you singlehandedly foiled the stagecoach robbery?" a man at the far end of the table asked.

"Did you really handle two pistols at once?" someone else asked. It was as if a dam had burst. Questions came at her from every direction.

Marty looked to Jake, who appeared as uncomfortable as she felt. He pulled on his collar and stared at his plate. Marty didn't know what to think or say, but the entire party awaited her response.

"I . . . I should say . . . no. I was only one passenger among many, and I had only one revolver. The driver and his associate were the heroes of the day." She fell silent, hoping she hadn't caused problems for Jake. Goodness, why hadn't he shown her the article in the paper? At least then she could have been ready for this.

"Well, I heard that the driver and his man were shot nearly to death," Mr. Morgan threw out.

Mrs. Morgan and her friends seemed appalled at the reference. She hushed her husband with a look. He shrugged. "I beg your forgiveness, ladies. I did not mean to be crude."

Marty would have laughed had the situation not been so important to her husband. So instead, she bolstered her courage. Amidst the fine china, silver, and crystal, she was the odd wooden bowl accidentally left in plain sight.

"I'm afraid it all happened quite fast. The men were wounded and because of that, someone had to get them to safety," Marty finally replied. "I did what anyone would have done."

"Few women would have known how to drive a team of stage horses," one of the men commented.

"Perhaps that's true, but I grew up on a ranch in Texas. We often found it necessary to learn . . . irregular duties."

"However could you manage climbing up that monstrous contraption?" Mrs. Cooper questioned. "I haven't ridden a stage in years, but I know them to be quite large."

Marty nodded. "It wasn't easy. It took all the strength I could muster. Even so, I'm just happy to know that my efforts helped those men."

"I should say so. The paper," Mr. Morgan said in a voice that suggested his approval, "said that if it were not for Mrs. Olson . . . pardon me, ma'am, *Mrs. Wythe's* actions, those men would have died and the stage occupants would have been left to the mercy of the bandits, who might have returned to the scene. Mrs. Wythe deserves our congratulations and admiration."

Mrs. Morgan agreed. "She does, indeed. She's a heroine, and we are glad to have her among us."

There was a great deal of murmuring and nodding. Marty offered them a smile. If the Morgans said she was a heroine, then these people were happy to conclude nothing less. The opinion of the Morgans mattered more than the shocking actions Marty had given the city to talk about.

After that, no one seemed inclined to comment, and the

guests returned to more private discussions. Marty found herself engaged in conversation again with Mr. Sheedy and Mr. Cooper. Sheedy, it seemed, had once been a rancher himself. Now, however, he was vice-president of the Colorado National Bank.

"Of course, I made my fortune in cattle and mining. Good money in ranching if you have the right people involved."

Marty nodded but said nothing. She was relieved when someone else spoke to Sheedy and drew his attention from her. Focusing on her plate—a beautiful gold-edged bone china—Marty toyed with her food.

"Do you not care for the fish?" Mr. Cooper asked.

Marty shook her head. "It's not that. With the excitement and all, I find that I'm not very hungry."

"These parties can be quite exhausting, so it's best to keep up one's strength—especially since there is to be dancing."

Course after course was served, and Marty did her best to nibble a little of each offering. She was momentarily relieved when the women were excused to ready themselves for the ball while the men smoked cigars and enjoyed a good brandy.

Finding herself in a room of strangers, Marty readied herself for the onslaught of questions she feared would come. Mrs. Morgan, however, was good to engage her first. She complimented Marty's gown, which prompted the other women to do so, as well.

"I find Mrs. Davies to be the most capable of seamstresses and designers. She is quick to understand exactly what I'm seeking," the woman introduced as Mrs. Katherine Sheedy commented.

"Personally, I'm spoiled," Mrs. Cooper started. "For formal

occasions, I must have Worth, or I'm completely out of sorts. The man is a positive genius of design. I believe his creations only get better each year."

"Oh, I agree wholeheartedly," Mrs. Morgan answered. "I daresay there will never be another designer quite so talented. It will be a sad day indeed when we lose Mr. Worth."

A rather mousy but opulently jeweled woman interjected, "He surely must have a great many students learning from his creative talents. It wouldn't be right to lose such insight—such vision."

"They can learn to emulate the man's designs," Mrs. Morgan replied, "but when Charles Worth dies, he will no doubt take his biggest secrets with him to the grave."

"Such a disparaging conversation," Mrs. Cooper said, *tsk*-ing her disapproval. "We are here to welcome Mrs. Wythe."

"Indeed we are." Mrs. Morgan stepped closer to Marty. "I believe we will all enjoy getting to know you better in the months to come."

Marty wasn't entirely sure that she could offer the same comment and so merely gave her thanks.

The women contented themselves with allowing maids to retouch their hair and help them into ornate gloves for the ball. Marty was assisted by a very plain young woman who knew her duty well. She had Marty fitted and buttoned in no time at all.

The beautiful gloves now gracing her hands were quite foreign to Marty. She had owned riding gloves most of her life, and in finishing school she had learned the requirements of wearing gloves for various occasions. Back on her ranch, though, gloves were used for work, and there were very few times she donned them for special occasions. Especially after she stopped going to church. However, her trip to Colorado had changed all of that. Now gloves were almost her constant companions—so much so, in fact, that she gave serious thought to giving them names. She looked around the room at all of the elegant pairs and couldn't help but smile at the thought of them each having names. What would the social etiquette be for introducing one's gloves?

She suppressed a girlish giggle at the thought and tried instead to focus on the conversation directed at her.

"I visited Texas once," Mrs. Keystone said. "I didn't appreciate the climate."

Marty nodded. "Many people don't."

"I also didn't appreciate the insects. You would think they could do something about that."

She wasn't entirely sure what the woman expected, but not wanting to make trouble, Marty only nodded again.

"I saw Texas as a dry and desolate place." Mrs. Cooper shook her head. "Mr. Cooper found it necessary to journey there several years ago, and I accompanied him. I was most miserable. The people were some of the strangest I've ever met." She looked at Marty. "At least your accent is tolerable."

Marty started to take offense at the remark. It was one thing that Marty found Texas an abominable place, but that this woman should insult the people was another matter. Mrs. Morgan spoke up just then, however, and Marty had no chance to interject her thoughts.

"It is time. Let us meet our men for the ball."

———————————— ★ ————————————

Jake smiled at Marty from across the room. The evening was nearly over, and soon they would return to their home and the imposed pretense of the evening would be behind them. So far, no one seemed the wiser about their arrangement.

Retrieving a glass of punch for his wife, Jake was joined by Mr. Sheedy.

"Wythe, I was delighted to converse with your missus over supper. She's a smart one."

"She is indeed, and beautiful," Jake said without the slightest hesitation.

"You did well for yourself. I understand she hails from a ranching background. I was heavily involved in cattle at one time. Hard work, but it can pay off."

"Marty grew up ranching—it's in her blood. Her sister and brother-in-law still have the spread where she spent most of her life. I look forward to seeing it one day."

Sheedy took a glass of punch offered by the servant and nodded. "I don't imagine that will be very soon, however. Times are difficult, to say the least."

"Yes, sir, they are. However, I believe we can weather this storm, just like the others that came before. Folks say that things haven't been the same since the war, but our great nation is exploding with growth and development. Those are the very things that will see us through."

"I hope you're right, Mr. Wythe."

Marty joined them at that moment, smiling warmly at Jake. "I hope you don't mind the interruption."

"Not at all, Mrs. Wythe," Sheedy answered before Jake could. "Your husband and I were just discussing your upbringing on the ranch and how he looks forward to one day visiting that very place."

Marty threw Jake a quick glance, looking hesitant to speak. He handed her a glass of punch, and she took a sip before addressing Sheedy. "I only hope there will be a ranch for him to visit. With recent hardships, I think my sister and brother-in-law are considering the possibility that they will need to sell."

This took Jake by surprise. She'd said nothing of the matter up until this time. "I had no idea things were so bad for them. Perhaps I should write to your brother-in-law and offer consultation. I know a great deal about ranching, and perhaps I could offer financial advice."

Marty shook her head rather vehemently. "It would shame him. Please don't mention it."

Sheedy nodded in agreement. "A man has his pride. Better not to step on it and cause more bruising than necessary."

Chapter 11

Fulfilling her social duties proved to be more and more exhausting to Marty. The endless visitations, gatherings, and changing of clothes left her feeling that her days were an utter waste of time, filled with pretentious people.

However, remembering Jake speak of Texas and his desire to one day return there made Marty more determined than ever to establish herself in Denver society. She always tried to receive her guests with the warmest of welcomes and even worked to tame her drawl and emulate the speech of her social peers.

Jake warned her there would be a great many responsibilities on her part, maintaining a presence at the social functions of the Denver elite. Marty would be expected to be seen at the proper events and reveal a knowledge of and interest in such functions in order to better fit into the social circles required for a woman of her position. Marty wanted to limit her participation, but she reconsidered every time she remembered how much Jake wanted to return to Texas. She vowed to herself that society and its façades would become as well known to her as ranching had once been. She would do her best to ingratiate herself with Denver's finest and prove to Jake that they belonged right where they were.

A little over a week after the Valentine's ball, Marty had attended yet another party celebrating George Washington's birthday. This one was hosted by the Sheedys and allowed Marty to see the interior of their elegant home. The house was palatial in size and was said to be a blend of Queen Anne and Richardsonian Romanesque architecture—although Marty wasn't entirely sure what that actually meant. The home had been completed just the year before, however, and was rumored to be one of the grandest in America.

As she had other events, Marty had endured that party rather than enjoyed it. Marty had found the house and its décor far more interesting than the people visiting it. The food, rich and overly abundant, had been delicious, but not to Marty's liking. It was only then that she realized just how much she preferred common things.

She awoke the next morning remembering the party and the unusual offering of multiple desserts. The dishes were lavish and presented in such a manner that they looked far more like pieces of art than dishes to eat. She sighed.

"I'd much rather have one of Hannah's good pies than whatever those concoctions were supposed to be."

Allowing Alice to guide her through the morning routine, Marty suppressed a yawn and wondered what was on her day's agenda. Alice was talking about something, but Marty didn't have any idea what the girl was saying. Already tired, Marty wished she could simply crawl back into bed.

She felt the same way much later in the day, when Alice helped her change clothes for the fourth time. Marty slipped into a stunning bodice that matched the skirt of green and blue tartan flannel. The simple cut of the skirt allowed her to wear a collapsible bustle, which would make it easy for Marty to spend time at her desk writing letters.

"I like the way the bodice lays," she commented as Alice did up the back buttons. The pleating was stitched into place with a rounded yoke trimmed in dark blue braid and a high lace neck.

"You look very pretty in it, ma'am," Alice replied. She secured a dark blue sash around Marty's small waist. "But you look lovely in most everything."

Marty could hear the longing in the girl's voice. "Alice, you are a very attractive woman yourself. That scar on your face does not take away from your sweet nature and spirit. The right man will come along one day and the scar will mean nothing to him."

"I pray that might be so," Alice admitted. She began to rearrange Marty's hair in a more intricate design. Taking up a curling iron, she carefully arranged some of the blond tresses around the rod. "As the pastor said at church just a few Sundays back, God isn't in the business of doing things without them having a purpose that will lead to His glory."

"Well, I don't know about that." Marty generally kept her religious thoughts to herself, but with Alice she felt she could be honest. "I've seen plenty of bad that has happened without any glory to God. There's a lot of suffering in this world. I find God cruel for not stopping it . . . or at best, insensitive to our pain."

"I beg to differ," Alice said, surprising Marty with her bold stand. "There will always be cruel and insensitive people, but those are not qualities that can be assigned to God. The Bible says that God is love. Love is never insensitive or cruel, so therefore I cannot believe God capable of such . . . human attributes."

Marty considered the younger woman's words. There was a time when she had accepted such thoughts herself. "So you believe God had you attacked and injured for His glory, and it wasn't an act of cruelty?"

Alice arranged a curl and pinned it in place before responding. "I don't think God had me attacked at all. I think the men who attacked me didn't much care what God wanted."

"But God could have prevented the entire situation."

"He could have," Alice agreed. "He could have done any number of things. And while I believe God did allow this to happen to me, I don't think it was His desire. I don't think He took any delight in the occurrence."

"Then why didn't He intervene to stop it? The Bible talks about how Jesus and the Spirit both intercede for us. Why not intercede to prevent an evil man from harming an innocent one?"

"Shall we receive good at the hand of God, and not receive evil?" Alice countered.

Marty studied Alice in the mirror. The younger woman seemed quite content in her beliefs and not at all shaken by Marty's questioning. "Isn't that Job?"

Alice nodded and continued to pin another curl. "It is Job. Second chapter, tenth verse. Job is suffering, and his wife wants him to curse God and die. That's how he answers her. To my way of thinking, evil will always be with us because of the sin of Adam. The world is not a perfect place."

"So your injury was just one of those things that happened because the world isn't perfect? Doesn't that alleviate God's responsibility in the matter?"

"And what would God's responsibility have been?" she asked.

"To keep you from harm. To save you."

"But He did save me, Mrs. Wythe. I very nearly died from loss of blood and then an infection."

Marty shook her head, causing Alice to jab a hairpin against her head. "Oh my. I apologize, ma'am."

"No, it was my own fault. I moved."

Alice gave a brief nod before her face lit up in a smile. "I suppose you could say that it was my fault or my father's for putting me in a position of danger. God didn't force us to go out that dark night. In fact, my father had commented that it wasn't a wise idea. However, he wanted to take care of business that evening. I decided to accompany him, even though he had suggested it would be better for me to remain home. So who is at fault?"

Marty was glad that the girl had gotten comfortable enough to debate such matters. "But my point is that if God truly is love, He would intervene and keep such bad things from happening to the innocent."

"Why?"

Marty turned and looked up at Alice. "Why? You ask why God should keep the innocent from harm?"

"Yes. He didn't keep Jesus from harm, and Jesus was completely innocent. He was beaten and spat upon and crucified. Does that mean God didn't love Him? Jesus is a part of God—how could He not love himself?"

Marty frowned as she considered the young woman's words. "You don't think that God . . . well . . . that He should keep the innocent from harm?"

Alice shrugged and moved toward the dressing room

window. "If you are suggesting that God somehow owes it to us, then no. I think God has given us a great many blessings beyond what we deserve and yet has withheld a great deal of the punishment we *do* deserve." Her words resonated with conviction, something Marty had not yet witnessed in Alice.

The young woman tied back the drapes one at a time. Marty thought her quite delicate in appearance, yet there was a fierceness in the younger woman that she couldn't help but admire—even if Marty couldn't agree with her spiritual reasoning.

"And what about your mother and brother?"

Alice said nothing, simply stared out the window as if contemplating the question. Marty continued. "Do you believe it fair for a child to lose her mother and brother, as you did?"

"There's someone out there." Alice jumped back from the window. "A man. He's sneaking around. I saw him cross from the stable to the yard."

Marty got up and walked to the window. "Where?"

"I'm not sure where he's gone, but he was there just a little bit ago."

It was clear Alice was upset, but Marty couldn't help but wonder if it was just her way of changing the subject so she wouldn't have to answer the question. "I don't see anything."

"I'm certain he was there."

"Did you recognize him? Perhaps it was just Brighton or Samson."

"No." Then Alice's demeanor seemed to change abruptly. She shrugged and went back to the dressing table to straighten up. "Oh, you're probably right. Maybe it was just Mr. Brighton. He probably took something out to Samson."

Just then Mrs. Landry appeared. "Mrs. Wythe, I have the

menus for the rest of this week for you to go over if you have the time."

Marty gave a quick glance toward Alice, who was now humming to herself and setting the vanity to rights. "I suppose it's as good a time as any," Marty said, turning to the housekeeper. "Shall we go to my sitting room?"

Mrs. Landry nodded and held out a large piece of paper. "Feel free to make any changes you wish. You asked me to prepare a menu much like those we'd had in the past, prior to your arrival. This is a typical arrangement."

Marty made her way back to the bedroom sitting area, studying the menu as she went. A wide variety of foods were listed, and while it was nowhere near the opulent affair of which she'd partaken at luncheons and suppers offered by society's finest, she found it appealing.

"I see my husband enjoys steak and ham."

"He does. He's not much for fish recipes."

Marty smiled. "Neither am I. My brother and brother-in-law were both quite fond of fishing and eating their catches, but I can't say I agreed. I'm glad Jake feels the same way."

"You will also note that he isn't much for desserts. However, I'm certain that if you wish to indulge in one each evening, Mr. Wythe would be amenable. He told me that he intended for you to adjust the menu in whatever manner would please you most."

Marty shook her head, amazed to have yet another thing in common with her husband. "I've not been one for them, either. Not that I don't enjoy a sweet now and then, but I hardly find it necessary at each meal." She continued to read the menu. "You haven't listed anything for Friday's supper." She looked to Mrs. Landry for explanation.

"That is the night Mr. Wythe plans to entertain Mr. Morgan and Mr. Keystone. I thought perhaps you would like to plan something special."

"He said nothing to me about this." Marty tried not to feel offended by her husband's omission. "Perhaps we should seek his advice."

"Oh, that wouldn't be proper. I can help you with some choices based on previous occasions, however. Mr. Morgan is fond of pork roast with a heavy sweet sauce. He also enjoys small roasted potatoes in dill, as well as asparagus in hollandaise sauce."

"I see. And will he desire a dessert?" Marty's tone was rather sarcastic. She wasn't sure why the subject matter put her at odds with her housekeeper, but it did.

"He does enjoy chocolate torte. Mrs. Standish has a delicious recipe, and I'm sure she will be happy to create it for the occasion. Other than that, I would suggest a cream of spinach soup and perhaps some fruit and cheese for those who would rather not partake of the torte."

"Whatever you think is best," Marty said, handing the paper back to Mrs. Landry.

The woman nodded and took her leave. Marty cast her gaze toward the writing desk. She still hadn't written to Hannah since arriving in Denver. She knew her sister would be most frantic for news, but she wasn't yet ready to tell her about the marriage. With a sigh, Marty made her way to the desk and took a seat.

"I'll simply tell her about the wonderful time I'm having in Colorado," she decided. Taking pen in hand, Marty consoled herself with the assurance that she needn't tell the entire truth. It seemed a reasonable compromise.

★

Alice Chesterfield pushed aside her fears and tried her best to focus on preparing for bed. The day had been long, and she had spent a good deal of time that evening reading a book given her by Mrs. Landry on how to be a proper lady's maid. Mrs. Landry told her that because Mrs. Wythe so desired Alice in the position, Mrs. Landry felt it important to educate her in her duties.

Gratitude didn't begin to explain Alice's feelings toward the older housekeeper. Mrs. Landry didn't hold it against Alice that she lacked training. Instead, she worked to teach the girl what was needed. Alice appreciated her kindness more than she could say. The employment company had been cruel in their assessment of her, chiding her for coming to them without any experience or references. Alice had tried to explain that up until a few months ago, she and her father had lived quite comfortably on their own. They'd even had a cook. The agency didn't believe her or else didn't care. Instead they had turned her away, suggesting that she get some type of experience working before returning.

If I'd had proper employment in which to gain experience, I wouldn't have needed to seek an agency's help in securing a position.

She carefully hung up the black dress that was her regular uniform. She had a variety of white aprons to protect the body of the dress, and that way she didn't need to wash the garment more than once a week. The Wythes had very generously provided two uniforms for her use, as well as three other dresses. One was a beautiful striped yellow gown for Sundays and the other two were for her time off from work.

But Alice doubted she would be using them anytime soon. She had no desire to leave the house. Especially now.

She cast a furtive glance at the window and shivered in the flannel nightgown she'd just put on. She'd seen a man out there earlier in the day. She knew he'd been there, and she knew that it wasn't Brighton or Samson.

Worried that her past was once again catching up with her, Alice dropped to her knees beside the bed and began to pray.

"Father in heaven, please deliver me from wicked men who seek to harm me. Deliver me from sin and from the temptation to do wrong. Please bolster my heart that I might not fear." She paused and gazed heavenward. "And please let my father know how much I miss him." She started to end her prayer and sighed. "My mother and brother, too. Amen."

She slid beneath the covers, grateful for the warming pan Mrs. Landry had suggested she use. The added warmth helped ease her weary body, and in doing so, Alice was able to put aside her fears and worries.

Sleep overcame her, but Alice's dreams soon turned to nightmares, as they often did. She remembered in detail the events of the night that took her father's life. . . .

She could feel the dampness around her. It had been rainy that night, and cold. Father had been so determined to make his delivery.

"It's critical that I get these papers to the right people. I don't want them to remain in the house overnight," he had told her. "Why don't you stay here at home? It isn't safe to venture out so late."

Father was nervous, but he always seemed so when working for the bank. She often wished he didn't have such an important job, for she knew it placed him in harm's way. She had begged him to leave it, but the money had been too good.

"One of these days we'll move away from Denver," he said as they walked. "We'll go somewhere warm. Somewhere special. A place where you can find yourself a good husband, and perhaps I'll even find a new . . ." He didn't finish his sentence, and Alice wondered if he might have been thinking of remarriage.

Father was never one to speak about such things. He wouldn't even discuss Alice's mother and the good memories . . . but why should he? He and Alice felt the same sense of betrayal.

The hair on her neck bristled at the sight of three men stepping out of the shadows to block their way. The largest one demanded Father's satchel.

"It contains nothing but papers," her father declared. "Now be gone with you."

"Give me the satchel, old man." The stranger moved closer, and Alice's father stepped to one side—away from Alice.

"You can look for yourself." He opened the case. "It's just paper."

"I don't care what it is. Hand it over."

"No." Her father was adamant.

Alice started to move away, thinking she might run for help. Her father's assaulter motioned to his companions, however, and they took hold of her. One man pulled her against him and held her in an iron-like grip, while the other pulled a large knife.

The man who faced her father smiled. It was a heartless and terrifying smile. "I think you'd better do what I say. Otherwise the boys might be inclined to persuade you."

"Don't hurt her!"

The man with the knife grabbed her by the hair and yanked her head back. The knife cut into her flesh without warning.

"Too late, old man. How much I cut her, however, will depend on you."

Alice was too stunned at first to even feel the pain. That moment, however, was short-lived and she cried out. Her father charged at the man in front of him, but the larger brute was able to easily push him aside.

"Here, take it. Take the satchel, but leave my girl alone," Father pleaded.

Her attacker breathed heavily against her face. He smelled of tobacco. "I skinned me a rabbit with this knife earlier today, and now I'm skinnin' me a little gal."

Alice, dizzy with pain, felt blood flow down her face. The warmth seemed strange against the cold night air. The man released her and stepped back as if to assess his handiwork. Alice's father took the opportunity to once again rush his assaulter. This time the man sent him flying backward.

Alice screamed as her father's head made contact with the edge of the brick building. She heard a terrible thud and watched her father crumple into the mud. It was the last thing Alice remembered before fainting.

"Wake up," Mrs. Landry said, shaking Alice by the shoulders. "Wake up, it's just a nightmare."

Alice opened her eyes, blinking against the light. "What . . . what's happened?"

"You were screaming," Mrs. Landry explained. "I came as soon as I could. Goodness, but you gave me a fright. Are you all right?"

Panting for air, Alice struggled to sit up. "I . . . I'm fine. I'm so sorry to have disturbed you."

"It's quite all right, dear. You seemed terribly fearful of something. Would you like to talk about it?"

Alice looked at the disheveled woman. Mrs. Landry's robe was open and her nightcap askew. Obviously the woman had made a mad dash for Alice's room without concern for her own well-being.

"I'm fine, Mrs. Landry. Truly. I was just remembering . . . that night."

"When your father died?"

She nodded. Mrs. Landry sat down beside her on the bed. "I suppose that night will always haunt you, but you can rest assured that God will never leave you or forsake you."

The words offered comfort. "I'm glad that you believe that. Mrs. Wythe doesn't, you know."

Mrs. Landry smiled. "Mrs. Wythe is dealing with her own demons. In time, I believe she'll come around, but we must make a special effort to pray for her. For Mr. Wythe, as well."

Alice agreed. "They both seem to bear heavy burdens."

"They do," Mrs. Landry said. "I don't know exactly what it is that causes them each such pain, but Jesus does . . . and He's the only one who can heal them of their hurt."

"I agree."

"So you'll join me in praying for them?"

"Of course," Alice replied. "I've already been praying for Mrs. Wythe."

Mrs. Landry nodded and got to her feet. "Good. Then we shall both continue in that way and add Mr. Wythe, as well."

Chapter 12

Supper that Friday night proved to be a bigger event than Marty had first anticipated. Word came earlier in the day that several of the board members would accompany Mr. Morgan and Mr. Keystone for the meal so that they might discuss business afterward. Mrs. Landry passed the information on to Mrs. Standish, who seemingly performed the miracle of the loaves and fishes and served a meal fit for a king.

Marty wondered at the audacity of people to just force themselves on an employee and his family in this unannounced manner. For all the rules of social etiquette, it seemed there ought to be one that precluded such impositions.

For a time, all the niceties were observed. Marty listened in relative silence as the men spoke of various happenings in the city.

"They are planning to dig up City Cemetery and relocate it," Mr. Morgan declared. "Plans are already in the works, and families have been asked by the city to cooperate and arrange to move their loved ones."

"Seems kind of odd that they would disturb a cemetery that way. What's the purpose?" Jake asked.

"Progress." This came from Josiah Keystone. "Progress, my boy. That area is prime real estate—much too close to the city and growing neighborhoods. They will move out the graves and expand the park. Some of the land will probably be developed, as well."

"There's really no doubt on that count," another of the men added.

Marty thought it appalling. How would she feel if they came to her with plans to dig up her Thomas's coffin? She would hate it. It would be like reliving his death all over again. She shook her head and decided to change the subject.

"Are you men aware that George Chesterfield, your deceased employee, has a seventeen-year-old daughter?" Marty interjected.

Everyone looked at her for a moment before Mr. Morgan replied. "I suppose I do remember something of that nature. It's been a while now since George passed on. You remember him, don't you, Josiah?"

"Of course I do. He was your bank manager before Mr. Wythe. He was murdered, wasn't he?"

Morgan cut into his roast. "Yes. He was murdered and bank papers were stolen. Caused me no end of grief, I assure you."

Marty despised his calloused response. "They severely wounded the man's daughter. She bears a scar along the right side of her face and will for the rest of her life."

"And how did you come by this knowledge, Mrs. Wythe?" Morgan's tone almost suggested he didn't believe her.

"Because she is my personal maid. Alice is a wonderful girl, but she was completely devastated at the loss of her father—both emotionally and financially. I wondered why the bank hadn't offered her some sort of support or assistance since her father died in the line of duty."

Morgan shrugged. "We can hardly be in the business of compensating every family member who loses someone in my employ. I'm sure relatives must have come alongside her in her hour of need."

"No, there were no other relatives. Her father was the only one she had," Marty replied. "I believe friends who attended church services with Alice provided her some short-term help, but they moved from the area, and the girl was again left with nothing."

"That is a sad story, Mrs. Wythe," one of the board members agreed. "So much violence and loss goes on all around us. In fact, I heard there was to be a new orphanage erected next year because of such sorrows. The girl was most fortunate to obtain employment with you."

Everyone murmured an awkward agreement and continued eating. Marty could see nothing more would be said or done about the matter and fell silent. These men had no idea how difficult Alice's life might have been if she hadn't obtained decent work. Or maybe they did know and simply didn't care.

Marty continued to listen to the discussions about new industry that would soon arrive to make Denver ever more successful. Apparently there were ongoing plans for everything from additional rail lines to a new mint.

"The mint is in desperate disrepair," Keystone told them. "Of course, they don't create coins there, but even for a glorified assay office taking in silver and gold from the local mines, it deserves better and safer quarters."

"I thought coins were minted there," Jake threw out. He hadn't said much that evening, and Marty couldn't help but wonder if this was a calculated move on his part. Jake was a smart man and probably knew well enough to listen much and speak little.

"Coins were only minted there for one year, although some $600,000 worth of gold coins were the result," Morgan explained. "I believe it was during the war, however, and they decided to forgo the expenses involved in continuing that project. We are hopeful that once we get Congress to agree to funds for a new building, they will also see the benefit of expanding operations to include minting coins."

Mr. Keystone hurried to add, "One would contend that with nearly six million in gold and silver passing through those doors, Congress would see the immediate need for better provisions."

The topic continued through dessert. Marty sampled the chocolate torte. It was delicious, but much too sweet. She pushed it aside and instead sipped her creamed coffee and waited for an appropriate time for her to leave.

"I suppose we have bored you with our discussions of civic plans and politics," Mr. Morgan said upon finishing his torte. "I do apologize if we made ourselves poor company."

"Not at all," Marty replied. This was the opening she'd been waiting for. "However, I am rather tired this evening, and if you do not mind, I would like to excuse myself." She got to her feet, and all of the men stood, as well. "Please, gentlemen, take your seats and enjoy your evening. I'm sure we will all meet again very soon."

"Good night, Mrs. Wythe," Mr. Morgan said, with the others following suit.

Jake came to her side with a smile. "Good night, my dear." He pressed a kiss upon her cheek.

Marty made her way upstairs as the men returned to their discussions of banking and the economy. She couldn't help but wonder if she should be more concerned about the state of the country. Earlier during the meal, Mr. Morgan had commented on several banks that might be forced to close. Nothing more was discussed on the subject, however. Surely if these titans were expecting Congress to hand over funding for a new mint, they couldn't be too concerned about local banks folding.

She decided it wasn't worth worrying about, but perhaps she would start reading the newspaper for more information. Maybe it would give her something more to talk about with Jake when they shared evenings together.

Later, after Marty had read for a time in front of her cozy fireplace, Alice helped her into her nightclothes. The beautiful white silk gown slid against Marty's body—a cold kiss against her warm skin. Alice then brought out a majestic white silk wrap. The set had been created with the new bride in mind. The shoulders were overlaid with a wide lace ruffle that cascaded down the right front side of the robe. There were buttons that lined the left side, but Marty waved Alice away from doing these up and chose instead to simply belt the garment closed. She sat at the vanity and toyed with the lace cuffs while Alice unbraided her long blond hair and began brushing it.

"Did I receive any mail today?" Marty asked.

"Not that I'm aware of, ma'am."

"Please, Alice, don't call me ma'am. At least not in private. Here we can just be informal. You call me Marty and I'll call you Alice and we shall be the best of friends."

Alice smiled at her in the mirror. "Mrs. Landry would have kittens."

Marty laughed. "Well, I happen to like cats."

"The book she gave me to read about being a proper lady's maid would also warn against it. Apparently it's a grievous error to allow employees and employers to have anything but a professional relationship."

"Yes, I'm sure that's how society sees it. But in the privacy of my dressing room, I don't see any reason for pretense. When I was growing up, we had a wonderful woman at our house who cooked and helped my sister. They were the best of friends, and she was quite dear to me. Goodness, she even prayed with us and told us stories about her life in Mexico. It never caused any problems, and I'd like to think it could be the same way for us. I want to be able to speak my mind, and I want you to do likewise."

"Truly?" Alice asked, continuing to work the brush.

"Truly. Why do you ask?"

"I just wondered . . . I wondered if you would tell me why you're so angry at God."

The question caught Marty completely off-guard. "I blame Him for not keeping my husband from death." Her answer was out of her mouth before she'd given it any real thought.

"What happened to your husband?"

"He was a rancher, and he had a longhorn bull that had been injured. Thomas nursed the animal back to health and was attempting to check the wound when the bull got spooked and went wild. Thomas was gored by the horns and died a short time later. On Christmas Eve."

"That must have been awful." Alice continued the rhythmic strokes.

"It was."

"And do you have any children?"

"No." Marty hoped that would be the end of it, but Alice wasn't through.

"And you blame God for letting your husband die." It wasn't really a question, but more an observation.

"For letting him die. For letting him get hurt. For letting us both down."

When Alice said nothing, Marty felt compelled to explain further. "You see, I was raised to put my trust in God. I went to church and learned the Scriptures. I knew what was expected of me by God, but I thought I could count on certain things from Him, as well. When that didn't prove true and Thomas died, I lost heart."

"How was it that you couldn't count on God?" Alice asked softly.

Marty shrugged. "I prayed for my husband's safety, and it didn't work. I prayed to have a child, and that didn't come about, either. I prayed for rain for the ranch, and we suffered on with drought. I prayed for so many things over the years, and so many things were denied me. It didn't seem that my faith was worth the effort."

"I'm sorry."

Despite the attack she'd suffered, Alice was still so innocent—naïve, really. Marty could see that she was genuine in her feelings, but it didn't help. In fact, Marty could see no purpose in continuing the discussion.

"Can I ask you something else?"

"Of course," Marty agreed, happy to move the conversation in a different direction.

"Did your husband Thomas hate God, too?"

"Hate God? I don't hate God. I would never do that." Marty turned around abruptly. "Thomas loved God." She smiled at the memory of him puzzling over passages in the Bible. "He used to sit in the evening and read the Bible to me. There would be times when he felt confused by something, and he'd continue to study and ponder it for days. He'd pray for understanding, and after a while he'd tell me he'd gotten some great epiphany." Marty met Alice's gaze. "Why do you think I hate God?"

"Well, I suppose because you're so angry with Him. Anger never seems to hold any love—at least not to my way of thinking. And . . . well, I just thought maybe in the absence of love, that anger had created hate."

"No," Marty said, shaking her head. "It's not created anything. It's left a void."

------------------------★------------------------

Jake was glad that Morgan concluded their business quickly. They had reached quick decisions on several pressing issues and agreed to proceed on Monday and spend no further time that evening on the matter. Jake bid the men good evening.

"Please give our best to Mrs. Wythe," Mr. Morgan said before climbing into his carriage.

"I will," Jake promised.

As he made his way up the grand staircase, the clock struck nine. The chime echoed through the large house and left Jake feeling rather lonely. He felt a sudden desire for Marty's company, and he wondered if she might still be awake.

He entered his bedroom and walked straight to the door that adjoined her dressing room, knocking loudly. The door opened almost immediately, and Alice jumped back in surprise.

"Mr. Wythe!"

Marty quickly stood up from where she was seated at the

154

vanity. Her long blond hair hung loose to her waist—something Jake had never seen before that moment.

"I'm glad to see you're still up. I wondered if we might have a conversation." He looked at Alice with a smile and added, "In private."

"Of course," Marty replied. She moved across the room in a swirl of white, leaving Jake to feel rather breathless at her beauty. The gown was the kind any man might desire his wife to wear.

"Alice, I can see myself to bed. Why don't you go ahead and turn in?"

"Thank you, ma'am," Alice said, giving a little curtsy. She hurried out of the room through the opposite door.

"What did you want to discuss? Should we go and sit in my room?"

"No, this is fine," Jake replied. "I was just curious as to why you brought Alice's situation into the conversation tonight."

"Was that wrong of me?" she asked plainly.

"No. It wasn't a matter of right or wrong. I was just surprised."

Marty shrugged. "I suppose I thought it intolerable that a man should be killed working for another and yet no one saw fit to see after his family. After all, these are men of means."

"That doesn't make them charitable."

"No, I suppose not, but it seems like common sense would place a reasonable obligation at their doorstep. Even on the ranch when a family man was killed or injured, we took care of the family. Even the single men were given proper care, and if they died, we helped arrange the burial and saw to it that their remains and final payment went to their folks."

"That was because you and your family are good people,"

Jake said. "The world, unfortunately, isn't populated with only good people. Many are self-centered and focused solely on what profits them most."

"Like Mr. Morgan and his friends?"

"I suppose so. But don't worry. Alice is welcome to work here as long as she likes. I'll even increase her pay if you tell me to."

Marty smiled, and the warmth of her expression caused Jake to feel weak in the knees. She inspired emotions in him that he had believed long dead. He hadn't expected to have these kind of feelings for . . . his wife.

Jake looked at her for a long moment. She was far more beautiful than he'd allowed himself to realize. The delicate design of her face was like that of a Grecian goddess—at least the statues he'd seen of the same. But instead of cold marble, Marty was all flesh and blood. Jake reached out and touched Marty's long hair.

He grinned. "It's like silk."

Marty said nothing, but her eyes widened, and Jake worried he'd gone too far. She didn't move, however, and this only seemed to entice him more. Reaching up, he put his hand against her cheek.

"Soft."

Still she didn't speak or move. A million thoughts cut loose in Jake's mind, and there was no way to make sense of any of them. He wanted more than anything to kiss her, but something warned him that this would only cause rejection on her part. He had made her a promise. They had agreed to a marriage of convenience, and now he was threatening the security of that agreement. Forcing himself to step back, Jake took a deep breath.

"I just wanted you to know that I'll see to it that Alice is taken care of." With that, he hurried back through the passageway to his room and closed the door behind him. Leaning hard against the wall, Jake berated himself for his lack of good sense.

"She didn't marry me for romance," he whispered aloud. "I need to keep that in mind and not allow my heart to get broken . . . again."

Chapter 13

Movement outside the window caught Marty's attention. She'd just bent down to retrieve her book when she spied someone hurrying away from the house. Alice had mentioned someone sneaking around the stable—could this be the same man? She strained to catch another glimpse in the fading light, but the man was gone.

A glance at the clock showed it was nearly time for Jake to return from work. Marty determined to speak with him on the matter to see what he thought.

Jake . . . The thought of Jake and what had happened last Friday evening between them had plagued Marty for nearly a week. She could still feel his warm hand against her cheek. Still see the desire in his eyes. She had never expected to have a man look at her like that again. Furthermore, she hadn't wanted one to. Until now.

"I'm being silly," she said aloud, straightening a piece of bric-a-brac on the nearest table. "We went into this arrangement fully aware that neither of us wanted a real marriage."

But Jake's touch had made her remember how Thomas would reach for her, and Marty found that she ached for someone to hold her—to offer a hug and the reassurance that she was loved. She frowned. Love had only served to deepen her pain. Why would she want to experience that again?

Taking up her book, Marty snuggled into her favorite chair by the fire and began reading. She had to keep her mind occupied with something other than the way Jake had looked at her. The way she longed to have him look at her again.

Jake climbed down from the carriage, anxious to see Marty. She'd been on his mind all day. In fact, she had been in most of his thoughts all week. Ever since he'd caressed her hair and cheek, Jake had found it impossible to forget the way she'd made him feel.

She doesn't know she made me feel that way. She would no doubt be upset to learn the truth, so there's no use in bringing it up. But maybe if I brought it up . . . things might change.

Change wasn't likely, however. They had both agreed to the parameters of their arrangement, with no provision for change. Despite this, Jake bounded into the house with no other desire than to see his wife and hear about her day.

Maybe I'm a hopeless romantic. Maybe I will always have a penchant for falling in love with any woman with whom I have more than a casual conversation.

"Mr. Wythe," Brighton said, receiving him in the entryway. "Let me take your coat." He helped Jake out of his overcoat and took his hat. "There is a small matter that I should speak to you about. It can wait until after supper if you wish."

"No, that's all right. What's the problem?"

Brighton nodded. "It would seem that the new groomsman found boot tracks in areas where no one should have been. He spied them coming from around the stable, which was the only reason he was intrigued to follow them. They led, I'm afraid, to the house windows on the south side."

Jake considered the matter a moment. "And everyone is certain the tracks did not belong to any of the servants?"

"Yes, sir. The tracks were made by a man's very large boot. The print was even larger than Samson's."

Rubbing his chin, Jake wondered what was to be done. "Does my wife know about this?"

"Yes, sir. It would seem she observed someone running away from the house. She couldn't get a good look, however. Also, she tells me that Miss Alice noted someone moving about the grounds the other day. It was thought that she was mistaken and that it was either myself or Samson, but that was not the case."

"I'll talk to Marty about this," Jake said. "Thank you for telling me. Keep your eyes open for anything unusual. I would guess it's probably someone looking for a house to rob. We need to be on guard."

"Yes, sir." Brighton moved toward the sitting room and pushed back the doors. "I believe you will find Mrs. Wythe in here."

Jake left the foyer and crossed the sitting room to find Marty comfortably ensconced before the fire. She was wearing a tawny gold-and-cream-checked gown with brown trim. She looked up and set aside the book she'd been reading.

"I see you're hard at it again," he said, pointing to the book. "What are you reading?"

"*The Picture of Dorian Gray*," she replied. "It's quite unusual. It's about a man who sells his soul to retain his youth, while his picture ages instead."

"Sounds intriguing. If I had the time, I would definitely give the book a try." He rubbed his eyes.

"Yes. I'm used to having more to do," she told him, sounding sad. "Sometimes I think I'm growing fat and lazy with all this idle time."

Jake gave her a smile. "Well, you look quite lovely being idle, and you'll be well-read." He plopped down on a red velvet chair near the fire. "Brighton tells me that someone has been sneaking about the grounds."

Marty's blue-eyed gaze never left his face. "Yes, that's right. I saw a man, but I cannot give you much of a description. The groomsman saw tracks, as well." Her voice lowered. "Alice saw someone a few days back, but I thought it was nothing. Now I'm not so sure."

Stretching out his legs, Jake sighed. "We are people of means, and as things continue to worsen financially, there will no doubt be those who will seek to take what they can from our blessings."

"Is it truly all that bad?"

"Worse every day, I'm afraid." Jake felt weary from the long day and suppressed a yawn. *She'll think I'm bored with her, but nothing could be further from the truth.*

"There are dozens of railroads in trouble—some have already folded, while others are trying their best to find a way to regain their profitability. And there's the second term of Grover Cleveland to face, as well as the aftermath of so many labor strikes last year. It's all bound to catch up and take its toll."

"So you figure that whoever was outside the window was looking to rob us?"

"That's my guess. I suppose I should hire someone to walk the grounds from time to time. Perhaps I could get a man who would be responsible for the gardens, and he could act as a guard. I hadn't figured to hire one until spring since Samson has been able to handle the snow removal."

"No need to rush it," Marty said. "Just buy me a double-barrel shotgun and I'll discourage window peepers."

He chuckled at this but could tell by her expression that she was serious. "I would happily buy you most anything your heart desired."

"Then a double-barrel shotgun is what I desire."

"What about your revolver?" His grin broadened at the thought of her wielding the weapon. "Wouldn't that be good enough?"

Marty shrugged. "It does its job, but I find men to be far more intimidated when staring down the barrels of a loaded shotgun. Perhaps it's realizing that even a poor shot has difficulty missing with that kind of weapon. Tends to make men rethink their choices."

Jake shook his head. "You amaze me. Just when I think I've come to know all there is about you, you surprise me. You are such a strong and capable woman—exactly the kind of Lone Star bride I'd hoped you'd be. You don't need anyone or anything."

"I need that double barrel," she replied with a hint of a smile.

He roared in laughter. "Then you shall have it. Goodness,

Marty, your reputation has already survived the stage rescue. I'm sure that being known for walking armed around the grounds of your fine Capitol Hill home won't damage your social standing a bit."

Marty couldn't resist joining his laughter. "I honestly don't care what society thinks. I know full well how to protect what is mine. I won't have Alice worrying about another attack or Mrs. Landry wondering if someone is going to steal her linens when they're hanging out to dry."

"You're a good mistress of the house, Marty, and you genuinely care about our staff. I think so many people treat their servants as unimportant. . . . I suppose that's why I enjoy the banter between Brighton and Mrs. Landry. I feel like they're just a part of my family."

Marty grew thoughtful. "When I was growing up, we always had help around the house, but Juanita and Berto were also our friends—we even ate together. Will and Hannah didn't hesitate to seek their opinion or advice. I suppose our isolation and dependence on one another made a difference, but even here I have difficulty considering the staff nothing more than servants."

Jake couldn't agree more. "We were the same. Our ranch had a great many people who worked in various jobs. My mother had a housekeeper and two maids, and it wasn't unusual at all for the four of them to quilt together or work in the garden side by side. They were more like sisters to her than employees. It's a different world in large cities and upper-class society. I saw it in California to be certain, and it's most likely no different back east. In fact, I think the folks living here are just doing their best to mimic those people."

"Frankly, I don't believe their way of living is anything

to emulate. Don't get me wrong—I am greatly enjoying the luxury here." She smiled and ran her hand down the front of her checked gown. "I've never had so many beautiful clothes, and my hands have never been this soft. Mrs. Landry and Alice have pampered and spoiled me. . . . But as I said earlier, I've become quite idle. And as my sister would contend, idle hands often lead to trouble."

"Perhaps you could involve yourself in some of the local charities. Maybe ask Mrs. Morgan about it. Which reminds me: Despite concerns about the economy, Mr. Morgan is giving me a bonus. I can't say anything about it, however. The board is afraid if it comes to light, the other branch managers will be upset because they didn't receive one, as well."

"That's wonderful news . . . I think. I know you've been working hard."

"It puts me that much closer to one day having my own ranch."

Marty frowned and looked away. "Was there a particular reason for your reward?"

Jake pushed back his dark blond hair and gazed upward at the ornate crown molding. "I have reviewed the bank books for the last three years and uncovered a number of problems. Most were poor bookkeeping and management mistakes, but there's also an amount of money that is missing. Strangely enough, it seems to change from time to time."

"Change? What do you mean?"

He was touched that she genuinely seemed to care. He appreciated having someone intelligent to converse with—someone not related to the banking business. "The amount of the missing money is never the same. It changes. Sometimes it's one amount, and then the next time I check, it might be higher or lower. I keep thinking it must have been a posting or accounting error, but I can't find it."

"Perhaps someone is taking money and putting it back," she said in a casual manner. "Then when they need more, they take it out again."

Jake straightened and looked at his wife. "You know, you may be right. I've never heard of an embezzler who puts money back, but . . ." He fell silent. Nearly a year ago there had been a substantial amount of money missing—several hundred dollars. Then a few months later the balance was only off by ten or twenty. In fact, when the bank audit took place, the amount was so small that Morgan himself agreed that it was a simple error and made the books right and the auditor a little richer to look the other way. So maybe it was Morgan who'd borrowed the funds? But why would he need to?

★

Alice had just finished doing up the buttons on the back of Marty's shirtwaist when a knock sounded on the dressing room door. Alice hurried to answer it and found Mr. Wythe holding a long wooden box.

"Good morning, Alice." He moved right past her without waiting for an invitation. "And how have you enjoyed your Saturday, wife?"

"We've been ever so busy," Marty declared. "I've changed into my second ensemble and am ready to face another few hours of boredom before lunch is served. What about you?"

"I was out shopping first thing this morning and brought you a gift."

Alice decided now would be a good time to see to the ironing that needed her attention. She walked to the far end of the room to gather the necessary articles of clothing.

"I think you'll like what I have here," Jake told Marty.

Alice heard Mrs. Wythe respond, but couldn't make out the words. How wonderful to have a husband who surprised you with gifts. *Mr. Wythe certainly loves her a great deal. His entire face lights up when he sees her. How I long for someone to love me like that.*

Touching her hand to her cheek, Alice couldn't help but be reminded that she was forever marred. The scar would fade a bit, the doctor said, but she would always bear the reminder. He had told her she was fortunate that the damage had been mostly superficial. Apparently the attacker knew exactly how deep to cut without causing greater damage to the nerves and muscle beneath.

"It's perfect!" Marty squealed in delight.

Alice turned to find her hoisting a shotgun out of the wooden box. She found it strange that her mistress should get so excited about a weapon. Trying not to eavesdrop, Alice focused her attention on the clothes, only to hear something that made her blood run cold.

"If that window peeper decides to return," Marty told her husband, "I'll brandish this in his face and see if he's still inclined to steal from us."

"I figure he'll forget about us mighty quick," he said, his southern drawl becoming more pronounced. "Once he sees that my little Texas wife can shoot, well, he'll mosey along and leave my womenfolk alone." They laughed together over this.

Alice froze at Mr. Wythe's comment. So the man had returned. Icy fingers went up her spine. They were looking for her, no doubt. But why? They'd taken the satchel from her father. What else were they looking for?

Her mind scrambled for an answer as fear welled within

her. These men seemed unwilling to leave her alone. They had come to the hospital asking after her. They had eventually located her with church friends. In fact, their threats were the biggest reason her hosts had left Denver. They had wanted Alice to come with them, but she knew the men would only follow. But why? What did they want?

"I couldn't help but pick this up for you, as well," Mr. Wythe announced. He drew out a small jewelry box and opened the lid. Alice couldn't see what it was, but from Marty's reaction, it apparently met with her approval.

"You shouldn't have. The shotgun was more than enough. It's not like it's my birthday," Marty declared.

"Speaking of which, I don't even know when that is."

Alice frowned. How could he not know when she was born? They were married, after all. Hadn't they shared all of these kinds of things with each other prior to the wedding? She couldn't imagine that two people would wed without knowing such details.

"It's in January," Marty admitted.

"Then I missed it. Good thing I bought the brooch." Alice thought he looked more than a little pleased with himself. Mr. Wythe continued. "I know you love just sitting around the house, but I thought we might take a carriage ride after lunch. You haven't seen much of the city, and since the streets are fairly dry, I thought it would be a good time to show you around."

"Oh, I'd love that," Marty replied. "And it will give me a good excuse to change my clothes again." She laughed and looked to Alice. "After we eat, I shall need an appropriate outfit for sight-seeing."

Chapter 14

"It's been a wonderful afternoon," Mrs. Cooper said, nodding to each of the women in her opulent sitting room.

"I should say so," Mrs. Morgan replied. "And I've decided that this new mauve color is lovely. Not really a pink and certainly not a true purple." She reached over to gently finger the damask draperies. "Very lovely."

"I knew when I first saw it featured in Byrant's store that I must have it for my sitting room. I'm quite pleased."

Marty tried to appear interested. The women had been good to include her, and she wanted to show them as much kindness and attention as she could. Unfortunately, there was little in their lives that appealed to her.

"So have you begun to redecorate your home?" Mrs. Morgan asked her.

Thinking of the house and how she could find little fault with the design, Marty shook her head. "I'm not entirely sure I will."

The other two women exchanged a look. Marty could see the hint of disapproval in their expressions. "I suppose," she continued, "that I'm still trying to adjust to living here and being married again. Besides, you arranged for it to be done so beautifully, Mrs. Morgan."

The women seemed to accept this as a valid excuse. Mrs. Morgan smiled and asked, "How long were you married before, Mrs. Wythe?"

"Ten years. Thomas was a rancher, and he was killed when a longhorn gored him." She added the latter, anticipating the women's curiosity regarding her husband's means of death.

"I'm sure that living as a rancher's wife in Texas was quite different from what you know today. Still, you were mistress of your ranch. Was it large?"

"The ranch?" Marty questioned, but continued before either could answer. "Yes. It was a decent size. My brother-in-law and sister gave large pieces of land to both my brother and me. By the time I returned from finishing school, my brother had already established himself on his portion and had purchased a homestead that abutted the property, as well. So my acreage isn't quite as large, but large enough."

"You attended finishing school?" Mrs. Cooper said, brightening. "Where, if I might ask?"

"In Georgia. Atlanta, to be exact. I have relatives there, and Hannah, my sister, thought it would do me good to get away from my primarily male world and engage with other young ladies and learn social etiquette."

"How wise of her," Mrs. Cooper said, looking to Mrs. Morgan for approval.

"Yes," Imogene Morgan agreed. "I knew there was a great deal of gentility to you, and now it's obvious as to why. Breeding always shows. In fact, when Mr. Morgan mentioned sponsoring you and Mr. Wythe in society, I was skeptical. I'm pleased that you have proven yourself to be a refined young lady."

Marty wanted to make a snide comment but held her tongue. What had the woman expected—savage behavior and unsavory conversation? Did she believe Texans to be social clods incapable of mingling among society's elite?

The footman arrived to clear away their dishes, and Marty took the opportunity to excuse herself. "I want to thank you for such a lovely time, but I really must be going. I have become interested of late in one of the local orphanages, and I want to stop there on my way home to see what I might be able to do to help."

Mrs. Morgan smiled in her tolerant way. "I'm certain a small donation would benefit them. I have several charitable organizations that provide assistance to such places. Perhaps you would care to join me for one of our meetings?"

Marty nodded. "I'd enjoy that very much. I'd like to be doing something more than holding teas and reading every book in my husband's library." She smiled and couldn't resist adding, "One day you and Mrs. Cooper must tell me how you endure this idle life."

She quickly got to her feet and the butler escorted her and helped her with her coat. Once Marty was in the carriage and headed down the street, she couldn't help but giggle. Those women were skilled in holding long conversations about nothing of importance—while believing themselves full of valuable information—and she couldn't help but feel bored in their presence.

Samson brought the carriage to a halt outside a three-story redbrick building in a poorer part of the city. Marty glanced around the neighborhood, noting the startling contrast to that of Capitol Hill. Spring weather was doing its best to brighten things up; the grass had begun to green rather nicely and the trees were leafing out. But where Capitol Hill prided itself on well-manicured lawns, it seemed this area of Denver did well to keep glass in the windows of its buildings.

She made her way to the door and noted a sign that read *Auraria Orphanage*. Before she could knock, a young man of about twelve opened the door. "Good afternoon," he said, sounding very formal.

Marty handed him her calling card. "I wonder if I might see the person in charge."

The boy took her card and nodded. "Mr. Brentwood is in his office." He knocked and opened the door to reveal a stern-faced man sitting behind a desk.

"Mr. Brentwood, this lady wants to see you," the boy said, some of his formality reverting to a more youthful tone.

The man stood and took hold of the calling card the boy extended. "Very good, Adam. Now return to your post." The boy nodded and scurried past Marty, pausing only long enough to give her a slight bow.

"I'm afraid Adam tends to forget his manners, Mrs. . . ." He glanced down at the card for a moment. "Wythe. Mrs. Wythe. Won't you be seated?"

Marty smiled and did as he bid. Already she felt the edges of her boredom give way. She was about to embark on a worthy project. At least she prayed it would be such.

———————————— ★ ————————————

"And he said that I might come and read to the children," Marty told Alice as she helped dress her mistress for dinner. "They are also in need of funds. The children seem to wear out their clothing so fast that I thought I might actually take up sewing for them."

"What will Mr. Wythe say?" Alice questioned. "That's hardly the kind of thing a lady in your position would normally do."

"I don't care," Marty replied. "I'm bored out of my mind most days. I'm not supposed to garden or make my own clothes. I'm not responsible for laundry or cooking because you and the other staff handle all of that. I can't care for the animals because that's not fitting. Honestly, I don't know how these ladies of leisure endure their existence."

Alice couldn't help but giggle. "Most women would love to be in your shoes, Mrs. . . . Marty."

Marty slipped her arms into the sleeves of her silk evening gown and smiled. "Well, I'm glad to be in my own shoes tonight. Mr. Wythe is taking me out for what he promises will be a lovely dinner and time of music. It's been quite a while since I've heard a concert. My sister and brother-in-law took Thomas and me to a wonderful performance in Dallas many years ago. Before that . . . well, when I was little, my sister, Hannah, always tried to expose Andy and me to music and art whenever possible. It just wasn't always available or timely. Ranch life is hard work and requires constant attention."

"I can only imagine," Alice said, doing up the back of the gown.

"I suppose that's why it's hard for me to sit and do nothing," Marty continued. "I'm used to pulling my weight. Seeing you and Mrs. Landry and the others work so hard . . . well, it makes me uncomfortable. Hannah said my mother was a fine lady, but she was always seeking to do good for others."

"My mother seemed to care about the good of others at one time," Alice admitted, not really wanting to allow the memories to resurface.

"You seem very bitter toward your mother. Are you angry because she died?"

Alice looked at the back of Marty's head as though carefully scrutinizing her coiffure. She thought about the question and then finally spoke. "My mother left me and my father when I was thirteen. She took my five-year-old brother and deserted us."

Marty turned to face her. "She deserted you? I thought she died."

"She did, but not until some months after she'd taken my brother and ran away with him. My father was devastated, as was I. I couldn't believe she'd just up and leave like that . . . no good-bye . . . nothing. She didn't even ask me if I wanted to go with her. Which I wouldn't have," Alice said in a tone that almost convinced her own heart.

"Did your father mistreat her?"

"No . . . at least I don't think he did. They did have some ugly arguments, but I never saw him hit her. My father could be rather indifferent at times, and he worked really hard to keep us in a lovely home. I think perhaps my mother felt his neglect, but that's certainly no reason to tear apart your family."

"I'm truly sorry, Alice. I didn't have any idea."

"Maybe I should have told you sooner." Alice shrugged. "I used to spend long hours trying to figure out why she left me. Right after it happened I would cry myself to sleep every night. I would ask my father every morning if they'd returned. Finally after several long months of this—maybe even a year—

my father told me he'd received word that they had died in an epidemic back east."

"That must have been hard." Marty's words were soothing and kind. "I know what it's like to grow up without a mother."

Alice went to the dressing table for the gown's sash. She returned and fitted it to Marty's waist and artfully tied it in a large bow. "I got very angry. Father would speak ill of Mother and I suppose that birthed anger in me—anger at her and even anger at him. I'm still trying to overcome it."

"I can imagine your hurt."

"I remember one of the first times Father and I attended church after learning that Mother had died. The pastor spoke about forgiving people the wrong they'd done you. He said that often the hardest thing to let go of was our disappointment in others, including God. That spoke straight to my heart. I'd like to say that I immediately forgave my mother and no longer felt anger toward her, but that wasn't the case. Forgiving Father was less difficult—after all, no matter his role in her desertion, at least he stayed."

"So you still battle your wounded heart?"

"Yes." Alice stepped back and admired her mistress. "You look so beautiful. That color of blue makes your eyes seem even brighter."

Marty didn't appear to hear her, however. The older woman had drawn her brows together, as if thinking hard on something Alice had said.

"Are you all right?" Alice asked.

Her mistress nodded. "I think part of my own trouble has to do with my anger at God. Maybe even anger at Thomas for getting himself killed. It's hard to accept that God could have stopped a bad thing from happening but didn't. I'm just not sure what to do with that knowledge."

"It isn't easy, I'll admit. I'm still struggling to forgive my mother, but every morning I wake up and tell myself that today will be the day—even if for just a few hours. Maybe you could try that, too, to help you forgive Thomas for dying and accept that God is good, even when He doesn't ward off the bad."

"Maybe," Marty said, not sounding at all convinced.

★

Jake stepped into one of the handsomely appointed lounges of the exclusive Denver Club. Mr. Morgan beckoned to him immediately and one of the footmen escorted Jake to where he sat. Men all around the room were puffing away on fat cigars, chatting about the day's events. Jake wasn't sure why Morgan had sent word for him to join him there. It was going to make Jake extremely late getting home, and he'd forgotten to send word to Marty.

"I received your note, Mr. Morgan."

"Good to have you join me, Mr. Wythe. Have you been here before?"

Jake shook his head. "No. I'm afraid this club has always been too elite for me."

"Nonsense. This is exactly where you need to be. If you want to get ahead in the banking industry, this is where business is done."

Jake didn't wish to tell him he had no desire to get ahead in the banking industry, so he simply gave a curt nod and took an offered chair.

"Cigar?" Morgan asked, holding one out.

"No, thank you." Jake noticed another footman had arrived.

"Would you care for something to drink, sir?"

Jake could see that other men in the room, including Morgan, were imbibing liquor. Since he'd made a fool of himself in Texas at the house of the Vandermarks, Jake had sworn off all alcohol. "No. I'm fine, thank you."

"My boy, you need to learn the importance of relaxing." Morgan smiled. "Business and pleasure are more easily enjoyed when a man is calm and not so anxious."

He wished Morgan would get to the point of this meeting. Jake had picked up a bouquet of flowers for Marty, which the doorman was now watching over. Jake didn't trust the man to watch them indefinitely, and besides, he was anxious to give them to Marty and see her reaction.

"So, what kind of business are we about today?" Jake asked.

Morgan laughed. "The business of getting your membership arranged in the Denver Club."

"That's hardly necessary," Jake answered. "The cost alone is rather prohibitive."

"Nonsense. It's a part of your duty as bank manager, and therefore the bank will pay your dues. Of course, I don't want that to get around to any of my other employees." He slid an envelope across the table. "I will sponsor your membership, and the board will also act as references. This will take care of your dues."

"But, Mr. Morgan, I assure you it's not necessary."

"But I say it is. I intend to see you in the position of vice-president by summer's end. That will only be accomplished by your working hard to bring in new accounts and see to it that this financial wrinkle doesn't cause us any setbacks."

"Vice-president?" Jake shook his head in surprise. "But what of Mr. Keystone?"

"He will assume the role of president for a time. Eventually, I intend to see you in that position, when he retires. But one step at a time. Keystone will be much too busy to tend to the daily operations of business. That's why you need to have a membership in this austere club. The wealthy men you need to entice to my banking organization will frequent this place. I'm counting on you, Wythe. I expect to get a strong return for my investment." Morgan gave him a pointed look.

"And I always get what I expect and then some," Morgan added, then lifted his glass in a salute to Jake.

Chapter 15

April arrived, and with it a growing concern in the financial world. Many people were now convinced that the problems were only going to get worse and because of that, were starting to pull back on investing. Jake had witnessed several customers, mostly those with smaller savings accounts, pull their money from the bank. They were inclined to trust their mattresses or other hiding places more than the bank's questionable future.

Jake had tried to assure each man that the bank was sound, but as he continued to look into the monetary backing of their branch, he felt less and less certain. Josiah Keystone only added to his concern on that early Friday morning.

"Wythe, good of you to see me," Keystone announced, entering the office. "I realize it wasn't in the best taste to send you a message so early in the morning. I appreciate your meeting me here."

"You said it was urgent."

"And so it is," Keystone said. "I won't take up much time, but I wanted to ask you to personally handle a matter for a friend of mine."

"I'll do what I can," Jake replied, still not knowing what Keystone needed.

"It would need to be kept quiet. I don't want Morgan hearing about it. He'll feel offended by our friend taking this path."

"What path is that?"

"He wants to trade in his gold certificates for gold. He's fretful about the economy, as are many. I tried to convince him otherwise, but he's convinced that this is what he must do. He said he'd rather have the gold itself on hand rather than a marker from the bank. I told him we would try to handle it with as little fanfare as possible. Not to mention we don't want to give the public any reason to make a run on the bank."

"Mr. Keystone, you know that this can't be kept from Mr. Morgan. All redemptions of gold certificates must have his approval. Besides, it will all depend on how much this man intends to cash in. You know as well as I do that the bank doesn't keep large amounts on hand and that the ratio of deposits to currency is severely declined."

"Surely this can be dealt with," Keystone all but growled. He clenched his jaw and pursed his lips as if trying to rid himself of a bad taste.

Jake hesitated, unsure of what to say. "I'll do what I can, Mr. Keystone. But again, it's all going to depend on the amount of withdrawal."

"Where is Morgan? I suppose I'll have to speak to him on this matter."

"I would imagine that he's still at home," Jake said, glancing at his pocket watch. "Perhaps you could catch him there."

"No, I don't want to make a scene."

"Well, he intends to be at the Denver Club around three. I'm to meet him there."

"I suppose it will have to wait until then." Tension laced his words, and he stormed from the office, leaving Jake to stare after him.

It seemed anyone with something to lose walked a narrow line these days, and there was an overwhelming sense that the financial world was holding its breath. Unfortunately, the daily newspapers were doing nothing to help the matter. Every time Jake picked up the paper, he read another story about a railroad facing bankruptcy or the rising unemployment. Such widespread problems, stated in the most alarming ways possible, served only to cause mass hysteria. It was a wonder they hadn't had a full run on the bank.

"Sir, this letter arrived for you," Arnold announced from the still open doorway. "It's notification of our upcoming audit."

Jake rolled his eyes. "Why not?"

Marty awoke after a restless night's sleep. Alice hadn't opened the drapes, yet there were hints of light playing at the corners. Silence cloaked the house in a sort of surreal, almost dreamlike state.

Getting out of the bed, Marty yawned and tried to ignore the fact that she was still exhausted. Glancing at her writing desk in the muted light, she could see the reason for her inability to sleep.

Hannah had written her a letter. Her unhappiness at Marty's last missive was quite clear. Hannah didn't try to hide her disappointment or pretend to understand Marty's desire to remain in Colorado for an extended visit. She wanted to know why Marty was being so vague with her information and when she intended to return.

There was more—comments about the ranch and Hannah's worry that Marty would get herself into trouble.

"If she only knew," Marty said, walking across the chilly hardwood floor. She picked up Hannah's letter and wondered how she could best reply.

Marty's first thought had been to just tell the truth—it would be the simplest way. But since when had she ever taken the simple way out? Her stomach growled. Perhaps a little milk and maybe one of Cook's good biscuits would stave off her hunger until a later breakfast.

Marty put the letter down and took up her robe. It was still early enough that she thought perhaps she could sneak down to the kitchen without notice. Cook was usually quite occupied first thing, and she and her assistant, Willa, would most likely be in the pantry or perhaps busy elsewhere.

Well, even if they're right there in plain sight, I am mistress of the house, and I have a right to the food that's in it.

Her reasoning did little to still the unease within. It wasn't the early morning raid on the larder, however, that had Marty tied in knots. It was knowing that she had to answer Hannah's letter and tell her about Jake.

Deciding to slip down the servants' stairs, which would lead her directly into the kitchen's back entry, Marty did her best to descend quietly. She was on the next to the last step when she heard a woman speak.

"Why don't we end our study with prayer," Mrs. Landry announced.

Marty frowned and halted, remaining still as one woman after another asked for God's provision and offered thanks for His blessings already received. It wasn't until Marty heard

Alice in prayer that she felt a strange sense of guilt mixed with irritation.

"And Lord," Alice prayed, "please help Mrs. Wythe. She has a wounded heart and needs to see that you love her and that you are there to comfort her. Help her with the decisions she needs to make."

Marty stepped back, shaking her head. She didn't want to listen to another word. She hurried back to her room, hoping that no one had known of her presence. She didn't know why the prayer had bothered her so much. She knew that Hannah prayed for her every day, but there was something about these women—her servants—praying for her that was unsettling.

Returning to bed, Marty tried her best to go back to sleep and forget about the letter from her sister and the women's prayers. But her mind kept returning to Hannah's missive, Alice's words. When Alice came into the room to pull back the drapes an hour later, Marty reluctantly gave up the battle.

"Good morning," Alice said with a bright smile. "Did you sleep well?"

"Not exactly." She slipped her legs over the side of the bed and stretched.

Alice went about the room attending to her daily chores until she came to the desk. "I see you had a letter from your sister. Have you told her yet about your marriage to Mr. Wythe?"

"That's none of your business," Marty snapped and immediately regretted it. "I'm sorry, Alice. Like I said, I didn't sleep very well. I'm afraid I'm acting like those snooty society women. I hope you'll forgive me."

Alice's expression changed from surprise to warmth. "Of course. Everyone has a bad day now and then. I'm sure this matter has weighed on you heavily."

"It has," Marty admitted. "I'm certain that's why I couldn't sleep. I don't know how to break the news to her without it hurting or alarming Hannah. She worries about me more than she should, and if I tell her what I've done, I know she'll probably load up and come here demanding to meet Jake and know everything about him."

"Would that be so bad?"

Marty grimaced at the thought. If Hannah came here, then the knowledge of Marty's ranch would be revealed. "I don't know," she lied. "I just don't know."

Alice moved into the dressing room. "I know you plan to go to tea this afternoon at Mrs. Keystone's. Would your lavender striped gown suit you?"

"As well as anything," Marty replied. "I have no desire to go to tea. No desire to make small talk with women of society. Perhaps I'll send my regrets and tell her I'm feeling unwell."

"Lie to Mrs. Keystone? Over tea?" Alice asked, popping back into the doorway. "Why ever would you sin in order to get out of tea? Just send her a note that says you won't be there and leave it at that."

Marty smiled. Alice really had gotten over her fear of talking back and offering her opinion. "I suppose I could, but you know how these society women are. They take offense at the smallest thing."

"So let them," Alice countered. "If not over this thing, then it will be another. No sense in being miserable over it. It seems to me that being firm in your convictions is something these women understand."

"It's just that every time I meet with them, they have yet another restraint or rule for me. Do you know that Mrs. Morgan was actually appalled by my idea to read to the orphans?

She said it wouldn't be fitting. She used excuses like how it would be unfair to the destitute motherless and fatherless children to see such obvious examples of money and know that they would never have such things. I told her I could dress very simply and have the carriage leave me off a block away, and that upset the poor woman further. I thought she might actually faint."

Alice smiled. "You have a good heart. I don't know those women, but it doesn't sound as if they value the same things. Now, I'm not judging them, mind you—I couldn't begin to say what's in their hearts. But their actions will speak for them."

Marty followed Alice into the dressing room and considered her maid's words. She'd never considered herself good or selfless. Alice's comment only served to vex Marty all the more. A good and selfless woman wouldn't treat her sister as Marty had. She wouldn't feel the need to lie and hide the details of her life—and she certainly wouldn't have gone into an arranged marriage and kept it a secret from the people she loved.

★

Jake smiled as he came into the house an hour earlier than usual. Despite the rainy weather, Jake felt more than a little excited. He had a surprise for Marty, and he could hardly wait to tell her about it. Brighton greeted him at the door as usual and asked after his day.

"It started much too early, as you will recall," Jake told his man. "I must say I'm glad that it's Friday." He handed Brighton his umbrella and outer coat.

"Yes, sir."

Just then Mrs. Landry appeared. "Goodness! Don't let that umbrella drip all over my freshly polished floor. There's a porch for such things."

"I apologize, Mrs. Landry," Jake declared before Brighton could speak. "It's all my fault. I was in such a hurry to get inside and see my wife, that it totally slipped my mind."

She gave an exasperated sigh. "It's not your fault at all, Mr. Wythe. If Mr. Brighton knew his job properly, he would have been waiting for you on the porch."

"But I came home early. Hardly his fault."

Brighton looked at Mrs. Landry with a rather smug expression. She jerked her chin high. Jake wanted to laugh out loud at the twosome, but knew better.

"A good servant anticipates his master's every move. If Mr. Brighton were American trained, he would know that. I seriously doubt the English ever do anything without a fixed schedule in place. Americans are far more spontaneous."

"I will admit the truth of being spontaneous, Mrs. Landry. However, I couldn't say if that is the case or not for the English. I've never been abroad."

"Mrs. Landry is rather ignorant of how a gentleman's manservant performs his duties." Brighton looked at the woman in a matter-of-fact manner. "The truth is, Mrs. Landry is woefully uninformed when it comes to understanding gentlemen."

"Ha! I know well enough, you rapscallion. You would think that the only people in the world who know how to keep order in a house are the English! I can tell you this much: I've been overseeing households for more years than I care to admit. I know perfectly well how to keep a house and how to keep the folks in it. And you still haven't removed that umbrella. I'm going to have to redo this entire foyer."

To Jake's surprise, she got down on her knees and pulled a cloth from her pocket. Wiping at the water, she shook her head and muttered about Brighton's inadequacies. Jake smiled at Brighton, who only gazed toward the ceiling and sighed.

"Do you know where Mrs. Wythe might be found?" he asked no one in particular.

"I believe she's reading in the small sitting room," Brighton replied.

"Of course she is," Mrs. Landry muttered from the floor. "Just as she is every afternoon at this time."

"Thank you." Jake headed off to find Marty just as Mrs. Landry started in once again on Brighton's failings.

"Marty?" he called, entering the sitting room. He looked around the room and thought perhaps she'd retired. Instead, he found her dozing by the fire. How pretty she looked, curled up with her feet under her. She was dressed simply but looked as fresh and beautiful as any grand dame of society.

"Marty?" he said again, not wanting to startle her.

She opened her eyes slowly and looked up. Obviously still drowsy, she smiled and closed her eyes again. Jake touched her cheek and at this, Marty's eyes flew open and she was fully awake.

"What's wrong?"

He laughed and took a seat. "Nothing. In fact, I have a surprise for you."

"A surprise? Goodness, you've done nothing but bestow presents and lovely things upon me since I arrived. I honestly feel spoiled." She straightened in her chair and the book she'd been reading dropped to the floor.

Jake picked it up and looked at the title. "*The Adventures of Sherlock Holmes?*"

She shrugged. "I found it in the library. It's really quite entertaining. Written by an Englishman named Sir Arthur Conan Doyle."

"Actually, as I recall from my days at school," Jake said, "he's Scottish. He just lives in England now."

"Ah, I see. Well, I enjoy his writing." Marty set the book aside. The clock chimed and she glanced at it as if something were wrong. Looking back at Jake she shook her head. "You're home very early."

"I went to work very early. I'd received a note from Mr. Keystone requesting we meet prior to the bank opening for the day. Therefore, I took it upon myself to close up shop early and come home with a marvelous surprise."

This made her smile. "Do tell?"

He leaned forward on the edge of his chair. "Well, it has come to my attention that you've not yet attended our new opera house. I was fortunate enough to secure tickets to tonight's performance of *Cavalleria Rusticana*. I thought I might entice you to spend the evening with me."

Marty's face brightened. "I would love to. Oh, what a treat. Thank you!" She jumped up and without warning leaned over and kissed Jake on the cheek. "I've been so bored. You have no idea."

Jake watched her for a moment, wondering if she would spoil the moment by apologizing. To his relief, however, she smiled. "I should go get ready." She paused at the doorway. "Will we dine in or out?"

"Why don't we make a complete evening of it. I'll take you to one of the best restaurants in town."

"That sounds wonderful. I'll let Mrs. Landry know so she can tell Cook."

He watched her leave and couldn't contain his smile. Not only was she pleased at the thought of an evening out with him—even if it was based on her boredom—but she'd kissed him. Never before had she originated such a sign of affection. His grin broadened. Tonight might very well be the start of something entirely new.

★

"I wondered if you'd like to go to church with me tonight," Mrs. Landry said to Alice. "Since the master and mistress are out until late, I thought you might enjoy it. I know it's not your regular church, but we're having a ladies gathering. There will be a speaker and good food. I'd love for you to join me."

Alice looked up from her ironing, pleased. "I'd be happy for the diversion. Do you suppose Mr. and Mrs. Wythe would mind?"

"Not at all. I will arrange it with them so you needn't worry." Mrs. Landry touched her hand to her graying hair. "I should go fix myself. It's been a very busy day, and I'm sure I look a fright."

Alice shook her head. "Not at all. You look fine."

"Beauty is in the eye of the beholder," Brighton murmured from where he sat polishing a teapot.

"What was that?" Mrs. Landry questioned. "Did I just hear a dog yammering?"

Alice smiled and turned back to her ironing.

Later that evening as they walked to Mrs. Landry's church, Alice couldn't help but ask the housekeeper about her deceased husband and whether she'd considered remarrying.

"Oh goodness, no. Not truly. I mean, there have been

thoughts, of course, but nothing of any substance," Mrs. Landry answered quickly, then fell silent. "Mr. Landry was quite a handful, let me tell you. That man was always in need of something. I wore myself out just trying to anticipate him. No, I don't think I'll marry again." She walked in silence a little longer before adding, "Of course, it would depend on the man."

"Of course," Alice replied, hiding her smile.

They continued their journey in silence. The chilly night air caused Alice to pull her shawl close, and she couldn't shake the feeling that someone was watching them. She glanced around, trying to be as inconspicuous as possible.

I'm being silly. I'm just remembering that night.

Of course. That was all it was. This night was so similar to the evening she'd been injured and her father killed.

"You remind me of my daughter, Meg," Mrs. Landry stated without warning. "She's a sweet girl like you. She's in her thirties now, but when she was younger, she could have been your sister in appearance."

"Except for the scar, I'm sure," Alice said.

"Alice, we all have our scars. Some are visible and others aren't, but they are there all the same. Your scar makes you no less worthy."

"I'm afraid it will make me less worthy of a man's love."

"Bah! If he's worth his salt, it won't matter to him," Mrs. Landry said. "You wait and see, Alice. You're but seventeen. In a short time, the right man will find you, and you will lose your heart to him and he will lose his to you. It will be just as it should be, and the scar will not matter."

"I hope you're right," Alice replied, not really convinced. Though she'd prayed for just such a thing, her heart doubted.

"Here we are," Mrs. Landry said, leading the way toward the large oak doors of the church. "Let's get in out of the damp night air."

Alice hurried to follow her, but just as she reached the door, she stumbled and dropped her small purse. Pausing to pick it up, Alice noticed movement across the street and straightened. She could see the outline of a man. The cherry-colored glow of a cigarette at his lips left her feeling shaken. The man who'd cut her had reeked of cigarette smoke.

The man didn't move, even though Alice was sure he knew she'd seen him. What was he doing there? Why was he following them? Or was he? Maybe this man was simply out for an evening stroll.

Swallowing back her fear, Alice picked up her purse and hurried after Mrs. Landry, whispering a prayer as she went.

Chapter 16

The following Monday morning, Marty looked at the paper on her desk. The blank page intimidated her in a way she didn't like to admit. Dipping her pen in the inkwell, she began to write a greeting to her sister.

Dearest Hannah,

I hope this letter finds all of you well. The weather is quite lovely here. I find it very different from Texas. The mountains are still covered with snow, which sends chilled air down over the city each evening after the sun goes down. The air is also much dryer. That, perhaps, is one thing I'm not certain of getting used to. My skin is always in need of lotions.

She put the pen aside and tried to think of what to say next. She had thought to speak about the new fashions she now possessed, but that would only cause Hannah to question how she could afford such luxuries—she knew that Marty hadn't taken much with her. No, there was little Marty could write about, if she was determined to keep her secret.

She thought again of her life in Denver and of Jake. The opera had been so enjoyable. Even now she found herself humming the intermezzo. The music had been glorious, and Marty found that it touched her soul like nothing she'd ever known. Perhaps it was because the story was one of love gone terribly wrong—of sacrifice and death.

Or maybe it was nothing more than the evening itself. She and Jake had shared a wonderful dinner together. He had been in such a happy mood, regaling her with stories of his youth. She could see the passion he had for returning to Texas, and though it concerned her, she couldn't help but recall her own fond memories of that state. More troubling, however, was that she was starting to feel things for Jake that she had only experienced with Thomas. And always, it came in unexpected ways. The touch of his hand on her arm. His hand at the small of her back. The way he looked at her.

She picked up the pen again and tapped it against her head. The time had come. She needed to tell Hannah about Jake. Perhaps she should ease into it, tell Hannah she had met someone and found him to be of great interest. Then again . . . maybe not. She dipped into the inkwell again.

I find Denver to be a marvelous place to live. In fact, I am giving strong consideration to making this my permanent home.

Marty frowned. *That alone is enough to send Hannah here. She'll wonder if I've lost my mind.* She sighed.

I know that might seem strange to you, given that I have no family here. But I very much enjoy the climate and the people. I have made good friends who are kind to me and have

She paused, wondering how much to put into detail.

taken me under their wings. They are well placed in society, and I find their lives to be quite interesting. The grandeur and opulence is unlike anything I've ever known.

She reread the last few lines. Hannah would know that Marty's simple taste would not be drawn to such finery. How could she make it sound more like her old self? A thought came to mind, and she smiled.

I find myself wondering just how much better the money might be spent on helping the poor or attending to the needs of orphans. Speaking of which, I have arranged to spend some time at a local orphanage reading to the children there. I've even decided I might take up sewing for them, as well.

Marty bit her lip and whispered the next words aloud before she wrote them. "Of course, the pay would not be much, but with my wealthy guardians insisting that I need not concern myself with the financial aspects of life, it will give me a small amount of spending money for extras."

It was a perfect way to ease any worries Hannah might have about Marty's well-being. She wrote the words, then wondered if she should go forward with her plan to mention Jake.

"Mrs. Wythe?" Alice called from the doorway.

Marty looked up to find the young woman with Kate, the household maid. "What is it?"

"Mrs. Landry would like to have Kate scrub the floors in here. Would that be acceptable?"

Marty nodded. "Yes, I need time to think about what else I want to say in this letter." She put the pen down and got to her feet. "I'll be downstairs if you need me."

Her mind overflowed with scenarios she could make up— stories that would sound completely plausible. She could mention meeting Jake at church her first week there. That would have an element of truth, but it would cause more questions, since Hannah knew she'd not attended church after Thomas's death. She could just say that she'd fallen head over heels and they'd gotten married. Or she could tell Hannah the truth . . . but she doubted her sister would take very kindly to having been duped.

No sooner had Marty stepped onto the first floor, however, when she noticed someone looking into the foyer from the porch window. She pretended nothing was amiss but went quickly to where she kept the shotgun.

"It might be nothing," she told herself as she moved back to the foyer. "But I'd rather not take a chance." Opening the front door, she peered out but didn't see anyone. She walked to the railing and looked out on the yard. Apparently whomever she'd seen was gone now.

A shiver went up her spine. She didn't like the idea of people sneaking around the house. But she also didn't want to jump to conclusions. She needed to make sure she hadn't mistaken one of their own workers for this mystery man. Marty made her way down the porch stairs and around to the back of the house, crossing to the stable.

"Samson?" she called, pausing just inside the doorway.

"Mr. Samson is fetching supplies for Mrs. Landry," Obed, the young groomsman, replied. He beamed a broad smile. "Can I help you?" His eyes widened at the sight of the shotgun. "You gonna go huntin', Miz Wythe?"

Marty smiled and shook her head. "Have you seen anything of Mr. Lawrence . . . the gardener?"

"No, ma'am. He ain't been here today. Leastwise not yet."

Marty nodded. It answered her question. She turned to go, but the boy called after her. "You want that I should have Mr. Lawrence come to you when he gets here?"

"No. That won't be necessary."

★

"It was good of you to come today, Mrs. Wythe," Mr. Brentwood said, leading her down the hall of the orphanage. "As I mentioned to you when we first met, we have only been open a month and already we have fifty children."

"Goodness. I had no idea there were that many orphans in the area," Marty replied.

Mr. Brentwood gave her a sympathetic look. "My dear Mrs. Wythe, these are but a handful of those out there. Denver has many orphanages. Some are run by churches, and others like ours are helped by the city or are funded by private individuals. Unfortunately, there are hundreds if not thousands of motherless and fatherless children in Colorado."

Marty couldn't begin to comprehend. "Where do they all come from?"

"A great many have come to us from the mining towns to the west. Parents left their homes in the East and came to find gold or silver. Unfortunately, most found starvation and death. Rather than see their children die, they leave them with us or one of the other institutions." He paused at a classroom door.

"This is where we school grades one through three. Miss Vernon is the teacher here."

Marty looked into the classroom and found a dozen or more children. It appeared the tall, willowy Miss Vernon held their attention as she showed them pictures of animals and asked the children to identify them.

"Then down the hall here, we have Mr. Cabot's classroom. He handles the fourth through sixth graders."

Marty followed him down the hall, noting the extreme cleanliness. From what she'd been told, each of the children helped in the upkeep of the house, as well as learned to handle laundry duties and other skills.

They paused a moment at Mr. Cabot's room, and Marty looked in. There were a couple dozen children—mostly boys. Mr. Cabot was directing their attention to a map of the United States. The children looked clean and well groomed, and most appeared content enough.

"You will do a great service to the teachers by offering the children your services. I know you had only in mind to read to the little ones, but since you are an educated woman, I wonder if you might also be willing to offer some tutoring. Some of our older children could benefit from having someone take a little extra time with them."

"I'll do whatever I can," Marty replied. "I want to be useful."

"Well, you are an answer to prayer for us. We don't get a great many volunteers—not like the church-sponsored or-phanages that have pastors and priests to request help from the pulpit." He smiled. "I hope this doesn't sound too forward, but I will admit I'm surprised that a woman of your social standing would even take the time."

"Social standings mean very little to me. I am where I am because of my husband's placement in Denver society. In Texas, I was a simple rancher's wife. I know, however, what it is to grow up without your parents. My sister and her husband were good to my brother and me, however. We were very loved."

"So many of these children will never experience the love of a family. We're the only family they have, and we do our best to encourage them, but it isn't the same."

He continued their tour. Climbing the stairs to the second floor, they looked in on the boys' dormitory first. Row after row of iron-framed beds lined the walls.

"We have more boys than girls at this point."

"And do you only have the younger ones—up to grade six, I believe you mentioned?"

The man shook his head. "We also have some older children. They attend the public school. We believe that will better prepare them for their life ahead. We're trying to find apprenticeships for them, as well. They very much need to learn job skills in order to support themselves as adults."

"And what do most of them desire to do?" Marty inquired.

The man chuckled. "Well, right now I have a great many would-be cowboys and a few who would like to attend military school. The girls mostly want to be nurses or teachers, wives and mothers, that kind of thing. Although I will admit we have one young lady who desires to be a suffragette."

Marty smiled. She thought of all the young men they had employed on the Barnett Ranch. Perhaps in time she could recommend some of these youngsters to Will and Hannah.

They often hired boys as young as fifteen. Maybe with a little bit of information on the plight of these children, they would agree to take them on at an even younger age.

"I must say I'm very impressed with the organization and cleanliness of your orphanage," Marty told Mr. Brentwood. "I suppose I had in mind a gloomy place where the rats ran free. Forgive me." She offered him a smile. "I'm glad to be wrong."

"There are such places, of course," the older man replied, directing Marty to the girls' dormitory. "We strive here to teach the children pride in their surroundings. We do not seek to make it all about work, however. You will note out back we have a very nice play area."

He drew Marty's attention to the window, and she followed him and peered out. There was, just as he said, a nice area for the children to play, complete with swings and a seesaw.

"There is a movement," he told her, "that has been encouraging schools and public facilities such as city parks to provide a variety of equipment to encourage physical activities. Fresh air is good for one's health."

Marty again thought of ranch life. Ninety percent of her day had been spent outdoors during the warm months. She couldn't imagine growing up in a city and having only limited sessions of outdoor play.

She finished the tour and returned home more determined than ever to do what she could to better the lives of the orphans. It grieved her to imagine thousands of children without the love of a mother and father. Perhaps she would consider adoption one day.

Later that afternoon, Marty picked up her letter and read

the lines she'd penned. She hoped that Hannah wouldn't overreact to her confession.

"It's silly. There's nothing wrong with the choices I've made. Jake's a good man." She looked over the final lines of the letter.

I have delayed far too long in finishing this letter. I wanted to share some news with you, however, and I hope you won't think me silly. I know this will come as a shock, but I have remarried. I have married a wonderful man, a Colorado banker named Jacob Wythe. Jake is a fine, upstanding man who has shown me great affection and consideration. He has generously provided an opulent home for me and has gifted me with more than you could imagine. We attend a wonderful church every Sunday.

She smiled to herself. That alone would entice Hannah to think twice before reprimanding.

I do hope you will be delighted for me and not angry. I didn't mean to be so covert. Well, I suppose I did, but not for the purpose of hurting anyone. Please be happy for me, because I'm happy.

Love, Marty

"Would you like me to post your letter for you?" Alice asked.

Marty turned, surprised to find the young woman there. The blond-haired girl smiled. "I hope I didn't startle you."

"Only a bit. And, yes, I suppose you can go ahead and post this letter."

"Did you tell your sister . . . about . . . Mr. Wythe?" Alice asked.

This time Marty didn't chide her for the personal question. "Yes."

"Do you think she'll be angry about your marriage?"

"I honestly don't know what Hannah will think or feel. She's always been very protective of me, but I know she would want me to be happy."

"And are you happy?"

Alice was the only one with whom Marty had shared the truth about her arrangement with Jake. As her personal maid, Alice was already well aware that the couple never shared the same bedroom.

"I'm content," Marty finally added. At least that much was true. "I prefer it here to Texas, and I find it's better for me to pretend there is no Texas and no family living there worrying after me."

Alice shook her head. "Pretending doesn't make it so."

Marty gave a heavy sigh. "No, but it does give me a little peace of mind. Very little, I'll admit, but enough for now. Hopefully Hannah and Will can accept my choices and will forgive me for my secrecy. Then there will be nothing more to worry about."

She met Alice's doubtful expression and knew the young woman didn't believe a word.

★

Jake put aside the newspaper and turned his attention back to the ledgers he'd been working on. It seemed that the missing money he'd been tracking had been returned very nearly in full. He frowned. How could this be happening under his nose?

Arnold came in with a stack of papers. "These letters will need your signature before they can go out."

"What are they?"

"Mostly notifications. The usual. Mortgage payments that are behind, loans that have been in arrears. We're calling in the notes on most."

"Foreclosing on the mortgages?" Jake asked. "Who arranged that?"

"Mr. Morgan himself. He brought this list in when you were at the Denver Club. You can review it to make sure there are no mistakes."

Jake nodded and took the papers. Looking through them, he frowned. Most of the notices were to homeowners who were behind on their mortgage payments. The addresses listed revealed homes from modest to lower income areas, suggesting the common man and his family.

"How can we foreclose on these people?" Jake asked aloud. He glanced up to find Arnold giving him a confused look. He shook his head and placed the papers on the desk. "I suppose the bank must have its money, but it seems heartless to put families out on the street."

"Indeed," Arnold agreed. "However, Mr. Morgan seemed to think it important for the health of his banks."

"I suppose." Jake drew a deep breath and blew it out. "Seems mighty unneighborly," he drawled.

This didn't sit right—but neither did the direction of his own life, especially in these uncertain times. Mr. Morgan was constantly speaking to him about promotion and an increased salary. He liked the way Jake handled himself and the bank and had even commented that he would like to put Jake in a position to oversee all of the branches. It sounded quite daunting to a man who longed only to be back in the saddle.

Arnold turned to go. "Please close the door on your way out," Jake called after him. The younger man did as instructed, leaving Jake to the quiet of his office.

"I'm not where I want to be," he whispered and glanced upward. His first love, Deborah Vandermark, would have told him he should pray on the matter. It had been a long time, however, since Jake had done any real talking to the Lord. He touched the scar on his right hand. He'd cut it while working for Deborah's family. She had been training to become a physician and had sewed it up for him. Whenever he saw the scar, he thought of her kindness to him and her faith. She was a strong woman of God. . . . How different from Marty, who obviously struggled when it came to the Almighty. He smiled. Hadn't he had his own issues? He couldn't fault Marty for feeling untrusting when he had some of the same problems.

"I suppose it wouldn't hurt to mention a few things to you, Lord." Jake got up and walked to the window. He couldn't help but wonder what Marty would think if she knew that he was beginning to wish for more in their marriage. More in his life.

Taking it to God in prayer was something his mother had always encouraged. He knew a Christian was supposed to pray, read his Bible, live a life pleasing to God. Jake knew, too, that he'd been focused only on survival—doing whatever it took to get one step closer to Texas.

Marty had been an important part of that, but the more time they spent together, the less inclined she seemed to be toward the idea of returning. He wasn't entirely sure why she held Texas a grudge. Maybe it had to do with the death of her first husband. She had loved him a great deal; that much was evident. No one had ever loved Jake that way, and it made him just a little bit jealous.

Pray about it.

The words seemed to burn deep into his heart.

"I wanna go home, Lord," he finally prayed. "I wanna go back to Texas."

Chapter 17

"The Morgans do love to entertain," Marty declared as they made their way home in the carriage. "And how interesting to have a May Day party complete with a Maypole. I have to admit I've never seen the dance involved, but it was quite lovely with all those ribbons."

Jake nodded but said very little. He seemed glum and restless, and Marty couldn't help but wonder what had been said or done to bring about such a mood.

"Did you have a bad time?" she dared to question.

He looked at her from across the carriage, but the dim street lighting did little to reveal his expression. Who was this man she'd married, and why couldn't she better understand him?

"I didn't have either a bad or good time," he answered her. "It was just one more party—one more meaningless day." The weariness in his voice rang clear.

Marty tried not to panic at his comment. Lately Jake was given to speaking more and more of his longing for Texas and the ranch life that he loved. "There are days here when I just want to pack up and walk away. I'm tired of bank ledgers and businessmen more concerned with their vast wealth than the condition of the people around them. I want more than this, but . . ."

He fell silent for a few moments, and then started in again. "You know how I feel about owning my own spread one day."

"I do," Marty said, keeping her tone neutral. She deeply feared what he might say next.

"I was speaking with Dennis Sheedy tonight. You'll remember he used to ranch a great deal."

"Yes."

"Well, he advised against any ranching or farming venture at this point. He said the markets weren't good for either. He said it would be a waste of time and money, and I would soon find myself in the same position my father was a few years ago."

Marty's heart skipped a beat. *God bless you, Mr. Sheedy.* She remained silent, hoping that Jake would tell her he was giving up on his dreams.

"I reminded him that folks will always need to eat, but he said there was already a glut of ranches and farms and that with the economy as it is, there have been a great many foreclosures, as well. I thought that would make it more reasonable for me to be able to buy in. After all, the places will sell dirt cheap."

"But you would be benefiting from another's loss. That doesn't seem like something you'd be comfortable with."

"I wouldn't like it, but better that someone continue the dream—don't you think?"

"I don't know," Marty said, though she had her own opinion about such dreams. "I do know that ranching is a dangerous business. There are things there that can take your life in a moment's notice."

"And there aren't here?"

She shrugged. "It's hardly the same. On the ranch a man can die from his horse taking a misstep or crossing the path of a rattler."

"And that can't happen here—to a banker?" He sounded irritated. "You weren't that far away from Denver when your stage was attacked. Someone's been creeping around the house, probably looking to steal us blind. There's always something or someone looking to do evil."

Marty knew she needed to rein back her negativity toward ranching. Perhaps changing the subject would help. "Oh, let's not dwell on the sad and bad. I very nearly forgot to tell you about my experience at the orphanage today. I was able to spend some time helping the little ones with their reading. It reminded me of how Hannah used to teach us when we were little." She paused and noticed Jake was lost in thought.

"There are a great many children in this city who have no one. Did you realize that? There are a dozen or more orphanages and all of them full," she rambled.

Jake, however, remained silent the entire journey home. She worried that her comments had left him overly discouraged.

"I'm sorry, Jake. I'm sorry if I sounded unfeeling in regard to your dreams," she said as they approached the house. Marty turned to find they were only inches from each other. The glow of the porch light made it easy to see the sadness in his eyes.

"I truly don't wish to see you hurt. I don't want to lose another husband the way I lost Thomas."

Jake's head cocked slightly. "Sounds as though you've come to care about me."

Marty trembled—grateful that Jake wasn't holding on to her arm or he might have felt it and wondered why. "Of course I care about you. We've been together now for more than three months. I've come to enjoy your company and thought you felt likewise."

"I do," he whispered.

She smiled. "Then surely you can understand why I don't want to see you hurt. I want to have you around for a good long time. I want to enjoy our life together."

"And you're content with this and nothing more?"

Marty hesitated, not sure of his meaning. They were so very close, and for just a heartbeat, Marty thought Jake might kiss her. Worse still, she wanted him to. When she said nothing, however, Jake apparently took this as a dismissal.

"I'm sorry. I shouldn't have said that. I appreciate that you care. I'm sorry if I've been poor company."

Disappointment flooded Marty's soul as Jake moved to the open front door, where Brighton awaited them. Why did she feel so out of sorts? Was she losing her heart to this man?

I swore never again. I never wanted to love another person like I loved Thomas—especially not a rancher.

She vowed then and there to guard her heart more carefully. She couldn't risk allowing Jake to make her care about him the way she would a husband. Theirs was a sensible arrangement—nothing more.

★

Brighton followed Jake to his bedroom and helped him with his clothes. "Will you need anything else this evening, sir?"

Jake shook his head. "Please feel free to retire. I will be fine."

"Very good, sir." Brighton moved toward the door with Jake's coat in hand. "I'll give this a good brushing and return it in the morning. Good night, sir."

"Yes, good night," Jake replied and all but closed the door in Brighton's face.

Pacing the room in his trousers and shirt, Jake couldn't stop thinking about Marty. She had looked so beautiful tonight. When they'd arrived home, she had mentioned caring about him and Jake had been certain she would have allowed him to kiss her.

So why didn't I?

He stopped and stared at the door that adjoined their rooms. It would be easy enough to open it and pass through to her dressing room. He could hear her in there. Alice was no doubt readying her mistress for bed, combing out her silky blond hair and braiding it for sleep. He could go to them on some pretense.

But why bother? Even if she has come to care about me, it doesn't mean she wants anything more.

Jake began pacing again. There had to be something more, however. He was so discontent with the way things were. He felt that life held no meaning. He had married because the bank had insisted he have a wife, but now he found himself feeling something more for his wife . . . and it stood to ruin everything.

Am I in love with her?

The question seemed simple enough, but Jake struggled to even allow the thought. He had been so certain that he would never love again. Of course, he'd been just as certain that he would never marry again, yet here he was . . . a husband.

At least there were no children to worry about. But that thought caused just as much anguish. He had wanted children, had always seen himself as fathering a large family. A family who could help him run the ranch and inherit the fruits of his labors.

Brighton had laid a small fire in the hearth—just enough to ward off the chill of the evening, but Jake couldn't help but feel cold. He was cold from the inside out. It was like sinking in quicksand and knowing you weren't going to get out.

Maybe it had been a mistake to marry Marty. He frowned. "But I can't imagine my life without her now."

He heard laughter from the room next door and longed to be a part of it. He went to the door and put his hand out to touch the polished wood.

If only you knew how I felt. If only I could help you see that we could have something more—something deeper—richer.

Jake spent the rest of the night in a restless sleep. He dreamed of Marty and how their marriage might be. He awakened several times almost sensing her nearness, only to realize it had been nothing more than his imagination at work.

He heard the clock chime four and wondered if he would ever again be able to enjoy a restful night. With that beautiful wife of his so close, yet so far away, it seemed doubtful.

I could woo her.

The thought seemed reasonable enough. Jake rubbed his jaw. *I could court my wife and show her that there could be a great romance between us.*

But what if that wasn't what she wanted? What if Jake put his heart and soul into winning Marty's affection, and she turned out to despise him for it? She might accuse him of altering their marriage agreement. She might even decide to have the marriage annulled, and he certainly didn't want that.

She said she cared about me. Jake wrestled with that thought. Wasn't that enough to build on? He'd never claimed to know much about courting and wooing, but he felt confident that the friendship they shared was a good foundation for something more.

We enjoy each other's company. We have a great deal in common.

Thoughts poured through his mind—all the reasons why this courtship should work. Jake grinned in the dark. He felt a surge of excitement and a rush of energy that made him feel like a youth again. He could be charming. He could make Marty fall in love with him. He was convinced of it.

He put his hands under his head and his smile broadened. "She thinks ranch life has its hidden dangers," he whispered to the night. "Wait until she sees what we Colorado bankers are capable of."

★

Trinity Methodist Church was beginning to grow on Marty. Or at least the music was. The organ's four thousand pipes were not to be ignored when sounding a hymn. Jake had once commented that this church made you *feel* the music deep within your soul. Marty agreed.

She listened only halfheartedly to the sermon. The minister was teaching from the book of Genesis, about Isaac and Rebekah. Abraham had arranged for his servant to go back to the country of his origin and get Isaac a wife. It was a story Marty remembered well from childhood.

Rebekah was rather like the original mail-order bride, Marty reasoned.

She listened momentarily as the Word was read. "'And they called Rebekah, and said unto her, Wilt thou go with this man? And she said, I will go.'"

Marty gave a quick side glance at Jake, who seemed completely caught up in the sermon. He was such a handsome man—more handsome than she'd even noticed when she'd first married him. And he was kind and generous. She couldn't fault him for much of anything. If only he would put aside his desire to return to Texas.

I can't go back there. There's nothing there for me—just memories. Even if she gave Jake the ranch and they started their life together there, the ghost of Thomas would always be between them. It wouldn't be a real marriage at all.

It isn't a real marriage, she reminded herself.

A longing stirred deep within her, and Marty did her best to squelch it. Desires, however, came unbidden, as they were known to do. She wanted a real marriage with Jacob Wythe. She wanted a lifetime of love and laughter—of children and growing old together. The thought brought tears to her eyes.

Why must I feel these things now?

"'And Isaac brought her into his mother Sarah's tent—'" the minister's voice broke through her thoughts—"'and took Rebekah, and she became his wife; and he loved her.'"

And he loved her.

The words echoed in her ears. Isaac and Rebekah were strangers to one another—arranged in a marriage not of their own doing—yet Isaac loved her.

Could Jake love me?

And what if he did? Could she set aside her fears and share

the truth with him? Could she tell him about the ranch and give him the choice of having his dream or remaining in Colorado?

I can't. I already know what he would choose.

She bit her lip and stared down at her gloved hands. If not for that stupid ranch, she wouldn't have to feel all this guilt. There would be no chance of love between them until she was free of that ranch. A thought came to mind: She didn't necessarily need to sell the place. She could just deed it over to William and Hannah. It had been their land to begin with.

She relaxed a bit. She could tell Jake the property reverted back to them—that she'd felt honor bound to return it after Thomas died. But how would she explain the delay? Maybe she could tell him that she hadn't been ready to move forward with her life, and they had been gracious enough to let her remain on the ranch. That made perfect sense. They were that kind of people.

Realizing she was once again spinning lies to save herself, Marty pushed the thoughts aside. There would be plenty of time to figure out the details later. No sense in using God's house for such underhanded purposes. She looked at Jake, and he turned to her and smiled.

She smiled in return. Maybe they *could* have a real marriage.

Chapter 18

"I heard someone at the door," Marty mentioned to Brighton as he entered the dining room.

"Yes, madam. A gentleman arrived to speak with Miss Chesterfield."

"Alice?" Marty put down her coffee. "Did he say why?" Alice had told Marty that she had no friends in the area—that she had led a very reclusive life after her mother had gone. Perhaps the bank had sent someone to offer her compensation.

"No, madam. He only said it was of some urgency."

Marty pushed away from the table, and Brighton hurried to assist her from the chair. "I think I'd better check on her. Where are they now?"

"I put them in the formal sitting room."

Marty nodded. "Thank you."

She made her way to the pocket doors of the front sitting room in time to hear the man speak. "You'd better figure out where they are—unless you want a scar on the other cheek."

Marty's blood ran cold. She hurried from the hall and went to where she had hidden her shotgun. Cocking it open, she checked the load. Both barrels were loaded and ready.

She started to snap it closed, then thought better of it. With a smile, she draped the open barrel over her arm, hoping to look casual but ready for action. The man might find it easy to intimidate Alice, but let him mess with a Texan and see what he thought.

Walking on tiptoes toward the large sitting room, Marty listened for the sound of conversation. Voices could be heard in muffled tones, though she couldn't quite make out what was being said.

She eased herself into position by the open pocket doors and waited for a moment.

"I told you," Alice said, sounding terrified, "I have no idea what you're talking about. My father was robbed that night and everything was taken. Everything he had from the bank was in that satchel."

"I don't believe you. See, I happen to know what was in that satchel. Or rather, what was supposed to be in there."

Alice gasped. "So you were one of the men who attacked us?"

"Not exactly." He laughed, and the sound made Marty's blood boil. "I'm the one who hired them. I happen to know that your father should have been carrying a large envelope that night. It would have had the bank's seal on it."

"I never saw anything like that. My father never included me in his business. He worked at the bank and that's all I ever knew." She sounded terror-stricken.

Marty could stand it no longer. "Oh! Excuse me," she said, entering the room. "I heard voices and couldn't imagine who it could be." She watched as the man darted a glance at the shotgun and then back to her face. He smiled as if knowing full well what Marty was up to.

"Ma'am." He nodded his head.

Marty looked to Alice. "You have a job to do. Don't let me catch you in such idleness again." She turned away from the man and gave Alice a wink. "You don't want to lose your position, do you?"

"No, Mrs. Wythe." Alice gave a curtsy and hurried from the room. "I'm sorry, Mrs. Wythe."

Marty snapped the shotgun closed and looked back at the man with a smile. "I do hope you will forgive me, but we have a busy schedule today. My maid isn't able to receive visitors on working days, Mr. . . . ?"

He gave her a smile that suggested he was less than impressed with her game. "Call me Smith. Mr. Smith."

"Of course," Marty said, not trying to hide the sarcasm from her tone. "Well, Mr. Smith, unless there's something I can help you with, I'll show you out. . . ." She let her words trail.

The man looked at her cradling the shotgun and nodded. "I suppose it can wait. I can catch up with her another time."

"I think not," Marty said, the smile never leaving her face. "I'm rather possessive of my help. I think it might be better if you were to leave Alice alone. Otherwise . . ."

"Are you threatening me if I don't?" he asked, narrowing his eyes.

"Did I say something threatening?" She batted her eyes in the same southern flirtatious style she'd been taught in finishing school. "Goodness, but I can't think of why you should feel threatened by little ol' me." She let her drawl thicken. "Why, I just never meant to suggest anything of the kind."

He laughed, but his eyes remained fixed and then they narrowed. "Of course not."

Marty sobered and pointed toward the door with the shotgun. "I'm glad we understand each other. Now if you'll be so kind as to leave."

"You might as well know, Mrs. Wythe, that this isn't the end of it. I intend to speak to Miss Chesterfield again. I've looked long and hard for her. Sent my men around to watch your place and her comings and goings. She has something that belongs to me."

"Alice is my employee, and she came here with nothing but the clothes on her back. If I see you or your men on my property again, I'll arrange a reception for you." She glanced at the shotgun. "And that isn't a threat—it's a promise. See, I'm not easily intimidated—unlike Alice."

"She knows what I'm after," he said, taking a step toward Marty. "And I will have it."

She raised the shotgun just enough to remind him of its presence. For just a moment, Marty thought he might charge her—and if that happened, she knew she'd have to make good her threat. But just then another voice called out.

"Miz Wythe, Mr. Brighton said you needed to see me."

It was Samson. For all the time she'd been married to Jake, Marty had never once seen Samson inside the house.

The stranger stopped midstep. His gaze traveled the full length of the hulking man. He looked back to Marty and gave her a knowing nod. "Good day, Mrs. Wythe. I will speak to you again . . . no doubt."

Marty didn't relax until the man was out of her house and on the back of his horse. From the porch, she watched him trot the mount down the street and wondered silently whether she'd handled things poorly. She had wanted the man to feel threatened, but she certainly hadn't wanted to stir him to take further action. In any case, the man was clearly an enemy now.

She went back into the house and found Samson gone but Alice waiting for her. One look at the girl told Marty she'd overheard the entire exchange between herself and Mr. Smith.

"I'm so sorry, Mrs. Wythe. I'm so sorry. I had Mr. Brighton fetch Samson. I hope it was the right thing to do."

Marty shook her head and lowered the shotgun. "It was exactly right, but never mind that. What in the world was he after?"

"Some papers—papers that apparently weren't in my father's satchel when we were robbed. He admitted to sending the men to attack us." Tears welled in the younger woman's eyes. "I'm so afraid. I don't know what he's talking about. When I recovered from my wounds, everything we owned was auctioned off to pay for my father's burial and my hospital fees. I was still in the hospital when they sold the house. There were only a few things that I even managed to hang on to, thanks to my friends, and nothing I have was of any value. Certainly there was no envelope of papers like he's after."

"Well, from now on, you stay close to me. I don't want you going out alone. If you need to go somewhere, I'll send Samson along with you. Folks will think twice about bothering you with him at your side."

"Thank you, Mrs. Wythe." Alice looked around the foyer and whispered, "Marty."

Marty embraced the girl, letting the shotgun dangle at her side. "I won't see you intimidated by him or anyone else."

"I should have told you." Alice moved away from Marty and shook her head. "I'm sorry."

"Told me what?" Marty asked.

Alice wrung her hands. "I . . . well . . . there's been some-one trying to get to me since the attack. They told me at the hospital that someone had come there searching for me, but the doctors wouldn't allow them to see me—especially since when they first arrived I was still unconscious. Then later, when I was staying with friends, they told me someone had come there looking for me. It just so happened that I was gone that day, but . . . well . . . the men who showed up threatened my friends. It frightened them so bad that they decided to leave Denver altogether rather than deal with that again. They figured I would go with them, but I reminded them that whoever it was would just follow, so I figured it was best to stay and let them escape."

"Well, Mr. Smith is going to find himself outnumbered here. You're safe with us. I grew up fending off Comanche and other marauders. You learn to be tough when you live out in the open range. In Texas you often have to be on your guard. That man doesn't worry me," she said gruffly. But truth be told, Marty had seen an evil glint in his eye that suggested he wasn't easily deterred from his plans.

"Will you tell Mr. Wythe?"

Marty nodded. "I think that would be best. He should know that the folks sneaking around the place were looking for you rather than stuff to steal."

Alice nodded. "I hope he won't be mad at me. I don't want to lose my position here."

"You won't. I believe he'll be just as protective of you as I am."

★

"He what?" Jake asked, his eyes narrowed.

"He threatened Alice . . . and in a way, me," Marty told

her husband later that day. "He told me he would get what he wanted."

"I don't like this one bit. I wish you knew where he came from. I'd like to pay him a visit." Jake looked at Alice. "Do you have any idea who he is?"

Alice shook her head. "He didn't give me a name, sir."

"He told me his name was Smith, but I think that's just made up," Marty added.

Alice stood visibly trembling. "He just started in on me. Kept saying how the punishment I'd already been dealt would be nothing compared to what was coming if I didn't cooperate."

"And you know nothing about what he's after?"

Again Alice shook her head. "He said it was a large envelope with papers, and that it had been sealed by the bank. I know from things my father told me that they only did that on very important dealings. If it was something that needed to go from the bank to the person involved without anyone else seeing the material, it would be sealed."

Jake nodded, already familiar with the process. He ran a hand through his hair. The thought of someone coming around with malicious intent caused him to feel more than a little agitation. The very idea that someone would send men to scout out his house and threaten his staff and wife . . . "I'll speak to the police about this. Perhaps they can help."

"They weren't of any help to my friends," Alice said bitterly. "I doubt they'd be any more help now."

"Well, you didn't have the backing of people like Morgan and Keystone. I do," Jake assured her. "We'll get to the bottom of this. I will personally go and speak with Mr. Morgan and find out what was in that envelope your father should have been carrying."

———————————— ★ ————————————

Two days later, Jake had his opportunity when Morgan appeared at the bank with an invitation for the Wythes to join the Morgans and others for a celebration.

"Mrs. Morgan delights in throwing me birthday parties, and she wanted to make certain you and Mrs. Wythe could attend. Now, there aren't to be any gifts, of course. Just the company of good friends for a nice lawn party."

"We'd be honored to attend," Jake said, having little interest yet knowing that if he accommodated the man he would be more likely to get some reasonable response to his questions. "I wonder, though, before you leave, could I have a word?"

Mr. Morgan nodded and took a seat. "If this is about your vice-presidency, be assured it is moving ever closer to fruition."

Jake moved to close his office door. "No, it's not about that at all." He came back to his desk and sat. "As you know, my wife's maid was the daughter of your former bank manager, Mr. Chesterfield."

"Yes. Yes, I know that. Is your wife pestering you again to have the bank offer the girl some form of reparation?"

"Not at all. Marty understands the situation. Unfortunately, however, we had a bit of an incident the other day. A man came to the house and threatened Miss Chesterfield in order to learn the whereabouts of a packet of papers her father should have been carrying the night of his death."

Morgan frowned. "What papers?"

"I was hoping you could tell me."

"The man didn't say what he wanted?"

Jake shook his head. "Only that they were in a bank-sealed envelope. A large envelope. It should have been in the satchel that was in Mr. Chesterfield's possession, and apparently this man knew that it was missing. I wondered if you might know what was in that envelope that made it worth killing for."

For several moments Morgan said nothing. He looked as if he were trying to remember. Finally he shook his head. "I'm really not at liberty to tell you the details."

"So you do know what was in it?"

"I do, but very few others have been told." He looked at Jake and seemed reluctant to share the information. "We were afraid of making a public scene. We didn't need negative stories to spread regarding the bank's security."

Jake could understand that, given the problems the economy was already starting to see in 1892. "So might you enlighten me? After all, my family and home seem to be under some threat."

"And your maid has no idea of what the man was talking about?" Morgan asked.

"None. She came to our employ with virtually nothing. If there were an envelope amidst the things she and her father owned, it was either destroyed or lost. All of their things were auctioned off to pay for the funeral and her medical expenses. Now, I'd like to know what this man is after."

"I suppose you're entitled." Morgan drew a deep breath and laced his fingers together. "It was full of gold certificates— worth a small fortune."

Jake startled at this news. "Why in the world was he carrying something as valuable as that?"

Morgan shrugged. "It was the way we handled it. We put on a fussy show of guarded couriers for those who might think to rob us, while sending the real goods with no escort whatsoever. It worked quite well, and we shipped money, certificates, stocks, and even some jewelry that way. In fact, Chesterfield was the first man we've ever lost."

"Let me get this straight: You gave Chesterfield an envelope with a fortune in gold certificates to be delivered as if it were nothing more important than business correspondence?"

"Exactly."

"And did he know what he was carrying?"

"Not to my knowledge. Oh, I mean he would have known there was value to the papers. He always knew that any delivery we entrusted to him was of vital importance. He was paid well, however. As for his knowing the contents . . . well . . . I can't imagine that he did. I certainly wouldn't have told him. There was no need."

"But gold certificates were included in his satchel that night, and someone knew they were supposed to be there."

"I don't know how they could have." Morgan shook his head. "There were only a couple of us privy to the information."

"Well, somebody talked," Jake said.

★

Marty dreaded opening the letter in her hand. Either Hannah had mailed it before Marty's missive arrived telling her about Jake and the marriage, or she'd hastily posted it after hearing the news. Either way, Marty wasn't in any hurry to discover what was within.

She thought to distract herself with a nice quiet lunch alone, but after studying the thin slices of rare roast beef on her plate, she sighed. "I might as well read it. My mind won't rest until I do."

Pulling the envelope from her pocket, Marty ran her dinner knife under the seal along the top to open it. The missive was short—one page. Marty drew a deep breath and perused the lines.

My dear sister,

How wonderful for you to have found love again. I'm surprised that you worried I would think badly of your choice. I've long hoped that you could find another man to love. You are much too young to be a widow. Perhaps now you will have a family of your own and know the happiness of motherhood, as well.

Please know that William and I are praying for you and that we are so very happy for you and Jake. You have made him sound like such a wonderful man, and I look forward to the day we can meet face-to-face. William said we could use a banker in the family.

I know that you never planned to remarry after Thomas, but now that you have, I pray you will be happy. I was delighted to read that you are attending church once again, and I pray, too, that this new adventure in life will allow you to once again draw close to God.

Faithfully yours,
Hannah

Marty let out the breath she'd been holding. Hannah didn't mind, didn't protest the matter in the least. It was a surprise—her sister had carefully tried to manage Marty's choices for most of her life. The announcement of her traveling to Colorado had completely upset that tradition, and Marty had been certain her news would cause Hannah a fit of apoplexy.

"Thank goodness that's done with." Marty folded the letter and put it back in her pocket.

She tried to think of what she should do next. She wanted to get the ranch matter settled and figured the best thing to do would be to write immediately to her sister and suggest that Will have the papers drawn up for her to deed the place back to him. Of course, Marty was married now and had no way of knowing if she'd need her husband's permission to conduct business. Laws were often funny about that, and married women didn't have the same rights that widowed women did. Perhaps she should seek the advice of a lawyer.

"But how do I go about that without Jake knowing what I'm doing?"

★

Jake noticed Marty's good mood that evening. She seemed more carefree and lighthearted than he'd ever known her to be. He had no idea what had caused the change, but he was glad for it. He thought back to his conversation with Mr. Morgan and wondered if he should spoil her happiness with the details of what he'd learned. Deciding against it for the time being, Jake chose instead to enjoy a quiet evening reading while Marty worked on some project of her own.

The clock chimed the hour, and Jake yawned. He stole a glance at his wife, who'd been quietly sewing. With her head bent over the garment, she looked completely content. Marty loved keeping busy, and he understood that.

She seemed to sense his gaze and looked up. Smiling, she rolled her shoulders. "I suppose it's time for bed. I tend to get caught up in what I'm doing."

"What exactly are you doing?"

"Making a pinafore. It's for one of the orphans. I wanted to do something more for them, and I figured I could sew as well as the next woman."

"Probably better, given your new circle of friends." He watched her carefully tuck the sewing back into a basket by the chair. "You truly enjoy working with the orphans, don't you?"

"I do," Marty replied. "They are so . . . well . . . they seem to thrive on my affection and attention. God knows they don't get much. The workers do their best, but it isn't the same as having a family."

"No, I'm sure it isn't."

"Speaking of family, I had a very nice letter from my sister." Marty reached into her pocket and handed it over to him. "I finally told her about us."

"You did?" Jake opened the letter and scanned the lines. He felt his chest tighten at the comment about Marty becoming a mother. The idea of having children with Marty had started to consume his thoughts more often than he liked to admit.

"She says you made me sound like a wonderful man," Jake commented, concluding the letter. "Whatever did you say to cause that kind of response?"

Marty gave a light laugh and got to her feet. Jake quickly followed suit. He handed her back the letter and waited for her to respond. For a very long moment all they did was gaze into each other's eyes, however. Jake longed to take her in his arms, but he forced himself to stand completely still.

Finally Marty replied. "I told her you were good to me—that you were generous and kind. I told her that I was happy and wanted her to be happy for me."

"And are you happy, Marty?" He was barely able to voice the words.

She smiled, and it warmed his heart in a way he'd never known. Neither Josephine nor Deborah had made him feel this way.

"Of course I'm happy. Especially now that my sister knows about our marriage and approves."

"Her approval was that important?"

She shrugged. "I suppose it was. Family has always been important to me. I guess I didn't make it seem that way, running off as I did without letting them know. I just wanted to make my own choices and be responsible for my life."

Her gaze held his. Jake wanted so much to tell her how he felt—how she had changed his mind about love. How he longed to alter their arrangement and start anew with a real marriage.

"I want to make you happy, Marty. I guess I want your approval, as well," he finally managed to whisper.

She surprised him by reaching up to touch his cheek. "You are an amazing man, Jake, and you do have my approval. I think together . . . we can be very happy."

He put his hand over hers. "I think so, too."

Chapter 19

Marty finished making her second pinafore when Brighton appeared with a large box. "This just arrived for you, madam," he announced.

"Goodness, what is it?"

"I do not know." He placed the box on a small table. "Would you like me to open it?"

Putting her sewing aside, Marty nodded. "Please." She got to her feet and joined him.

Brighton opened the box, revealing a dozen red roses. The fragrance wafted through the air, and Marty inhaled the sweet aroma. She hadn't been given roses since long before Thomas's death.

"They're beautiful," she murmured, gently touching one of the blossoms.

"There is a card, madam." Brighton reached in and pulled it from among the flowers. He handed it to Marty.

Marty opened the card. *To my wife. Thank you for the trust you've placed in me. You make my life so much better. Affectionately, your husband.*

The sentiment surprised and disturbed Marty. Already

uncertain and confused by her own feelings for Jake, she didn't need this to further complicate matters.

But it's not such a complication if he feels the same way, is it? Should I be afraid of falling in love with a man who clearly feels something for me?

"Would you like me to have Mrs. Landry arrange them in a vase?" Brighton asked.

Marty nodded. "Yes, please do."

"Very good, madam." He took up the box, leaving Marty with the note.

In the hallway he apparently ran into Mrs. Landry, because Marty could hear the two begin to pick at each other.

Mrs. Landry commented in a rather loud voice, "I know very well how to arrange flowers, you ninny. Don't be trying to tell me how to do my job."

Marty looked down at the card again and frowned. Why was this happening now? And why did it bother her as much as it did? Surely she should feel a sense of relief that the man she'd married was a good match—that they both enjoyed each other's company and had found some semblance of happiness in the aftermath of losing their prior mates.

So why do I feel so uncomfortable?

Marty tucked the card into her sewing box and moved back to her work. She tried to calm her mind, telling herself it was a kind gesture, nothing more. But there had been moments of tenderness lately that stirred her heart. . . .

Jake had made it clear in his letters prior to their marriage that he didn't want a romance. Had he changed his mind? Had she changed hers?

Marty had to admit the aching in her heart was evidence that something was afoot. She had thought herself incapable of loving again—Thomas had been the love of her life. Wouldn't it be a betrayal to his memory if she were to give her heart to another?

Folding the pinafore carefully, Marty tried to reason through her feelings. Thomas was dead. There was no one who could bring him back. Thomas himself would have been the first one to tell her to be happy—to find something in life she could enjoy and live for. He would have wanted her to remarry and have children.

"I saw the flowers," Alice said, entering the small sitting room. "They're beautiful."

"Jake . . . Mr. Wythe sent them," Marty replied.

Alice looked at her for a moment. "Is that a bad thing?"

"Why do you ask?"

"You seem troubled. I just wondered, given your . . . arrangement . . . if it made matters difficult for you."

Marty shrugged. "I've been asking myself the same thing, to tell you the truth." She put the pinafore into her sewing basket and frowned. "I never figured to have these feelings again, and now that I do, I have to say they're making me most uncomfortable."

"What feelings are those?" Alice asked in her innocent way.

Marty met her maid's gaze. The girl was young enough to have been Marty's daughter. Her blond hair even resembled Marty's own thick tresses. For reasons Marty couldn't even begin to put into words, Alice touched a special place in her heart.

"I suppose . . . love," Marty finally answered. "I'd hardened my heart against it until I came here. Then I found myself moved by you and your plight, touched by the orphans and theirs, and . . ."

"And you're falling in love with your husband?" Alice dared to ask.

Marty wasn't yet ready to admit that idea aloud. "I don't know."

Alice smiled. "I think you do, and that's the problem. You just don't know how to face the truth."

Marty heard male voices coming from the hallway and glanced at the clock. It was only half past two. Had Alice's tormenter returned? She looked to Alice, who seemed to wonder the same thing—if the look on her face was any indication.

"Don't worry," Marty said. "You're safe."

Jake marched into the room with an expression of grave concern. "There's been an unexpected board meeting called at the bank this afternoon, and I've been asked to attend. I expect it will run well into the evening, and I wanted to let you know."

"What's wrong?" Marty questioned. The tone of his voice and his countenance were most severe.

"The president has called for an emergency session of Congress. He hopes to repeal the Sherman Silver Purchase Act. It won't bode well for anyone, but especially not this state. We rely heavily on silver holding its value, and this will change everything."

"Is it really that bad?" Just last week she'd dined at one of Denver's finest homes, and the wealth there flowed like an undammed river.

He stopped in front of Marty. "It is. Colorado is responsible for over 60 percent of this country's silver. It's not right that the president should imagine silver is the culprit for all our financial woes, but apparently he does. This is only going to make matters worse, the way I see it."

Marty longed to offer him comfort. "I'll wait up to talk

with you. Perhaps once you know more about it, things won't seem so bad."

"It'll probably be late. You might as well go to bed."

"I don't mind waiting," she said softly. "I'm sure it will be important for our future."

He nodded. "I'm afraid it's going to completely alter the future of a great many folks."

Marty had never heard him sound so grave. She knew at one time she would have encouraged solace with prayer. A sparking in her heart told her she should again suggest such recourse, but bitterness quickly snuffed out the ember. Why ask God for help? If He cared, wouldn't He have already offered His protection?

Another thought came to mind. "Should I send someone with a meal for you and the others?"

Jake smiled. "I doubt anyone else has thought of that."

"I could have Cook put together some sandwiches and cookies. Food that would be easy to eat without benefit of table service."

"That sounds like a grand idea, Marty. Thank you. Why don't you send Samson over with it at about six?"

"That will give us plenty of time to arrange it," Marty replied, smiling. She was glad to be able to do something to make things easier for him. "Try not to worry," she added. "These things have a way of working out."

"I hope so. God knows this isn't going to be pleasant for anyone. We may well watch the collapse of our entire country's financial foundation."

★

The evening passed in relative silence. Alice helped Marty dress for bed early.

"Are you sure you don't want me to keep you company for a while?" Alice asked.

Marty shook her head. "No, go enjoy an evening to yourself. You work hard, and I appreciate all that you do. Besides, I'm just going to sit here and read."

"I think I'll do the same," Alice told her. "It'll be nice to just have the time to myself." She picked up the rest of Marty's clothes and smiled. "I'll take these to the laundry first. Good night."

"Good night."

The day had been warm, so Marty opened one of her bedroom windows and breathed deeply of the night air. She could smell the scent of flowering trees and marveled at the slight chill to the air. The weather here was so different. The day could be hot and dry, then often in the afternoon a brief rain would come down from the mountains and by night the air would be cool. She marveled at the glow of electric lighting coming from the neighboring houses. Folks in this elite community wouldn't know how to function without their wealth. If things were as bad as Jake thought, Marty couldn't help but wonder what would happen to these people.

Of course, she knew that the rich usually had contingencies for such things. They wouldn't suffer as much as those poor souls who relied on the generosity of the wealthy.

Rubbing her arms, Marty closed the window again and took up her book. She heard the large grandfather clock chime the hour. Nine o'clock. And still there was no sign of Jake. Marty wondered how the meeting was going—what it would mean for them.

She couldn't help but think of the ranch. She knew that

Jake had put aside money for what he hoped would be his future purchase of a spread in Texas. She knew that this tragedy could prevent that from ever happening. Maybe that was the answer to her problems.

Am I hopelessly greedy in wanting things my own way? Is it wrong to hope that the financial situation will keep us right here in Denver?

Marty had read nearly half of her book by the time she heard someone at the door to Jake's bedroom. She listened and waited. She'd left both of her dressing room doors open wide in hopes that he would come and tell her all about the meeting. Voices were soon evident.

"I won't need anything, Brighton. Go ahead and retire. I'm sure that anything I have to see to can wait until morning."

"Very good, sir."

Marty heard the exchange and noted the weariness in her husband's voice. Maybe it would be better if they didn't speak. Maybe the news would be so bad that she'd be unable to sleep.

But maybe if I share the load with him, Jake will rest better. Given her guilt over the ranch, Marty wanted to push aside her own selfish needs and reach out to Jake.

"Marty?" Jake called from the dressing room.

"I'm in here. Please join me," she called back. She put the book away, then adjusted her robe to make certain she wasn't being immodest.

Jake entered the room in a state of undress. His tie was gone and shirt unbuttoned partway but still tucked into his trousers. He'd shed his shoes, coat, and vest and looked more tired than Marty had ever seen him. It gave Marty a start. He looked far more like a Texas cowboy than a Colorado banker.

He plopped into one of the wingback chairs by the fireplace and began to rub his neck.

"Let me," Marty said, pushing his hands aside. "I'm pretty good at this. Years of milking and toting gave me strong hands." She began to knead his tight muscles.

"Oh, that feels so good. Thank you." For several minutes he said nothing more. Marty remained silent, as well. It was one of the most intimate moments she could recall having with him. They were like an old married couple at the end of a busy day. The thought made her smile.

Finally, after nearly ten minutes had passed, Jake stilled her hands and motioned her to sit. "The news is better taken sitting down."

"That bad—already?"

He nodded. "They fully expect that hundreds of banks will close almost overnight in anticipation of what's to come. Ours isn't one of them—at least not yet. We're strong enough to survive for a time, but there's no way of knowing how long that will last. Morgan has in mind to close a couple of the branches and consolidate all his efforts into just a few banks. Ours would be one of them, and he wants me to oversee the reorganization."

"So you won't lose your position?"

"Not yet. But who knows what will happen in the months to come. There's no way of estimating just how bad this is going to get, Marty. Most of the silver mines are going to close. The value of silver has dropped already. This will send property values sliding. I feel bad because I promised you pleasantries and a life of ease, and now this is going to change everything. We're going to have to let some of the staff go and tighten our belts."

"That's all right. We can manage." She tried to not think of what Alice might do. The poor girl needed protection, as well as a job. Perhaps she could send her to Hannah.

"I figure we'll keep Samson, Brighton, Mrs. Landry, and Alice for now. Oh, and Mrs. Standish. Unfortunately, the others will have to go."

"If need be, Jake, I'm a pretty fair cook and I know perfectly well how to care for horses and hitch my own carriage, although I'd hate to lose Samson. I can also wash clothes and clean house. I am, as you have always said, quite capable."

Jake nodded. "You've proven that again and again. You know how to handle yourself and you don't need anyone."

"I wouldn't say that." Marty's voice dropped to almost a whisper. "I'm becoming rather dependent on you. I rather like our time together."

He gave her a weary smile and his drawl thickened. "Yup. I do, too." A sigh escaped his lips. "I just don't know how bad this is gonna get. I figure we should know better in a few weeks, but for now it's a mystery."

"Then we hunker down and ride out the storm," Marty replied. "We're young and strong. I've even got a few things— things I left in Texas that I can sell."

"No, I don't want you doing that. At least not yet. There's no need. I have money set aside—at least as long as the bank is solvent."

"Is there a chance it won't remain so?"

"There's no way of knowing, and I can't very well pull my money out. Even though I might want to." He laughed. "Imagine that—the bank manager, soon to be vice-president, pulling his savings out for fear that the bank will collapse. That wouldn't go over well."

"I suppose not," Marty agreed. In the back of her mind she thought again of the ranch. She could sell it and give the money over to Jake or at least use it for their day-to-day expenses. That would resolve several problems at once. Maybe Will would buy it from her rather than just take it back. She could ask him for a pittance of what it was worth.

"I'm gonna need you to watch your spending—not that you've ever given me reason to worry. Seems like the only time you have spent money has been for someone else—like the orphans."

"That won't be a problem. I already have a good bolt of broadcloth for the projects I'm working on. Otherwise, I don't need anything."

"I'll speak to Mrs. Landry about the household budget, as well."

"We can certainly eat in a simpler manner. Unless you need to entertain, I can do quite well on beans and tortillas." She grinned. "Of course, I doubt Mrs. Standish knows how to make tortillas, but I could teach her."

Jake nodded. "I would enjoy some tortillas myself. It's been a long time."

She leaned forward. "Seriously, we can weather this together. I'm not worried about social status or fancy baubles. Although I will say the roses you sent today were beautiful and most appreciated."

"You deserved them. That and much more. You've been a good wife and done everything you agreed to. You even go to church with me, and I know you've had a difficult time with that."

Marty felt her heart squeeze at his words. "Maybe it's time to stop having such a hard time of it." She got up and walked to the fireplace. "I know my anger at God needs to end. I know the truth, and I can't just go on ignoring it."

"I feel the same way, Marty. Maybe it's time we repented and let the past go."

She met his eyes. Such wonderful eyes.

Getting to his feet, Jake came to where she stood. "There's been a lot of things I've done wrong in life, Martha Wythe, but you aren't one of those things. I think you're probably the best thing that's ever happened to me."

Marty didn't know what to say. She was touched at his declaration and hoped with all her heart that Jake might seal his statement with a kiss. She offered what she hoped was an inviting smile. Jake just held her gaze for a few silent moments, then let go his hold.

"I'm gonna get some sleep before I fall down. You'd better do the same. No tellin' what tomorrow's gonna bring."

★

Marty slept restlessly, and by the time dawn cracked the horizon, she was up and pacing. A thought had come to her: Alice said she read her Bible and prayed every morning before work. Would she be doing just that at this hour?

Making her way to the third floor, Marty crept along the hallway to the room Mrs. Landry had assigned Alice. There was light coming from beneath the door, so Marty gave a light knock.

Alice opened the door, her eyes widening in surprise. "Marty, is something wrong?"

"May I come in?"

"Of course. It's your house." Alice backed up and pulled the door open.

Marty went into the simple room and noted the furnishings. The bed had already been made and the side table revealed an open Bible. "I remember you said that you spent this time in prayer and reading the Word of God."

"I do. I was just getting ready to pray when you knocked."

"I . . . well . . . I've not been right with God for a very long while now, as you know," Marty began. "I blamed God for taking Thomas from me, and I know it was wrong. It just hurt so much to lose him. Seemed easy to blame God for most of my miseries."

Alice nodded. "I know how much it hurt to lose my father and mother. I can only imagine the pain of losing a husband."

"My sister, Hannah, shared the plan of salvation with me when I was just a little girl. It seemed so easy then to accept that Jesus would come to earth and give His life to bring us into right accord with His Father—God. I remember Hannah telling me that Jesus loved me so much that He would rather die a horrible death on a cross than spend eternity without me." She smiled. "Isn't that a sweet way of putting it?"

Again Alice nodded, but this time she said nothing, as if sensing that Marty needed to get something off her chest.

"I asked Jesus to forgive me my sins, just like Hannah told me to do. I was a terrible liar at that time . . . I still have trouble with lies." She frowned. "Hannah told me lying was a sin just as much as killing was—that sin was sin in the eyes of God. All sin would keep us from Him."

Marty toyed with the belt of her robe. "I know the truth, and I've ignored it these last four years. Well, maybe not in whole, but in every way that mattered. I put a wall between me and God, and frankly . . . I'm tired, and I think it's time for that wall to come down."

Alice smiled and nodded. "Would you like to pray . . . with me?"

Marty felt a sense of relief and warmth of comfort pour over her. "I would like that very much."

Alice took hold of her hand. "I think God would like it, too."

Chapter 20

The weeks slipped by in a nightmarish sort of madness. Marty continued her work with the orphans, feeling that it offered her some semblance of order. But in truth, life in Denver verged on chaotic.

Daily the papers told of the financial collapse and all the problems that the state was bound to face. Women's suffrage was mentioned in the background, with some people claiming it would pass on the ballot come November. Marty had never concerned herself much with politics or the idea of voting, but given the state of the country, perhaps women did need to have a voice.

She considered the day laid out for her that June morning, and while the morning's activities were to her liking, the afternoon's were less favorable. She would first go to the orphanage; Marty loved getting to know the children, and today she planned to take pinafores for all the girls. Samson had already loaded them in the carriage. And, lest the boys feel left out, Marty had managed, with the help of Mrs. Landry, to secure a good number of donated shirts. She figured the sizes would be questionable, but since there hadn't been time to measure and sew for each boy, this would have to do. Those, too, awaited her in the carriage.

She ate breakfast alone that morning, as she often did of late. Jake had been forced to arrive at the bank earlier and earlier. Just as Jake had predicted, many banks were folding, though Mr. Morgan's banks seemed to be managing. Jake served faithfully to see that they continued to keep their place in the business world, but who could say where it would all end. Often he was gone until late at night, and Marty noticed that he'd begun to lose weight.

Soon after Jake had mentioned his concerns for both the banks and the silver market, Marty had written to Hannah. In the letter she had requested that Will sell her ranch. She told Hannah that she would prefer they buy the land so it would remain in the family.

Marty was anxious to hear what her sister would have to say, but feared Hannah would brush aside her concerns for the banks and her husband's job and instead chide Marty for not simply returning to Texas. But for Marty, Texas was still a thorn in her side.

The children at the orphanage welcomed Marty with open arms that morning. The kids had come to recognize her carriage and would eagerly await her arrival. Since it was summer, school was concluded for the time, and Marty had taken the opportunity to volunteer her time to read with them more often.

"Children, Mrs. Wythe has come with gifts this morning," Mrs. Staples announced. She was one of the caretakers of the children and although strict, was quite pleasant. "You will have a chance to receive a present later—if you listen well to the story and do not give Mrs. Wythe any trouble."

"What's the present?" one of the boys asked.

Mrs. Staples smiled. "Robert, you will have to wait with everyone else until after story time. Mrs. Wythe cannot spend all day with us. She has other appointments to tend to after this."

Marty waited until some of the other children posed their questions before pulling out her book. This signaled the children to take their seats on the floor around her. She waited patiently until everyone was positioned where they wanted to be.

"Good morning, children," she said, smiling. "I've brought a new book today, just as I promised. This one is called *The Adventures of Tom Sawyer*."

"Who's that?" a boy named Clyde asked.

"He's an energetic young boy who has many great adventures along the Mississippi River," Marty replied.

"Is he a big boy?" one of the little girls asked.

Someone else called out, "Does he swim in the river?"

Marty laughed. "Why don't I read the book, and then you'll see for yourself what kind of boy our Tom is and how he lives his life."

She opened the book and thumbed to the beginning. "Chapter one."

The children settled in and Marty, in her animated way, began to read.

After entertaining the children for over an hour—without a single one wanting to leave or do something else—Marty had to bid the children good-bye. She didn't want to leave. Leaving meant she would have to attend the luncheon being hosted by Mrs. Carmichael. The pretentious rich woman gave Marty a case of hives. Well, very nearly.

Samson waited faithfully to help her into the carriage. "There's lots of folks out today," he told her. "Might be late."

"That would be fine with me," Marty murmured. "I wouldn't even be attending if it wasn't important to keep up appearances."

"Yes'm."

She settled against the leather upholstery and sighed as Samson merged into traffic. Marty couldn't help but feel like she'd left a part of her heart behind. A half dozen of the youngest had given her hugs before she'd departed. It made her want to load them all into her carriage and take them home. The children gave meaning and purpose to her life, and she was starting to consider speaking to Jake about adoption.

Of course, the timing wasn't exactly ideal; it might be difficult to care for children in an uncertain future. Still, Marty knew that the children needed love and attention whether the economy fell apart or not. They couldn't comprehend the devaluation of silver or the insolvency of banks. Nor should they have to. Children were to be loved and protected, and Marty found herself stirred to do both.

Mrs. Carmichael's butler met Marty at the door with a curt nod. He ushered her to the garden, where tables had been laid for their luncheon. Mrs. Carmichael greeted Marty in her cool and composed manner. She always had a way of making Marty feel substandard, no matter the gathering.

"Mrs. Wythe." She peered at Marty as if she were something the cat had dragged in. "We feared you weren't coming."

"Mrs. Carmichael. It was kind of you to invite me." Marty smiled and nodded her head toward a group of society matrons seated around a table.

"Please have a seat. I believe we can finally get started."

Marty nodded and hurried to take an empty chair. She felt overly conspicuous with everyone else so carefully assembled. She had clearly committed a grave error in her late arrival. She had thought to offer an excuse and tell the women about the traffic, but they'd only want to know where she'd been. Marty knew they'd never approve of her work with the orphans.

"Ladies, as you know, our city is in peril," Mrs. Carmichael began. "Our very society has been altered in the wake of this new economic injustice." The women seemed fixed on her every word, while Marty wished they'd get to serving the food. She was starved.

"I wanted to host this luncheon in order to review the situation and to determine what, if anything, is to be managed by our number. I believe Mrs. Morgan would like to speak first."

Mrs. Morgan stood. "As you know, I am not one to frequent these occasions. However, I felt that the circumstances of our dear city necessitated my presence. Several of our former friends have found themselves completely stripped of their financial status. Thankfully, they have taken their families and left the city, so there is no need to feel uncomfortable in their presence."

Marty tried not to roll her eyes. These women—these so-called dear friends—were as fickle as they came.

"In addition to that, we are faced with a grave concern. There are a great many homeless arriving into Denver on a daily basis. As you know, a good number of the silver mines have closed, and this has put many men out of work and onto the streets. I believe this situation will only worsen as time goes on. In turn, it will cause many dangers for the people of our town."

Marty listened with only halfhearted interest. The women who inevitably attended these affairs bored her. Unlike some of the women she'd befriended in Texas, these women seemed to have no real understanding of or concern for humanity. They were wealthy and spoiled, and the only thing that seemed to concern them was remaining exactly so.

"I have spoken to Mr. Morgan on this matter and have suggested that these unemployed men be sent elsewhere to look for work. Obviously, the city cannot accommodate them, and their presence will only lead to a sullying of our environment."

Marty frowned and couldn't help but interject. "Where would you have them go? As I understand it, the entire country is struggling with this financial crisis." The women at her table looked aghast that she had dared to interrupt.

Mrs. Morgan smiled tolerantly. "That's true, but the rest of the country isn't my concern. Denver is. I would have them go anywhere but here."

The other women nodded and murmured their approval. Marty knew she should just keep quiet, but she couldn't help herself. "Seems rather selfish. What if we were to figure out ways to help those poor folks instead?"

"There are institutions and churches for such things, and the larger eastern cities would be better suited to see to their needs," Mrs. Morgan replied. "I'm sure that given your background, it's difficult to understand our position. However, people of means are the guardians of their surroundings. That instills in us a responsibility to oversee the welfare of our people and properties. Our men rely on us to practice wisdom in this matter, and this city is dependent upon such sacrifice."

"I understand that. And, given my background," Marty said in a somewhat sarcastic tone, "I know what it is to help the needy. I'm suggesting that rather than try to rid ourselves of them, we give assistance—perhaps offering shelter and teaching them new trades. After all, if their work as silver miners is over, they will need to be reeducated to work in another field."

There were gasps from several women, but Mrs. Morgan was patient. She gave Marty a look, however, that left the younger woman cold.

"It is not the responsibility of our society to provide such things."

"Maybe it should be," Marty replied. She could see she was alienating every woman at the luncheon, but she didn't care.

"Such matters are better left to the churches," Mrs. Morgan insisted.

"Are we not the church?" Marty could have heard a pin drop. "Does the Bible not show that it is our responsibility to care for the body? I'm not suggesting mere handouts. I'm not even saying that we need deplete all our wealth. I'm merely stating that sending these people away isn't going to solve anything."

"Well, you are entitled to your opinion, Mrs. Wythe. However, my husband would disagree with you. When I mentioned that these homeless and jobless people should be sent elsewhere, he agreed. He and some of our other good men are making plans to arrange for just that."

The other women nodded their approval. "Do tell," Mrs.

Keystone called out. "Let us know how this is to be accomplished and what role we are to play."

Mrs. Morgan turned away from Marty to smile at her friend. "I suggested that these people be given a train ticket to leave the city. Let them go to friends and family elsewhere." She glanced back at Marty. "After all, we are not without heart. If they have no one to go to, then let us send them to one of the larger cities where help might be more readily available. Chicago, Kansas City, New York, and so on. All of those places would be better suited to assist the downtrodden than Denver."

"But Denver *is* a large city," Marty protested. "Maybe we should focus on making it a better city by incorporating ideas to help the downtrodden, as you put it."

"Mrs. Wythe, I believe your country manners might well be acceptable in some settings, such as the wilds of Texas," Mrs. Carmichael interjected. "But here, we rely on a better society—a way that affords us a protected life. I think perhaps you believe your Texas ways better than ours, and if that is the case, then might I suggest . . . you return to Texas."

"Hear, hear," many of the women called out. Mrs. Morgan nodded her agreement.

The women who had pretended to be Marty's friends had now made their true feelings clear. Marty stood and shook her head.

"I feel sorry for you. I thought you were women of means, but instead I find that you're simply mean women. You have, but you've no desire to share. You know comfort and full bellies, but you would send others away hungry. I would remind you that it was Jesus himself who said that whatever we do unto the least of these . . . we do unto Him."

With that, she left the murmuring dissension and made her way back through the house and out the front door. Samson looked up in surprise as she stormed to the carriage.

"Get me out of here, please. Those women have seen the last of me."

He grinned, seeming happy for the news. "Yes'm."

★

Marty fretted the rest of the day, worrying about what Jake would say when he heard what she'd done. She feared she'd be the reason he'd fall from the good graces of his employer. She agonized over whether they'd be put out on the street for her behavior.

Perhaps I should send a letter of apology to Mrs. Morgan. I shouldn't have been so cantankerous, I suppose. I could have handled the situation with better judgment.

But the women had been so calloused and unfeeling. Maybe it was their fear of change that made them so, but to Marty, they bordered on cruel. She thought of all the orphans in the city—would the elite put them on a train and rid their precious Denver of their presence, as well?

I won't apologize. For once I did speak the truth, and they didn't want to hear it. They were much too worried about their town being dirtied with the poor and needy. And they call themselves Christians! How she seethed. It made her want to march right over to the Morgans and give them both a piece of her mind.

It was past eight before she heard the carriage arrive with Jake. She panicked. What if he was livid over her actions? What if she'd ruined everything? Marty began to pace in the sitting room. Jake cared for her, but he also cared about keeping his position at the bank.

It wasn't long before she heard Brighton greet her husband at the front door. There was a quick exchange that she couldn't quite hear, and then footsteps sounded on the hardwood floor outside the sitting room pocket doors.

The doors slid back, and Jake walked wearily into the room. Marty could see he was exhausted. She had arranged a very simple dinner for them that evening and hoped he wouldn't even feel the need to change his clothes.

"You look spent," she said. "Why don't you sit here and I'll rub your shoulders."

He shook his head. "I'd rather eat. I'm famished."

"I waited dinner for you. It's simple fare, so you needn't redress. It's just you and me and we could even take it upstairs if you'd like."

"No, that's all right. We can eat in the dining room, but I will take you up on the suggestion of not changing. I doubt I'd have the energy to return if I climbed those stairs."

She smiled. "I'll let Mrs. Landry know." She pulled the cord and waited until the housekeeper appeared. "Mrs. Landry, we'll have dinner in the dining room—right away, please."

The housekeeper smiled. "I figured as much. Well, not the exact location, but I had Cook get to it when I heard Mr. Wythe's carriage."

"Thank you. We'll be right in," Marty said. "Oh, and please have Brighton ready a hot bath for my husband. I'm sure he'll need to soak a bit after he eats." She looked to Jake, who smiled in spite of his exhaustion. "What are you smiling about?"

"You. The way you're taking care of me. Feels good. You're a real asset, Marty."

She thought of the way she'd acted at the garden party. "You might not be inclined to say so after you hear about my day," she said in as nonchalant a manner as she could manage. "But that can wait. Let's eat first."

Chapter 21

Jake awaited Marty's arrival at breakfast the next morning. She had told him of her falling-out with the society women, and he wanted to assure her that she needn't fear—at least not on his part—any repercussions. He couldn't care less about the social side of life. At one time it had seemed important, but financial crashes had a way of leveling the playing field, and Jake was beginning to see what a fool he'd been to even worry about such matters. Just looking back on the choices he'd made to please Morgan almost made him feel sick.

It seems all my life I've been trying to please someone rather than figure out what God desired for me in the first place.

"I didn't expect to find you still here," Marty said as she entered the dining room. "I was so glad you sent Alice for me."

"I thought you deserved to see your husband in a rested state." He held out her chair and helped seat her at the table. "Not only that, but I wanted to reassure you."

Marty's expression changed to one of confusion. "Reassure me?"

"Marty, I haven't wanted to say anything, but I think our days in Denver are numbered anyway. Your falling-out with

Mrs. Morgan and the other great ladies of society may simply coincide with a progression of changes that cannot be stopped."

"What do you mean?"

"I mean that I feel confident, given the problems going on in the country, that it will only be a matter of time until our bank collapses. There are all manner of problems at our institution, and I cannot begin to figure them all out. I can say without a doubt, however, that changes are upon us."

"It can't be that bad," Marty declared. She shook her head when Brighton offered to pour her a cup of coffee. He retreated to Jake's side of the table and refilled his cup instead.

"I'm afraid it is. What you experienced at the garden party is just the tip of the iceberg, I'm afraid. The few ladies that were mentioned as having left the city with their families are only the start of what may well become a mass exodus."

"But things aren't any better anywhere else, are they? I mean, my sister has even talked about how awful things are in Texas. Cotton prices have dropped so low that farmers aren't even considering replanting another crop."

"I know, but it would seem that folks of means are tightening their belts just as we are. Instead of having three or four homes at their disposal, they're consolidating and selling off some of their holdings and real estate. At the very least they are closing the houses in an effort to save money. I heard Mr. Morgan speak of selling his seaside place in California. He may move back east if he finds it necessary to close down the banks here. All I'm saying is that I didn't want you to fret over what happened with the ladies. You aren't to blame. You've a kind heart, Marty. That's something most of them can't understand."

"And you believe we'll need to move, as well?"

Jake nodded. "I never wanted this house in the first place. For now, Mr. Morgan told me to sit tight. He's not even requiring I make the mortgage payment on it since he's had to cut back on my salary."

"I didn't know that he'd done that," Marty said, the worry in her tone obvious.

"I didn't want to scare you."

"What will we do if you lose your position?" she asked.

He shook his head. "I don't know. I do know, however, that there's little we can accomplish by being afraid. We'll take this one step at a time."

Marty looked unconvinced but said nothing more on the subject. They made small talk over a light breakfast of eggs and toast, but Jake could tell her heart wasn't in it. He finally pushed back from the table.

"I'd best get down to the bank." He moved to where Marty sat and gave her a kiss on the cheek. In the past he'd only done this for show, but now he felt his heart beat a little faster at the mere touch of his lips to her face.

"Will you be late?" she asked. Her gaze lifted to meet his.

"Probably. But don't worry about me, Marty. You need to take care of yourself."

He rode in silence to the bank and arrived twenty minutes before the doors were to be opened to the public. Jake tensed at the sight of Mr. Morgan's fine carriage. There was another carriage parked in front of Morgan's, and Jake guessed it belonged to Mr. Keystone.

Making his way into the bank, Jake spotted the men waiting for him in his office. "Good morning, gentlemen," he said, walking to his desk. "Did we have a meeting this morning?"

"No," Morgan replied. "But we need one. I've been going over the papers you sent me. It would appear there are problems with some of the numbers being duplicated, just as you stated."

Jake felt a sense of relief. He'd almost worried that the men were there because of what Marty had said and done at the garden party. "Yes, it's clear that there are duplicated numbers and a lack of inventory to back up what's been declared."

Morgan smiled and lit a cigar. "Well, I know we'll get to the bottom of it in time. I just wanted to tell you that you've done a fine job here. I'm going to turn it all over to Mr. Keystone, and he will take care of it."

"I'm glad to hear that. I've enough on my agenda to keep me busy. Is there any other news out of Washington?" Jake asked.

"Not per se," Morgan replied. "Although I read this morning that Lizzie Borden will most likely be acquitted of murdering her parents."

Jake had read about the Massachusetts woman who had been accused of killing her parents with an ax. He nodded but had no desire to discuss it. "I thought maybe something related to the economy and the well-being of the American people."

Morgan gave a laugh. "Oh, there is news out of Washington, but it's from last month. However, it continues to amuse me. It would seem the Supreme Court has finally ruled that a tomato is a vegetable."

"Well, that's a relief," Keystone said sarcastically. "At least now waiters will know the proper place setting for it." He and Morgan roared with laughter, and even Jake couldn't help but chuckle. The world was falling down around them, but at least they now knew that a tomato was officially a vegetable. And because the Supreme Court had declared it such—it must be so.

★

"Mrs. Wythe?" a little boy said in a questioning tone.

Marty looked to her left and found the little waif looking at her with great expectation. "What is it, Wyatt?"

"Do you have children of your own?"

The seven-year-old's question threw her for a moment. Marty finally shook her head. By now several other children had gathered at her side. "No, I don't have any . . . yet."

"Maybe I could be your little boy." His eyes were filled with hope, and it made Marty want to snatch him up and pledge her undying love.

"Well, right now all of you are my children," Marty replied. "I so enjoy getting to be with you and share our stories together."

"But it ain't the same as havin' a real ma and pa," one of the older boys stated.

Marty caught his look. She saw betrayal and hurt in his eyes. This was a child who had been gravely wounded. "You're Adam, aren't you?" The boy nodded. Marty wondered how best to answer the lad. "You know, when I was a newborn baby my mother died. My father died when I was five, and my sister raised me. I know it's not the same as having to live in an orphanage, but I think it's important to find love wherever we are."

"Do you love us?" a little girl Marty knew as Nettie asked.

Marty smiled. "I do indeed. I love each and every one of you. You make my day brighter."

"So couldn't you 'dopt us?" Wyatt asked.

How she wanted to tell him yes. She knew these children were afraid of their future. They only had the employees of the orphanage to show them affection and love. She hated that she couldn't just tell them to line up—that she'd take them all.

"Children, it's time for lunch," Mrs. Staples called from the door. Most of the children made a mad dash for the dining room.

Wyatt gave Marty one last hopeful look, then ran after his friends. Marty knew that as long as she lived, she would never forget that face.

"Are you all right, Mrs. Wythe?" Mrs. Staples asked.

Marty looked up and met the woman's questioning gaze. "I suppose so. I . . . well . . . what are the chances these children will find homes?"

Mrs. Staples shook her head. "Not good. Especially now. The wealthy have never been inclined to take in poor children—except as servants, of course. The families who would be likely to adopt are now doing without daily provisions for themselves. So many are out of work and can't feed the folks already reliant upon them. And of course the poor are the ones who brought us most of these youngsters to begin with. They found themselves unable to raise children even when the economy was booming."

The woman gave a sigh. "I'm afraid in the very near future, most of the older children will simply be put out from the orphanage in order to have enough money to tend to the younger ones."

"Put out . . . where?"

"On the streets." Mrs. Staples shook her head again. "It isn't what any of us want, but there aren't very many options.

We encourage the children to seek out the churches for help. We encourage them to find places where they can work for room and board. Sadly, it's only going to get worse before it gets better." She glanced over her shoulder and then back to Marty. "I'd best get in there. Miss Hayden has a difficult time handling the older boys."

Marty let the woman go without another comment. Her heart ached at the thought of Adam being turned out of the orphanage. She had no idea what age classified a child as "older," but surely it wouldn't be that long before Adam would be on that list.

Gathering her things, Marty walked to Mr. Brentwood's office and knocked on the door.

"Come in," he called, and Marty opened the door.

"I was about to leave but wondered if I could speak to you."

"Of course," he replied, standing. "Won't you have a seat?"

"Thank you. I heard today that you will have to release some of the older orphans."

He frowned. "I'm sorry to say that is true. Given that our support comes from private funds and donations, I'm afraid we can no longer afford to keep everyone. In order to see to it that the little ones have a minimal amount of care, we have no choice."

"I wonder if you could delay long enough for me to contact my sister in Texas. She and her husband own a ranch. They might be able to provide work for some of the children. I know you said that there were several who wanted to work with cattle."

He looked at her for a moment and rubbed his chin. "How long would this delay take?"

"Only as long as it takes to get a telegraph off to Texas

and receive an answer," Marty replied. "A letter would be better, as I could explain in more detail, but I think I can get my sister to understand the situation with a telegram."

He nodded. "I don't know why it couldn't wait a day or two—maybe a week at most. We haven't yet spoken to the children."

"Good," Marty said, getting to her feet. "Don't. I will check with my sister and see what she can offer. Perhaps there will be other ranches in the area who can take on a boy or two."

Mr. Brentwood stood. "Mrs. Wythe, you are a saint. I know that God sent you to us in our hour of need. No one else has posed any kind of solution for helping these children—just you."

"Well, I don't know how much of a solution it will prove to be, but I'll do what I can."

As she made her way to her carriage, a heaviness settled on her heart. Marty wanted to make life better for the children, but she was just one woman. What could she do? Save Adam? Wyatt? But what of the others? John and Tim were in their teens, nearly adults. Nettie and Willen were each twelve. Would that be enough to send them from the safety of the orphanage? There didn't seem to be any reasonable answer. Even if Hannah and Will could take a good number of them—there were hundreds left.

"Samson, I need to stop by a telegraph office."

"Yes'm." He helped her into the carriage and by the time Marty had settled in, Samson had the horses in motion.

She mentally composed the message she would send. *Numerous orphans to be turned out on the street. Can you take some for ranch work? Need answer immediately. More to follow in letter.*

With the telegram on its way, Marty felt that she had done at least a small thing for the welfare of the orphans. Of course, Hannah and Will might say no. But she doubted it. They were just as concerned about assisting the helpless as she was. Maybe even more. It saddened her to imagine children trying to live on their own, begging passersby for food.

Upon arriving home, Samson helped Marty from the carriage. He beamed a smile, but it didn't change Marty's mood.

"Thank you, Samson." She didn't even try to hide her sorrow.

"Them children are mighty lucky to have you come there to read to 'em," Samson said. "Mighty lucky."

Marty wanted to contradict him, but thought better of it. Samson was just trying to help. She approached the front door, and Brighton, ever vigilant, opened it before she could even reach the handle.

"You have company, Mrs. Wythe."

"Company?" She looked at the grandfather clock. "I don't recall having extended an invitation."

"No, madam. Mrs. Davies, the dressmaker, arrived unexpectedly. I put her in the formal sitting room."

Marty nodded. "Thank you, Brighton."

She made her way to Mrs. Davies and could see that the woman looked quite upset. "Mrs. Davies, what a pleasant surprise."

As Marty got closer, she could see the woman had been crying. "Whatever is wrong?" she asked.

"Mrs. Wythe, I'm not usually one to gossip, but truth be told I don't see it as such since it involves you."

Marty's eyes narrowed. "What involves me?"

Mrs. Davies dabbed her eyes with a handkerchief. "The reason I'm here."

Taking a seat, Marty hoped her silence would encourage the woman to continue. It was obvious that the older woman didn't like what she had come to say.

"It would seem that certain . . . ladies . . . have informed me that they will no longer bring me their business . . . if . . . if . . . I'm also doing business . . ." She couldn't seem to finish the sentence.

Marty immediately understood. It was her punishment for speaking out at the garden party. "If you're also doing business with me? Is that it?"

Mrs. Davies broke into tears anew. "I didn't know what else to do. I didn't want to offend you, nor did I want to lose their patronage. There are so many of them . . . and . . . I need the income."

"Don't worry," Marty said, hoping to ease the woman's conscience. "I have no need for new gowns anyway." She smiled. "Would you like refreshments? I could have tea brought in or perhaps a small lunch?"

"No." Mrs. Davies got to her feet. "I only stopped by to tell you in person. I felt it was only right. You've been a wonderful customer and a good woman. You've always treated my staff so well. I'm sorry that it's come to this."

"Please don't fret over it, Mrs. Davies. Denver's well-to-do have spoken, and we mustn't defy them." She gave a harsh laugh. "Otherwise, we'll both pay for our indiscretion instead of just me."

★

That evening Marty ate alone in her room. She thought about the troubling day and all she had encountered. The children were still uppermost on her mind, and she wished she would hear back from Hannah. Then a thought came. Even if Hannah and Will would take them, how would she get them to Texas?

Perhaps Mrs. Morgan could give them all a free train ticket. She calmed a bit. *Why not? Why not get the woman to put her money behind her mouth. She's so anxious that the poor should leave the state—so let her pay to transport the orphans.*

Alice entered the room as silent as a mouse. She came to collect Marty's tray, but stopped. "You've hardly eaten anything. Would you like me to leave it?"

"No. I'm not hungry. It's been a difficult week." She sighed. "You see, I have been ejected from the elite society of Denver's wealthy matrons. I said some things the other day when we were together, and it didn't set well."

"And that troubles you?"

"No, not exactly. I think what troubles me is that for the longest time, I actually thought I could be happy in their world. Now I know better. They don't even approve of my work at the orphanage."

"Of course not. They don't understand it."

Marty nodded. "I suppose that's true enough, but they should. What's so hard to understand about children needing someone to love them?"

"For some people," Alice replied, "love is the one thing they never understand."

Chapter 22

"You've had a ranch all this time, and you didn't tell me?" Jake questioned. "How could you do this? How could you betray my trust like this?"

Marty felt her blood run cold. "I couldn't tell you. You would have insisted we move there, and I didn't want to be a rancher's wife. Thomas was killed working with cattle—do you suppose I want to be a widow a second time?"

"You lied to me. You are nothing but a lying, scheming woman. I've nothing more to say to you. You ruined my life, Marty. Ruined it and all my dreams." Jake turned to leave.

Marty called after him, begging him to come back. "Please don't leave me—I love you! I can't lose another husband." Then all at once the scene began to shift and Jake was in the middle of a cattle pen—with an angry bull charging at him.

"No!" she screamed over and over. "No, Jake—watch out!"

"Marty, wake up! Marty!"

She opened her eyes and realized it had all just been a nightmare. Jake sat beside her on the bed, his hand casually resting on her shoulder. Without thinking, Marty threw herself into his arms. She was so glad to see that he was there—that nothing had changed. He was safe and her secret was, too.

Sobbing, Marty clung to Jake as though she might be pulled back into the dream should he let go. She drenched his bare chest with her tears.

"It's all right, Marty. You're safe and nothing can hurt you," he whispered. Stroking her hair, he held her close. "It was just a bad dream. Nobody can harm you. I won't let them."

Marty felt terrible. The entire nightmare was because she'd refused to tell Jake the truth about the ranch. It was time to just face her demons. She pulled back just a bit. "Oh, Jake. I . . . I . . . should tell you . . ."

"Shhh, there's no need to go relivin' the dream. You just take it easy and get yourself calmed down." His lazy drawl filled the night air and her heart.

Jake hadn't bothered to turn the lights on, and Marty couldn't see the details of his face, but she felt the wonderful warmth of his arms about her. Cheek against his chest, Marty focused on the steady beat of his heart. It comforted her. She could remember a time so long ago when she had laid her head upon Thomas's chest and listened to his heartbeat.

I cannot lose another husband. The thought was the same as the words she'd spoken in the dream. The idea of Jake dying sent a shiver through her. The trembling only caused Jake to tighten his hold on her.

Marty calmed but refused to leave his embrace. She loved this man. She'd told him so in her dream, and now she could admit to herself that it was true. She loved him most dearly, but her lies stood between them. She felt tears come anew. How could she ever make this right?

"I figure we'll be all right, Marty. No matter what happens. I'll take good care of you. Whatever happens, we have each other."

Marty raised her head again. She could feel Jake's warm breath against her face and knew his lips were only a few inches away. She ached for him to kiss her. "I'm glad we have each other," she whispered, wanting to speak of her love. Instead, she could only bring herself to add, "I need you."

Jake said nothing for a moment, and Marty couldn't help but worry she'd said the wrong thing. He hadn't pulled away, but neither had he replied. Could it be that her words had made him rethink his feelings for her?

She felt his hand at the back of her head before realizing that he was guiding her into a gentle kiss. Their lips met and Marty wanted the moment to go on forever. Then as quickly as it had started, Jake put an end to it. He dropped his hold on her and got to his feet.

"I'm sorry, Marty. I'm so sorry."

"Don't . . . don't . . . be."

"It wasn't right. You've been so good to honor our arrangement. You've demanded nothing of me, and you've been content to do all that I've asked of you—and this is how I reward you. I'm such a dolt. I was never the kind of man to take advantage of a woman's emotions, yet here I am. Please forgive me."

He stalked from the room, leaving Marty stunned. She wanted to call to him—beg him to return—but something told her it would do little good. She heard him slam her bedroom door closed behind him, then the dressing room doors and the one to his own bedroom followed in rapid pace.

A part of her wanted to run after him—tell him that he'd

done nothing wrong. That she loved him and wanted to be a real wife to him. Another part warned her that it would only serve to ruin everything. They had both gone into this marriage of convenience knowing the truth—at least most of the truth.

I should have told him about the ranch, and every day that goes by makes it just that much harder to be honest. Oh, God, please help me. I don't know what to say or do to make this right. I keep thinking if only Hannah will just write to tell me the ranch has been sold or that William has reclaimed it, then it wouldn't be so bad.

But wouldn't that just be another lie?

She pounded her fists against her pillow. *Why do I always choose a lie to get me out of trouble?*

Lies had always come easily to her, and if not lies, then omissions of truth or exaggerations. These had always been Marty's downfall. She could remember Hannah praying that she not give in to such temptation, but Marty didn't see it as a truly sinful thing. At least not until now. Now she could see the full implications of this sin. She could see the potential damage and pain it would cause.

"I want to do the right thing," she said. "I want to tell Jake the truth." She buried her face in the pillow. *Please, God, show me what's right and give me the strength to do it.*

★

Jake leaned out his open bedroom window and drew in deep breaths of night air. How could he have been so stupid? He should never have gone to Marty's room. He should have just left well enough alone.

"But she was scared. She was screaming and crying out. What kind of husband would I be to ignore that?"

The kind of husband I signed on to be.

He wrestled with his conscience. He should never have married Marty. It wasn't right that they had pledged faithfulness to each other and to God. Jake had even promised to love Marty. Was this his punishment for such blasphemy?

"God, I never meant for this to happen. I never meant to lie to you. It seemed reasonable to marry and pledge to love and honor. Without a real wedding it didn't seem wrong—it felt like just a bunch of words." He pulled back into his room and buried his face in his hands.

He tried to figure out how to fix the mess he'd made. It would be best to just come clean and tell Marty the truth. Tell her that he'd fallen in love with her, that he wanted her to be his wife for real. If he just told her the truth, they could work through it. She might get angry about it, but Jake could promise to just love her from afar. Love her until she was ready to love him back.

"But what if that never comes?"

He lifted his face and stared across the darkened room. What good was any of this now? He'd thought to make a new life. Thought he could actually endure this life and be happy until he had enough money to return to Texas. Now, even Texas seemed a foolish desire compared to wanting Marty to return his love.

★

By six in the morning, dawn was starting to brighten the horizon and Marty gave up trying to sleep. She could still smell Jake's cologne in her hair. She could still feel his arms around her. The rest of the night she had done battle with her conscience, and now she was completely exhausted. No answers offered comfort.

"If I tell him the truth," she whispered, "he will never come to care for me. I would be effectually ending our marriage."

The truth shall make you free.

The Bible verse seemed to ring like a bell in the air. It was one Hannah had quoted to her on many occasions. That and the commandment about not bearing false witness.

"But I'm so afraid." She looked toward the ceiling as if she might see the face of God in the ornate plaster. "I'm afraid that you aren't listening. I'm afraid I've strayed too far and you can't . . . won't reach out to me."

The truth shall make you free.

Ye shall know the truth, and the truth shall make you free.

Marty remembered that this was the day Alice and the others would be having their Bible study in the kitchen. She could join them and ask them to pray for her. *I'm not strong enough to face this on my own.*

Pulling on her robe, Marty wondered if the women would be offended by her presence. After all, she was the mistress of the house. Maybe they wouldn't want her to be a part of their gathering.

She paused at the door and swallowed hard. What if they refused to let her join them? What would she do?

None of her worries stopped her, however. Marty knew she needed someone to reassure her—to help her with the truth. She made her way down the back stairs, not even trying to be quiet. When she entered the kitchen, Mrs. Standish, Mrs. Landry, and Alice were all anticipating her entry.

"Are you all right, Mrs. Wythe?" Mrs. Landry asked. "Are you ill?"

Marty shook her head. "I'm just . . . I'm . . ." She paused to gather her courage. "I wonder if I might join you. I know you don't approve of the help mingling with their employers, Mrs. Landry, but we are all equal in the sight of the Lord."

Alice smiled. "Of course we are, and of course you can join us. We're studying the life of Abraham."

Mrs. Landry got up and retrieved another chair. "Sit right here. You are quite right—spiritually we are equal."

The housekeeper sounded hesitant, but Marty sank into the ladder-back chair with a sigh. "Thank you. You don't know what this means to me. I've been tossing all night."

"Can you speak to what is troubling your heart?" Mrs. Standish asked.

Not knowing how much to say, Marty shrugged. "Everything. The world is in such a fix right now, and so am I."

"Then perhaps we should spend time in prayer," Mrs. Landry suggested.

Alice nodded. "I think that's the perfect place to start."

★

With the afternoon post came Marty's answer to prayer. A letter from Hannah informed Marty that William was happy to take back the ranch. He would weigh out the situation—the assets would be assessed, and he would send her a fair price for the entire property.

"Well, that's that," Marty said, feeling a little of the pressure ease from her heart. "I have no need to ever return to Texas, and if Jake insists we leave Denver, then I will suggest we look elsewhere for our new home. I can mention the ranch sometime if it comes up and explain that the land reverted to Will. I'll tell Hannah not to mention otherwise." No, that would never do. Hannah would see that as evading the truth.

Must I tell him? Must I admit to having the ranch all this time? He'll hate me, just like in the dream. Because the truth is that I have wronged him. I have lied and kept from him the only thing in life he really wants.

She caught a glimpse of herself in the foyer mirror. Marty thought she looked tired—not even the least bit pretty. The lies and worries had taken their toll. She wished fervently she could start anew . . . and perhaps that's exactly what was happening. Maybe she could just explain to Jake that she had once owned land and now it was held by her brother-in-law. Maybe if Jake demanded they return to Texas, he could go as a banker or bookkeeper. That was a nice safe job. But could she live again in Texas?

It's not Texas, she told herself. It's the ranch and the dangers there. It's all the terrible things that happen. She remembered her brother and Will suffering broken bones and nearly losing their lives in multiple incidents. They had lost ranch hands to kicking horses, stampeding cattle, and even one to snakebite. Life on a ranch was an unforgiving world. She could never risk living—and loving someone—in such a place.

Why did I even think of sending children there? As if in answer to her thoughts, a knock sounded at the front door. Disregarding Brighton's duties, Marty opened it to find a young man.

"Telegram for Mrs. Martha Wythe."

"That's me." Marty pulled some coins from her chatelaine bag and handed them to the boy. "Thank you."

The boy handed her the telegram, then turned to run back down the porch steps. Marty immediately opened the reply from her sister.

Happy to have them. Send as soon as you like. Look forward to hearing more. Hannah.

There it was. Only now Marty felt guilty. What if she was only sending these children to their deaths? She heaved a sigh. Leaving them to face an uncertain life here was no better. At least under Hannah and Will's care they wouldn't go hungry.

"Madam, I heard someone at the door," Brighton said.

Marty hid the telegram behind her back and smiled. "It was nothing."

She closed the door and made her way to the kitchen, leaving Brighton to stare after her. She knew most likely he hadn't believed her, but his manners wouldn't allow him to challenge her.

Marty checked for Mrs. Standish. Seeing that the cook had gone out back to the small herb garden, Marty hastily tossed the letter and telegram from Hannah into the stove and watched a moment while they burned. She couldn't risk keeping either one. If Jake saw the telegram he'd know that things were apparently going well enough for Hannah and Will that they could take on a bunch of children. And if he saw the letter . . . well . . . he mustn't ever see the letter.

When the papers were nothing more than ash, Marty closed the door and stepped back from the stove. Just then, Mrs. Standish returned and upon seeing Marty held a wide smile.

"You don't look nearly so tired as you did this morning. I hope you had a bit of a rest."

"I did," Marty replied. "Now I find myself in need of tea. I just thought I would make it myself rather than disturb you or Mrs. Landry."

"Nonsense. 'Tis my job," the older woman declared. "You go right on to your sitting room, and I'll bring you a good hot cup in three shakes of a lamb's tail."

Marty smiled. "I've seen lambs shake their tails, Mrs. Standish, and it's quite speedy. You needn't rush that much."

The woman chuckled, and Marty made her way to the sitting room she'd come to love. But upon entering, she was surprised to come upon her butler and housekeeper in each other's arms.

"I'm so . . . sorry," Marty declared. "I was only passing through."

"Nonsense, Mrs. Wythe," Brighton replied, dropping his hold on the older woman. "Mrs. Landry learned this morning that her sister has died."

Mrs. Landry looked up, and her tear-stained face revealed her grief. Marty embraced her. "I'm so sorry. What happened?"

"She's been ill for some time." Mrs. Landry sniffed and stepped away. "Even so, it comes as a shock."

"Of course it would," Marty agreed. "I want you to take the rest of the day and weekend off to rest. Where does your sister live? Will you need time to travel there for the funeral?"

"No. She lived in Michigan. I won't be attending the funeral. It's too far and too much expense."

"I'm certain that we can find the funds if you desire to be there," Marty insisted.

"No. I'd rather remain here. We weren't all that close . . . it's just . . . well, I thought we'd have time to settle our past."

"I'm sorry, Mrs. Landry. I didn't realize there were problems."

The housekeeper nodded. "That's why Mr. Brighton was so good to console me. I felt I had failed as a good Christian woman to help my sister see the truth about God. She called herself an atheist, and we had many a fight over it. Funny, isn't it, that something as wondrous as God's love should cause families to fight?"

It was difficult to see the pain in the woman's eyes and not feel moved. Marty reached out and touched her housekeeper's shoulder. "I still want you to take some time to yourself. I want you to know how very sorry I am, but that I'm certain you planted seeds in the life of your sister. Maybe one of them took root. You can never tell."

Mrs. Landry nodded. "It's my fondest wish that she would have accepted the Lord. I don't know why people reject Him— the truth seems so evident to me."

Marty knew why people rejected Him. From her own personal experience, she knew that often they did so for no other reason than to harden their hearts from the possibility of more pain in their life.

She looked to Brighton and smiled. "I'm so glad you were here to comfort Mrs. Landry. She's fortunate to have a good friend like you."

Brighton flushed red and looked away. "Thank you, madam."

Marty couldn't help but think of Jake holding her in the night. That comfort had meant more to her than anything he could have bought her or done for her. The troubles of the world were upon them, but in his arms she felt completely safe—at ease. Somehow, she had to convince him that this was where she belonged.

Chapter 23

Alice hated waiting outside alone for Mrs. Landry, but neither did she want to frighten or upset the children inside the
church. She'd been the recipient of too many ugly comments
about her face; she couldn't bear to see the repulsion and hear
the whispers from the little ones. Mrs. Landry had scoffed and
insisted Alice come inside, but Alice simply shook her head.

"I'll take this bundle of cookies in and then come back
for yours," Mrs. Landry said in exasperation. They'd baked
cookies for the children's fair that the church was sponsoring,
and Mrs. Landry had needed Alice to help carry the cookies because the carriage was in use. Samson had taken Mrs.
Wythe to the orphanage.

A few minutes later, Mrs. Landry returned and took the
bundle from Alice. "I don't know why you worry so much
about your face. That scar isn't as noticeable as you think."

She touched the scar on her cheek and tried to forget how a
child had once screamed in terror at her face. Of course, that
had not been long after the attack, when Alice was barely up
and around the hospital grounds. The scar didn't look as bad
now as it had then, but it was still puckerish and very evident.

"With adults it's not so bad, but it scares the children," Alice whispered.

Mrs. Landry gave a heavy sigh. "Very well. I'll try to hurry, but I have to speak with the pastor." The older woman disappeared inside the church, leaving Alice alone once again.

Pacing the small walkway, Alice glanced at the door of the church and tried to calm her nerves. It was broad daylight and no one would—

"Well, I see you're finally alone."

She whirled around to find the man she feared most in the world. "What do you want?" She moved toward the church, but the man reached out and held her fast.

Smith gripped her arm in a painful manner. "You know very well what I want."

"I told you before and I'm telling you now: I don't know anything about a bank envelope. I told you that. I had very little left me after I got out of the hospital. My friends had to sell off our things to pay for my hospital bills and Father's funeral." She pulled against his hold. "Not only that, but you and your thugs frightened them so much, they left town without a chance to even tell me all that had transpired while I'd been in the hospital."

"They were only questioned about the envelope. If they were afraid, that was their problem."

"No, it was your fault. Your friends threatened them. They told me how awful it was."

He shook his head. "Not nearly as awful as it's gonna get if I don't get that envelope." Alice tried again to move away from him.

"You're a fool if you think you can escape me." He grinned, forcing her closer. "That scar does mar your face, but it doesn't steal all your beauty. I might have use for you. I have gals uglier than you making me a good living."

"Leave me alone!" Alice pulled even harder.

Smith slapped her across the face, and Alice fell backward from the blow and crumpled onto the ground. She had hoped he would leave her there, but instead he reached down and yanked her back to her feet.

"That's just a sample of the kind of pain I can cause you. You have something that belongs to me, and I intend to have it back. I'm watching you all the time, Miss Chesterfield. There's no place you can hide and nothing you can do to escape my reach." He let go his hold. "Even if you think you can. Now, I suggest you write a letter to your friends and find out what they did with your father's personal papers. That ain't something you can sell."

Alice frowned. She'd not really given that much thought in the aftermath of the attack. Her father hadn't had many personal business dealings, and he wasn't one for corresponding with anyone. Alice did recall there were a few personal things he kept in a box—among them her mother's wedding ring, which she had left behind. He'd once showed it to Alice and told her it was a reminder to him of how the devil can appear as an angel to fool man. Alice had never thought about what might have happened to that box.

"It's been nearly a year. I honestly have no memory of him keeping any personal papers." Alice was silent a moment. "I suppose there might have been things that wouldn't have been sold. . . ." She shook her head and let the words trail off.

The man loosened his hold, to her surprise. "Write to your friends. I'll be in touch." He hurried down the road and had already turned a corner by the time Mrs. Landry appeared.

"They were ever so glad for the refreshments. Thank you for helping me get them here." She stopped and looked at Alice oddly. "What happened?"

Alice shook her head and struggled to keep her hand from covering the cheek where Smith had hit her. "What are you talking about?"

"Your cheek, it's red—and there are grass stains on the sleeve of your blouse."

She swallowed hard. "I fell, that's all."

"Alice, don't lie to me. You have the perfect imprint of a hand on your face."

Alice lowered her gaze. "That Mr. Smith showed up."

"Here? Why didn't you scream for help?"

"I was too surprised. I never imagined anyone would attack me outside a church in the middle of the day."

Mrs. Landry frowned. "We must tell Mr. and Mrs. Wythe immediately. That man is a menace."

Alice nodded and felt her every hope dissolve.

------------------ ★ ------------------

"You must know this is an answer to prayer, Mrs. Wythe." Mr. Brentwood slapped his hands atop his desk. "An answer to prayer."

"My sister and her husband are quite generous. I know they will see that the children are well provided for. There may be other ranchers and farmers in the area who could take a few on, as well. I will write to her and let her know your situation. There are some very good people in our circle of friends."

He let out a heavy sigh. "This has weighed so heavily on my heart. I immediately went to prayer and fasting after you mentioned the possibility. So now my question is, how do we arrange for their travel?"

Marty smiled. "I've already thought of that. You see, I happen to know that Mrs. Morgan has petitioned her husband and his friends to provide free rail passage to the poor in order to rid our precious city of their presence. She is no longer receiving me, because of my response to her ideas."

Mr. Brentwood frowned. "I am sorry, Mrs. Wythe. I don't see how this will help us."

"She won't see me, but she would no doubt see you. I think you have only to go to her and request train passage for the orphans. Tell her you thought you would have to put these children on the streets, but instead you have found a location for them in Texas—if only you can transport them there."

He smiled. "I think I understand. She would rather get her husband to pay the passage than to have additional homeless milling about her fair city."

Marty nodded. "Exactly."

"I don't think that will be a problem," Brentwood replied. "I will go and see her this afternoon. I won't ask for an appointment ahead of time, lest she refuse me. I'll simply show up and explain our plight."

"I think that's best." Marty felt a deep sense of satisfaction. "If my time spent with her has taught me anything, it's that surprise will work to your advantage. When anything threatens their way of life, they can't help but respond quickly."

★

Jake thought so often of Marty and their kiss that he had to refigure a column of numbers four times to get it right.

Everything balanced. The money that had been missing, though comparatively small, was now all accounted for.

When Jake had repeatedly mentioned the missing money to Mr. Morgan, the bank owner had been unconcerned. And now that it appeared the matter had resolved itself, Morgan felt certain the money had just been mislaid or accounted improperly. At least that's what he'd told Jake earlier that morning.

Still uncomfortable about the matter, Jake closed the ledger and stretched. He felt weariness settle over him. He thought again of Marty and the way she'd felt in his arms.

He grinned. She didn't seem to hate the kiss so much herself. Maybe, just maybe, she had wanted it as much as he had. After all, she did call out to him and ask him not to leave.

But that could just have been the fact that she was afraid. Something had caused her great worry in her sleep.

"Sir, Mr. Keystone is here to see you," Arnold announced.

Jake nodded and straightened his tie. "Send him in."

Arnold gave a nod and left the doorway. Keystone quickly entered and Jake got to his feet. "Mr. Keystone, this is an unexpected surprise."

"Yes, well, it would seem a most necessary one." He seemed bothered by something, so Jake only motioned to the chair and said nothing more.

Taking the seat, Keystone wasted no time. "Our funds are short. The banks are not doing at all well here in Colorado. We held a board meeting just a short time ago. I'm here to report on our decision."

"Decision about what?" Jake could only pray they hadn't decided to close the bank.

"We're going to start refusing to cash depositors' checks.

Instead, we will issue them bank checks that they can use in lieu of money."

"Won't that signal a problem and cause a run on the bank?" Jake asked.

"Not if it's handled properly," Keystone replied. "We must assure the depositor that this is merely a safety precaution and point out that we've remained solvent while other banks have collapsed—but only because of implementing such measures. If we focus on the fact that their money is still safely available to them in this form, I believe they'll understand."

Jake was less inclined to think so. "I've seen these people daily," he began. "I'm not convinced it will work. After all, we're talking about the life savings of some of these folks."

"I'm well aware of that, Wythe," Keystone said, clearly irritated. "It's a sound measure and we're not the only bank doing this. If folks want to be able to access their funds, they'll do it through a bank check or not at all."

"And what of the larger depositors? The businesses?"

"It will work well for everyone. You'll see. We have this all figured out. I only stopped here to let you know what was decided. You needn't approve or disapprove. It's done."

Jake nodded. "Well, I thank you for letting me know."

"Honestly, Wythe, the customers will be glad just to have the ability to purchase goods and pay their mortgages. You'll see. This is the only way it can work right now."

"I suppose so." Jake thought to change the subject. "What of the gold certificates being duplicated? Did you get to the bottom of that?"

"I'm still working on it," he assured Jake. "It won't be an easy matter to resolve. After all, each of the gold certificates is backed by gold marked with the same identifying number.

With the banking system in the mess it is now, we will be hard-pressed to get anywhere with this investigation for some time. It falls low on the priorities we have."

"And if those people come to get their gold?"

"That's exactly why we are resolving matters this way with the bank checks. There's obviously been a moratorium placed on cashing out for gold. Hopefully the bank checks will ease the worries of those who had thought to redeem their silver certificates."

"I hope you're right," Jake said, still uncertain it would satisfy the customers.

On his way home from work that night he very nearly had Samson stop by the florist's shop. Though he wanted to bring Marty flowers again, he put aside the idea, when considering the cost. He knew they would have to be very careful with their limited funds. He was thankful that Morgan continued to waive their mortgage payments, but that was only a short-term solution.

Samson slowed the carriage to round a street corner, and Jake heard a young boy calling out with the new edition of the *Evening Post*. Jake tapped on the roof of the carriage. "Samson, would you stop so I can buy a paper?"

"Yes, sir," the man called back, drawing the carriage to a halt. Jake jumped out and went to where the boy was announcing the headlines and waving a newspaper in each hand.

"I'll take one," Jake said. The boy exchanged the paper for coin and continued hawking the news.

Jake returned to the carriage and read the paper as Samson headed for home. One headline caught his attention: *Big Failure in America*. He read the first paragraph.

The Chamberlain Investment Company, of Denver, the largest real estate company in Western America, has suspended payment. The liabilities exceed $2,250,000.00.

Neither Morgan nor Keystone had said anything about this, but Jake knew it had been anticipated and would send the city spiraling further into fear. He blew out a heavy breath and continued to read the article. Elsewhere in the paper, Jake read of hundreds of people demanding the governor grant them audience to discuss what was to be done about Colorado's severe depression.

Samson opened the door to the carriage before Jake even realized they had stopped. He looked out at the tall man and shook his head. "The times are truly getting worse, Samson. I wonder, do you have family somewhere?"

"I gots me a sister in Kansas City."

Jake climbed down and looked up to meet the man's questioning look. "I may very well need to let you go, and if so, I want to be able to send you to family if need be."

Samson smiled. "Don't you go worrying about me none. The good Lord done already took care of my needs."

Jake looked at the man. He seemed genuinely unconcerned. "Aren't you worried?"

"Sakes, no. What good would that do me? Been without money all my life and don't 'spect this time around gonna make a bit o' difference. I'll jes go on like before."

"But what will you do if I have to let you go?"

Samson shrugged. "Good Lord ain't told me that yet, 'cause you ain't let me go."

Jake smiled. "I suppose that makes sense. I have to say, I wish I had more of your faith in the matter."

"You don't go gettin' faith by wishin' it, if you pardon

my saying so, sir. The Good Book say that 'Faith cometh by hearing, and hearing by the word of God.'" He smiled again.

"Thank you, Samson. I think I needed to hear that. It's easy enough to hear the world crying out its problems." He held up the newspaper. "People are only too happy to bemoan all that's going on these days. I guess I need to put that aside and put my mind on the Bible."

"Yes, sir," Samson said, climbing back atop the carriage. "You can't go wrong by lookin' to the good Lord."

Jake knew the man was wiser than he'd ever given him credit for. Oh, to have faith like Samson—not to worry about the future or where he'd get the money to feed and care for his people. To stop fretting over whether he'd ever get back to Texas. If God wanted him there, then surely God would make a way for it to happen.

I want to leave it all in your hands, Lord. Jake looked heavenward. "Help me to have faith—to trust you more."

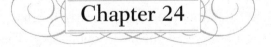

Chapter 24

"I've asked Morgan to meet us here," Mr. Keystone told Jake. "I had the opportunity to do some further digging on your discovery of the duplicated gold certificates. Unfortunately, what I've found leads us to a major betrayal."

Jake frowned, his brows knitting together. "What do you mean . . . betrayal?"

Keystone shook his head. "I mean that there was a great deal more to this than you can imagine. By my own calculations, it must have been going on for several years, and there is no way of knowing to what extent it will affect this banking institution. Or for that matter, our country."

"I don't exactly follow you. What did you find?"

"Counterfeiting," Keystone replied.

For a moment Jake said nothing. He sat down at his desk and considered the full implications. "Counterfeit gold certificates? It wasn't just an error."

Keystone nodded. "I can't even begin to tell how far-reaching it is or who all might be involved. I met with Morgan and filled him in on everything I knew—that's why he's coming here today."

"I don't understand." Jake leaned back in his chair. "It would have to be an awfully large group of folks to pull something like this off—wouldn't it?" His drawl thickened. "Seems to me that it couldn't be handled by just a man or two."

"Exactly." Keystone pounded the arm of the chair. "That's why this is a betrayal of the most serious sort. This would have to involve not only men on the outside, but obviously men on the inside."

"And the only inside man who could have been responsible," Mr. Morgan said, entering the office unannounced, "was George Chesterfield."

Jake rose, but Morgan waved him to return to his seat. Taking the chair beside Keystone, Morgan sat stiffly. "Chesterfield," Morgan continued, "is the only one who would have had access to the original gold certificates—besides me, of course."

"You mentioned that the night he was killed, he was supposed to be transporting certificates, didn't you?" Jake asked.

"Yes. It was presumed they were lost in the robbery. But now, according to what you've told me, it would seem they weren't in the satchel, which leads us to this question: Where are those gold certificates?"

Keystone nodded. "And how many counterfeits were created?"

"And how much of the original gold has been redeemed without the actual owner realizing the loss?" Jake threw in. The entire matter was a colossal mess. It would most certainly ruin Morgan Bank.

"We must handle this discreetly," Mr. Morgan continued.

"I can tell by the look on your face, Mr. Wythe, that you've already come to realize the ramifications. We cannot, under any circumstances, let this become public knowledge."

"But how will we keep it quiet?" Jake asked. "People are already clamoring to redeem as much as they can for gold. No one believes in paper or silver—it's all about the gold."

"Granted, but we have put an end to that. We must have some measures in place to keep the country from falling into bankruptcy. And now, with this matter of counterfeit gold certificates, I hesitate to even stir the pot for fear of what might rise to the surface."

Jake looked at the newspaper on his desk. "What will happen once the Senate finally approves the repeal of the Sherman Silver Purchase Act?"

"Mass chaos. The panic will only deepen," Morgan promised. "The stock exchange crashes back in May and June will pale to the problems we will see. Already thousands of businesses have collapsed and banks have closed. It's only the beginning, Mr. Wythe. Mark my words."

Jake nodded. The hopelessness of the future was made all the more clear with each conversation he had with Morgan. He seriously considered cashing out what he could of his savings, letting the house go back to the bank, and hightailing it back to Texas. Of course, what would they do there? People were hurting in Texas just as they were everywhere else—though maybe not as much as Colorado, which had come to depend on silver as a standard.

"I'm here today because we have no choice, Mr. Wythe. There is to be absolutely no cash given out—no silver exchanged for gold. Nothing but loan certificates that can be used in lieu of cash. If the people ask why this is happening, remind them the president has caused this fuss and nonsense. The collapse of this country rests on his shoulders."

Jake considered the matter another moment before speaking. "And what of you gentlemen? What will you do to weather this storm?"

Morgan looked at Keystone, then back to Jake. "I can't speak for Josiah, but for myself, I took measures long ago when I saw the problems that were upon us. I would imagine most sensible men did."

"At least if they were wealthy enough to have something set aside," Keystone countered.

"But most of the savings in this bank were put here by men who were poorer than you two," Jake replied. "Like myself. They put their savings here, hoping for a future."

"Your future is safe enough, Mr. Wythe," Morgan declared. "Have I not taken good care of you, my boy? I can see that this situation might seem overwhelming to you, but I assure you that so long as you are in my employ, you needn't worry."

Jake nodded. "And I appreciate all you've done. But what happens when this bank folds and you no longer need my services? My savings are here just like every other depositor, and now you're telling me I can't have it."

Morgan smiled, but it didn't quite reach his eyes. "I suppose for the time, you are dependent upon me."

★

Marty and Alice sat discussing the latest visit of Mr. Smith. "Will you write to your friends?" Marty asked.

"I suppose I must. After all, Mr. Smith brought up a good point. Where did my father's personal things go after the sale of the house? I don't know why it never occurred to me to question it."

"Shock and loss will do that to a mind," Marty declared. "I know from personal experience. After Thomas died, I couldn't have managed such matters on my own. Hannah was the one who helped me and she made a very neat and orderly inventory of the things she packed away. It was a godsend, but I don't suppose everyone is quite as well organized as my sister." She heaved a sigh. "Jake . . . Mr. Wythe believes that we should speak to the authorities about this."

"But what can they do?" Alice questioned. "The man has threatened me—even struck me—but I don't know who he really is, nor can I tell them where to find him. We are at his mercy.

"If I just knew where that envelope was," Alice said, "I would hand it over to him in a heartbeat—even knowing that it doesn't belong to him. I'm weary of the entire matter and desire only that this madness end. It took the life of my father and left me . . . like this. What more will it demand before it's settled?"

Marty wasn't used to seeing this side of Alice. For all the time she'd known the young woman, she'd been reserved but joyful. Now her fear and frustration were overriding any potential for happiness.

The sound of the clock chiming altered Marty's train of thought. It was nearly time for supper. Jake had plans to stay late at the bank, so Marty had already decided to take her meal upstairs.

"I'll leave you now," Alice said. "I need to spend some time praying on this, and I know Mrs. Landry will be coming with your tray. She said she wanted to speak to you about something, so I don't want to be here and make her uncomfortable."

"Oh dear, that sounds most grave."

Alice shrugged. "I really don't know what she wants to discuss, but she didn't seem upset. But happy or sad, I just don't feel up to answering her questions. She's as worried about this as you are, and I don't think talking about it more is going to help at this point."

Marty nodded. She could understand Alice's desire to sequester herself away, but in the girl's departure, Marty felt all the more lonely. Ever since Jake had kissed her, she'd not been the same. Everything had changed with that kiss. It had awakened in Marty a desire and hope for a future she had never thought possible.

The day had been unbearably warm, but thankfully a nice breeze blew in through the open window now. Marty relished the fresh air and prayed that the evening would cool off considerably. Just then she heard a knock on the bedroom door, and Mrs. Landry entered with supper.

"Mrs. Wythe, I hope you have had a pleasant afternoon," Mrs. Landry stated, placing the tray on the small table beside Marty.

"I have, and you?"

Mrs. Landry smiled and reached for the teapot. "I have enjoyed a very fine day, thank you, ma'am." The housekeeper appeared quite content, even joyful. Perhaps she'd come to discuss something good, rather than bad, as Marty had worried.

"Alice tells me that you wish to speak to me about something."

Mrs. Landry poured the tea and replaced the pot before

straightening. "Yes, there is an important matter I wish to discuss. I came to make an announcement and offer a request."

"I see." Marty nodded. "Continue."

"Well, you see . . . Mr. Brighton and I . . . we . . ."

"Would like to marry?" Marty interjected.

Mrs. Landry's face flushed. She gave a little nod and smiled. "We would, Mrs. Wythe. He asked me just this morning. I've been fit to be tied waiting to discuss it with you."

"What is there to discuss?" Marty asked, laughing in relief. "I'm delighted, and Mr. Wythe will be, as well. We've long thought the two of you belonged together."

The housekeeper smiled but appeared completely flustered. "We plan to marry early next week, and that brings me to my request."

"Please, whatever I can do to help make this happy occasion happen, I am very glad to assist."

"Oh, there isn't anything you need to do, Mrs. Wythe. We simply . . . well . . . we wanted permission to . . . uh, share the same room once we are wed."

Marty couldn't help but giggle. "Of course you may share the same room. Goodness, I would never keep two people in love from being together as they should be. Do you anticipate how this might work?"

Mrs. Wythe nodded. "Neither of our rooms is very large; however, there is a more spacious room that was designed to house four servants. It's at the far end of the third floor. I wondered if we might take that room."

"Of course. I'm certain Mr. Wythe would approve. If I see him tonight, I will insist upon it, so feel free to start arranging it as you'd like."

"Oh, thank you, ma'am. You have no idea how happy this has made me."

Marty got to her feet and surprised the older woman by embracing her. "I think I do, and I'm glad to be a part of it. Please give Mr. Brighton my congratulations."

"Oh, I will, Mrs. Wythe. I will." Mrs. Landry started to hurry from the room, then halted. "I apologize, ma'am. I didn't uncover your supper." She started back for the tray, but Marty waved her away.

"Never mind. I will see to it myself. You go and speak to Brighton now. Let him know how much we approve." She smiled broadly and motioned the housekeeper to leave.

Once Mrs. Landry had gone, Marty pulled the cover from her supper plate. There rested a simple but adequate meal of roasted meat and potatoes. Mrs. Landry had included a thick slice of homemade bread, as well as a fruit tart that Mrs. Standish delighted in making.

Marty settled in to enjoy her meal, but all the while her thoughts wandered back to Mrs. Landry's announcement and Jake's kiss. It would seem the house was full of romantic hearts. She longed for Jake to throw off his fears as Brighton had. She longed for him to come home and tell her how much he wanted them to enjoy a real marriage—a true love.

Nibbling at the bread, Marty couldn't help but consider the older couple's future. There would no doubt be the same good-natured quibbling, but now they could kiss and make up at the end of every day. With a sigh, Marty wondered if it might ever be the same for her.

Tell him the truth. Set yourself free.

The words echoed in her heart, and whether they were simply remnants of Marty's guilty conscience or the Lord himself speaking to her, she didn't know. She did know beyond a doubt that until the truth of the ranch was disclosed, there would be no hope of a real marriage.

"But what do I do, Lord?" she asked, putting the bread aside to take up the teacup. "He's already so deeply distressed by the bank and all the problems they are facing. I can't bear for him to be disappointed—betrayed, angry—with me, as well." She didn't know if he'd be able to trust and forgive her after hiding the truth for so long.

Marty knew that the only place she could go was to prayer and the Scriptures. She'd avoided both for such a time that now it felt like she was learning to walk all over again.

With the meal concluded, Marty picked up her Bible. Hannah had sent Marty to the Scriptures whenever a lie had been revealed. Marty was pretty sure she knew every verse in the Bible that dealt with truth or lies.

Proverbs 12:19 was one of the first that came to mind. *The lip of truth shall be established for ever: but a lying tongue is but for a moment.*

The lip of truth shall be established forever.

That's what I'm afraid of. If I tell the truth, it will forever be established and divide me from Jake.

She flipped to 3 John 1:4 and read aloud. "'I have no greater joy than to hear that my children walk in truth.'" She sighed.

I want to please you, Father. I truly do. I know that means I need to be honest. I know that you hate lies. Please help me. I want so much to make this right.

Marty fell to her knees and prayed in earnest. *Father, I love him. I love him so dearly, and I never thought I could love another. I know I've done wrong. I know I should have told him about the ranch the first time he mentioned his longing for Texas. Oh, Father, I just don't know if I can endure that again. I fear that Jake might be injured or killed if we take up ranching. And now that Hannah and Will are taking the ranch back—I know it's really too late.*

She paused and shook her head. *No, that isn't right. They would quickly return the ranch to me. It's not too late, and that's what makes this so hard. With everything falling down around us, Texas seems to be the answer to all our needs. But I don't want it to be the answer.*

Tears came to her eyes. Was a ranch in Texas the price for love?

Marty lost track of the time as she prayed and wept before God. She paused occasionally to pace the room or read the Scriptures, but she always ended up back on her knees. And that was where she was when Jake knocked on her open dressing room door.

"Marty?"

Without reserve, she rose and at the sight of him flew to his arms. Jake's surprised expression said it all, but Marty didn't let that stop her. "I love you, Jake, and I want to be your wife." She pressed her lips to his, not letting him respond.

But it was clear Jake didn't need words. He wrapped her in his arms and kissed her with all the pent-up passion they both felt. Marty melted against him, hoping the moment might never end. She knew she still needed to tell Jake the truth, however.

Pulling back, she met his gaze. "I need to tell you . . ."

He put his finger to her lips. "Tell me later." He lifted her in his arms. "Much later."

Chapter 25

Jake looked at the woman sleeping by his side and smiled. Marty loved him. It was amazing that he should know the love of such a woman. She had given him a new reason to face the day, and despite all the problems that awaited him at work, Jake was inspired to forge ahead.

Careful not to wake her as he slipped from the bed, Jake couldn't keep himself from gazing at his wife for just a moment longer. He was in love and nothing else mattered. He would have whistled a tune if not for disturbing her peaceful slumber. Without waiting for Brighton, he gathered his things and dressed by himself. He was halfway downstairs when Brighton met him on the landing.

"Good morning, sir. You are up very early. I'm sorry to not have been ready to assist you."

"No problem." Jake glanced back at the upstairs hall. "Uh, you might want to wait to make up my room until later. Mrs. Wythe is still sleeping."

Brighton glanced upward but said nothing. He gave a professional nod and continued as if nothing were amiss. "Sir, I wonder if I might have a word with you."

"Of course. Let's do it while I eat, however. I'm pert near starved to death."

In the dining room, Jake was pleased to see breakfast already waiting on the sideboard. He helped himself to scrambled eggs, which Cook had blended with green peppers, ham, and onion. It was one of his favorites. The day was looking better all the time.

By the time he sat down, Brighton had toast and coffee waiting for him. Jake offered a quick silent blessing. *Father, I don't know quite what to say or how to thank you, but . . . thanks a lot. Amen.*

He looked up to find Brighton waiting. "So, my good man, what can I do for you?" Jake asked in an animated tone. He dug into the egg concoction.

"I wanted your . . . permission to marry Mrs. Landry."

Jake nearly dropped the forkful of food. He couldn't contain his grin at the stately announcement. "I'd give you a good ol' Texas whoop, but I'm afraid it might wake up Marty. That's wonderful news, Brighton, and of course you don't need my permission."

The man gave a small smile. "Thank you, sir. Mrs. Landry spoke to Mrs. Wythe last night and I thought perhaps you two had discussed the matter already."

"No," Jake said, lowering his face so that Brighton couldn't see his grin. "We didn't have much of a chance to . . . talk last night."

"Mrs. Landry, it would seem, has asked Mrs. Wythe's permission to claim the larger room on the servants' floor for us to use after our vows are said. Would that be acceptable to you, as well?"

"Of course. If Marty said it was all right, it's fine by me. When will you two marry?"

"I believe next week, sir. So long as we can put everything in order."

"I would love to be there," Jake said, finally feeling able to meet Brighton's gaze. He smiled. "I know Mrs. Wythe would want to, as well."

"We thought only to see a justice of the peace, sir."

"That's fine. Marty and I would be happy to stand as your witnesses."

"Very good, sir. I would like that."

Jake could see a twinkle in the older man's eyes. "I can't tell you how happy I am for you both. It's been a time in coming, but I'm happier than a dog with a new bone."

Brighton covered what sounded to be an amused chuckle with a cough. When he'd cleared his throat a couple of times, he excused himself.

Jake finished his breakfast and was out the door before anyone else appeared to speak with him. The joy of the night and morning fled, however, as Samson pulled up to the bank. There were people lining the walkway outside the bank and the line stretched clear around to the side of the building. Jake waited for Samson to open the carriage door, wondering if he might need the man to assist in making a way through the crowd.

As he stepped out, a chorus of cries erupted. "We want our money!" "Let us have our money—it belongs to us!" "You thieves aren't gonna take my savings!"

Jake looked to Samson, who seemed to understand. The big man stepped forward and the people parted like the Red Sea for Moses and the children of Israel. When Jake reached the locked bank door, he paused and turned. Raising his hands, he called to the crowd.

"Folks, if you'll quiet down, I'll hear you out. But not if everyone just keeps talking over the other."

"This bank is failing," a man close to him said. "We know it, and we want our money. I heard you folks weren't of a mind to let us have it."

Jake shook his head. "I've not heard anything of the kind. However, I am to attend a meeting this morning. Most likely they are awaiting me now. I would very much appreciate it if you'd give me time to speak to my board, and then I can better understand what's going on."

This did little to calm the crowd, but there was nothing else Jake could do. With Samson at his back, he turned and unlocked the bank's front door. "Thank you, Samson. Come for me at five. I'm not staying late tonight."

"Yes, sir."

With that, Jake closed and relocked the door behind him. He turned and found a wide-eyed Arnold standing near his office door.

"They started coming at eight. I've never seen the likes."

Jake nodded and noted the time was half past. "Quite a crowd for just half an hour."

"Yes, sir. And they aren't at all happy. They've been out there yelling and demanding they be let in here the entire time."

"I can well imagine. Tell me, have the board members arrived?"

Arnold nodded. "They're assembled in the back room away from the noise. They weren't any happier than you are about the scene."

Jake handed Arnold his hat and made his way to the back of the bank, where the board had assembled. He opened the door hesitantly and peered inside. Already the men were arguing and pointing fingers.

He slipped in and found an empty seat at the table just as Morgan slammed his fists down on the hard oak wood. "I won't have this kind of insubordination. You may be the bank's board of directors, but I'm its owner and you will listen to me."

"Those people indicate otherwise," Mr. Cooper declared. "It would seem we will have to keep the bank closed or face a riot."

"We'll face a riot if we keep the bank closed," Keystone threw out.

"I've telephoned for the police," Morgan replied. "I didn't build up this business just to watch a bunch of dim-witted fools tear it apart."

"They've cause to be worried," one of the other board members declared. "I can't say that I don't have my own concerns. Especially given that we're facing the complete devaluation of silver. Most of those people know the truth, and they aren't going to be easily reassured."

Morgan eyed Jake as if just realizing he had joined them. "What say you, Mr. Wythe? I realize you are only the branch manager, but I'm sure you have dealt with these customers."

"I have," Jake replied. "My guess is that they won't be put off. You have a lot of folks out there who live nickel to nickel. Now that they know you aren't planning to let them have their cash, but instead are giving them bank checks, I think they're going to panic. They'll figure the money could be lost to them."

"That's my take, as well," Keystone agreed. "They are like children. It only takes one to start raising a ruckus until all of them join in."

A knock sounded on the door. It was Arnold. "Mr. Morgan, sir, the police have arrived. They are working to disperse the crowd. However, they want a word with you."

Morgan got to his feet. "Very well. Keystone, carry on."

Josiah Keystone didn't look excited to take the helm of this sinking ship, but he did nevertheless. "We will suspend all cash transactions, as Mr. Morgan has explained. Instead, we will be issuing bank checks. If this is not agreeable, the people will either need to await further notice to get their money in cash, or they will have to do without it altogether."

Jake listened to the discussion of the members, with talk centered on the fall of stocks and gold reserves and the role of the government.

"The president of the United States will get his repeal—of this we can be sure. The House has already passed it, and the Senate is just concluding their discussion on the matter. By summer's end we will face a devastating situation in this city. The western states' economy will collapse like dominoes," Mr. Cooper declared. "There will be no stopping it. We might as well close our doors now and keep them closed."

And that was the way the rest of the meeting continued. Finally Jake had stomached all he could. When Morgan returned, he asked if he could be excused to attend to daily business, and Morgan quickly agreed.

Jake slipped from the room and made his way to the solace of his office. Unfortunately, he was not to find peace of mind there, either.

Jake had barely sat at his desk when Winfield Mays appeared in his doorway. The older man, a longtime teller at the bank, looked almost sick. "Mr. Wythe, I must speak with you." He twisted his hands and looked to the floor. "It's important, Mr. Wythe, or I wouldn't have bothered you."

Jake nodded. "Come in and take a seat, Mr. Mays. What can I do for you?"

Mays closed the door, then walked slowly to the desk. He didn't sit, but instead continued to twist his hands as he glanced up a bit. "I've wronged you, Mr. Wythe. I've wronged the bank, but I tried to make it right."

Jake couldn't imagine what the old man was talking about. "Go on."

Mays nodded. "You see, Martha—she's my wife—has been very sick."

Jake immediately thought of Marty and smiled. "I didn't realize you were married, Mays. I am very sorry to hear that she's been sick."

"It's been going on over a year now—closer to two. The doctors have tried all sorts of things, but nothing much has worked. It's been hard on me to pay all those bills, and some of those newfangled medical procedures . . . well . . . they are expensive."

"I can imagine," Jake replied. "But what does this have to do with me or the bank?"

The old man cleared his throat. "I know you've studied the books. I know you saw the discrepancies in the bank's listed assets. It's my fault, Mr. Wythe, and if you want to put me in jail, I ask only that you wait until my Martha passes. It shouldn't be long now."

Jake finally understood the direction the conversation was taking. "You took the money?"

"I did. Put it back, too. See, I knew I couldn't get a loan with the bank. I didn't have any assets to put up as collateral.

One day when the doctor told me he had a new procedure that he thought would save Martha's life, I just lost all sense. I took the money that I needed. Only for the procedure, mind you. I knew in time I could pay it back, and I did."

"So why are you telling me this now? Surely you know that Mr. Morgan told me to just consider it a fluke—money mislaid and refound."

"I know that, sir, but I also know that things aren't going well for the bank. I've found it hard to live with myself. . . . Now that my Martha is passing on, I don't much care to live in this world without her."

"I'm sure her loss will be difficult," Jake replied. "Even so, you can't give up on life, Mr. Mays. The good Lord will let you know when your time has come.

"As for the money," Jake said, shaking his head, "I am sorry you felt that you had to take it in such a manner. There should have been a provision for a bank employee to receive a loan against his wages. However, it was a crime, and your confession puts me in a difficult position."

"I know that, sir. Like I said, my Martha won't be here more than another day or two."

"Then why are you here?" Jake asked, moved by the man's situation and need to come clean.

"I have to keep my position for as long as possible," the old man replied. "I . . . have a funeral to pay for."

Jake got to his feet and pulled out his wallet. There wasn't a great amount inside, but definitely as much as the old man made in two days' time. He handed the cash to him. "Take this and go home to your wife. Be at her side. That's where you belong. The bank will most likely not even open today."

"I can't take your money, sir. It wouldn't be right—especially now." The old man had tears in his eyes as he tried to push the cash back into Jake's hands.

"Mr. Mays, I am your superior here, am I not?" Jake asked with a gentle smile. "I have told you to take this money and not return to work for at least two days. You take all the time you need. For as long as this bank is solvent, you will have a job. I will fight Mr. Morgan and anyone else to see to it."

"But after what I did—"

"You've confessed your sins and made restitution. Now I ask that you say nothing more about the matter. That's the end of it. Even Mr. Morgan declared it so, and I see no reason to contradict him."

Mays looked at the cash in his hands and then back to Jake. Without another word, he simply nodded and left the office. Jake sighed and reclaimed his chair. At least now he understood what was going on with the missing and replaced money.

At five o'clock Samson picked Jake up at the bank. They had kept the doors closed and the crowd had finally given up and gone home. Jake knew they'd be back on Monday morning, however. What he didn't know for sure was how Morgan intended to handle it. Josiah Keystone had come to see him after their meeting concluded and indicated they would open as usual on Monday at nine, but Jake feared the crowd would no doubt storm the place without regard to anyone's safety or well-being. It would be mass chaos.

Despite this, Jake couldn't keep a smile from his face as he approached home. Marty would be there waiting for him. He knew it would be a little awkward to face each other after last night, but he was eager to see her again. He wanted to tell her how much he loved her—how glad he was that God had put them together. It seemed that his prayers had mattered to God after all.

Brighton met him at the door. "Welcome home, sir."

"Brighton," Jake said, barely taking time to hand the man his hat. "Don't worry about helping me with my clothes. I'll manage for myself. Where's Mrs. Wythe?"

"She's in her room, sir. I believe she's been unwell."

Jake frowned. "I'm sorry to hear that. I'll go to her right away."

He bounded up the stairs, taking them two at a time. He hated to think of Marty sick and prayed silently that it wasn't anything serious. He knocked on her dressing room door but didn't receive a response. Opening it just a crack, he could see that no one was in the room. He quickly made his way to her bedroom door and knocked again.

"Come in," she said in a voice that suggested she'd been crying.

Jake entered and noted that only a sliver of light from the window penetrated the darkness of the room. He reached for the lamp, but Marty halted him.

"Please don't. I have a terrible headache."

"I'm so sorry. Brighton told me you were sick."

"I'm not really so much sick—I'm . . . I'm worried."

Jake crossed the room and pulled up a chair to where she was sitting. "What's wrong?" Fear edged his soul. "Is this about last night?" He closed his eyes, dreading her response.

"In a way," she whispered. "I shouldn't have let it happen. I should have . . . I needed to tell you something first. Something that may alter . . . no, I'm sure it will alter your feelings for me."

His eyes snapped open. "That's impossible. I love you. I've loved you for some time, but I couldn't bring myself to tell you for fear of your rejection."

"Just as I fear yours now," Marty said. She turned her face to his, and he could see that her eyes were swollen from crying.

"You don't need to fear me, Marty. You can tell me anything. I love you."

"I hope you'll feel that way after you hear what I have to say."

———

Marty hesitated a moment before continuing. She could see that Jake was surprised by her statement. "I want you to know that I've tried several times to tell you the truth. But for one reason or another, I've always backed down. Mostly because I'm a coward. But I cannot live with this lie between us. Not now. Not when I know I love you more than I ever dreamed possible."

Jake reached out and took hold of her hand. "Marty, there's nothing you can say that will make me love you less."

She wanted to believe him. She had spent the day in tears and prayers, and now that her moment of confession had come, she felt unable to continue. Her lies had finally caught up with her . . . and she feared the cost would be more than she could bear.

"Jake, I've kept something from you. Something that I knew would have pleased you. Something that you had hoped for."

He looked at her, puzzled. "What are you saying?"

"I own a ranch, Jake. That is, I owned a ranch until a short time ago. My brother-in-law has reclaimed it, as it was his gift to me to begin with. I gave it back to him, however, because I couldn't bear the idea of returning to ranch life. I couldn't bear the thought—no matter how much it meant to you—of losing you as I lost Thomas."

Jake looked at her without saying a word. The light seemed to go out of his eyes, and he released her hand. Marty knew the impact of her confession was only now starting to hit him. She hurried to continue, praying he would understand her pain.

"I'm so sorry. I know I should have told you the first time you mentioned your dream of returning to ranching. Each time you talked about it, however, I felt my fears get the better of me. I answered your ad for a wife mainly to get away from Texas and all that it stood for, yet you wanted to take me back to that life. I just couldn't bear the thought of it."

"So you lied to me? You lied about something that you knew was important to me—was my very heart and soul?"

She bit her lower lip and nodded. "Yes."

He rubbed his hand over his mouth, staring straight ahead at the cold fireplace. For several minutes he said nothing at all. Marty wished he would speak. She'd rather have his rage or even his sorrow rather than this silence.

When he got to his feet, Marty jumped to hers as well and took hold of his arm. "Jake, I'm so very sorry. I don't know what else to say. I want our marriage more than you'll ever know, but if you feel you . . . have to . . . to . . . send me away . . ." She gave a heavy sigh. "I'll understand." She bit her tongue knowing that, too, was just one more lie. She wouldn't understand.

He looked at her for a long time, his face betraying his anguish. "I can't talk to you about this right now. You've near broken my heart, and all I can think about is getting away from you." He turned and left without another word.

Marty collapsed on the floor and sobbed. Once again she'd lost a man she loved more than life itself. Why couldn't God just end her life now and be done with it? Why wouldn't He just show mercy and put her out of her misery?

Chapter 26

Alice found Marty on the floor, weeping as if her life were over. She knew of her mistress's plans to tell Jake everything, and apparently it hadn't gone well. With a gentle hand, Alice helped Marty up from the floor and directed her to the bed. Marty stared aimlessly at the wall as Alice undressed her and replaced her tear-soaked dress with a white lawn nightgown. She helped Marty into bed, then surprised herself by sitting down beside her.

Taking up Marty's hand, Alice told her, "The truth will set you free. You may not believe that, but you've done the right thing, and God will bless it."

"He said that all he could think of was getting away from me," Marty said in a hushed, weak voice.

Alice patted her hand. "He's shocked and hurting. Give him some time to pray through this—to think on it."

"I crushed his spirit, Alice. I wounded him more deeply than he could bear." Marty shook her head slowly, her blond hair spilling out across the pillow. "I never thought a lie could hurt anyone that much. It seemed such a simple thing—an easy thing."

"But a very harmful thing," Alice added.

Marty continued to look away. "I can't bear the way he looked at me. He knew I'd betrayed him in the worst possible way. He could have forgiven me had I been unfaithful in our sensible arrangement, but not this. Not keeping him from his dream of ranching. Not keeping him from his beloved Texas."

She turned to Alice and gripped her hand tightly. "I've lost him. The truth set him free from me, and now I'm alone again."

"No," Alice said, shaking her head. "You are never alone with God."

"Why would He do this to me?"

"Marty, listen to yourself. God didn't lie, nor did He make you lie. You made that decision. I don't say this to hurt you, but you have to see the truth of it. God loves you, Marty, and He wants you to give Him your life—your love—your all. You had to tell the truth, otherwise things would never be right between you and God or you and Jake."

"I know," Marty whispered. She closed her eyes. "I can't bear who I am—what I've done. I'm a wretched creature. A sinful, wretched creature."

Alice smiled. "Well, now that you realize what you are . . . maybe you can let God show you what you can be. I'm going to pray for you, Marty. Just as I have been doing for the entire time I've worked for you. I'm going to pray that you and Jake will both seek God's healing in this and trust Him to help you both know what to do about it."

She released Marty's hand and stood. "I'm going to get you some hot tea and lemon—maybe some headache powders, too. I'll be back shortly."

After she got Marty settled, Alice went to her room and

sank to her knees. "Oh, Father," she began to pray, "please hear my prayers."

★

Marty lay awake throughout the night waiting and listening for some sound that might indicate that Jake had returned home. Alice had checked on Jake's whereabouts several times, only to have Brighton tell her that he had stormed from the house, not even stopping to take up his hat.

Tossing and turning in her bed, Marty did her best to pray, but the words seemed stuck in her throat. She had no desire to go back to being the woman she'd been before—bitter and angry at God. She desperately needed God's love at this moment, probably more so than any other time in her life.

Even in losing Thomas, Marty had not felt so alone. Back in Texas she'd had Hannah and Will at her side. Hannah had stood by Marty and cared for her. Marty had known that her family loved her and that love would get her through the loss. Now, however, she had betrayed everyone—even her family.

She knew that in the days to come, she would write to tell Hannah everything. If Jake insisted she leave—if he annulled their marriage—Marty had already decided to remain in Colorado. She would ask Alice to be her friend, to find a place where they could live together. She would get a job.

I know how to work hard. I can do any number of jobs. If Jake won't have me anymore . . . I'll find a way to live my life.

But she doubted the truth of that. She might be able to survive the blow, but she seriously doubted life would be worth living.

Closing her eyes, Marty imagined life without Jake and tears formed anew. It wasn't a life she desired—at all. When sleep finally came, Marty endured one nightmare after another. She relived her confession to Jake and felt the cut of his rejection over and over.

She dreamed about Thomas at one point, and instead of seeing him attacked by the longhorn, he stood in accusation, telling Marty that she had disappointed him. That was worse, in some ways, than watching him die.

Waking, Marty brought a hand to her forehead and noted it was beaded with sweat. She felt the damp perspiration all over her body and longed for a cool bath. She got up and sponged off with the water that Alice had left in her room. It helped a little, but not enough. She went to the window and leaned out as far as she dared. The cooler night air hit her damp skin. It felt good, and Marty lingered there for some time.

She noticed a hint of the darkness lessening. *It must be close to dawn. In a few hours I'll have to face another day. But how?*

For a moment she gave serious consideration to just packing up the things she'd brought to Colorado and leaving. She could stay with her brother, Andy, in Wyoming for a time. Maybe that was the answer she sought. If she left and gave Jake time to consider the situation, it might do them both good.

Oh, Jake. I'm so sorry.

Marty turned toward her closed bedroom door and wondered if Jake had ever come home. Without much thought she opened the door and passed through the dressing room. She hesitated a moment at the passageway that would take her to Jake's bedroom. Dare she continue? If he wasn't there, she would worry all the more. If he was there, he might be awake and waiting to speak with her.

She opened the first door and tiptoed through the hall to the second door. Opening it just enough to glance inside, Marty could see that the room was dark. Even so, she could hear Jake's even breathing. He'd come home. Relief and dread washed over her in equal parts.

Entering the room, Marty made her way to the bed. She could see his outline in the darkness, but little more. The urge to pray overcame her and Marty knelt beside the bed. At first she prayed silently, but then her heart grew much too heavy, and the words just seemed to pour from her mouth.

"Oh, God, please help Jake not to hate me. Please let him know how sorry I am. I never knew my lies could cause such pain. It wasn't my desire to hurt him like I did—I was just a coward. I kept thinking of how Thomas had died, and it was more than I could bear. Forgive me, God. Please forgive me, and help Jake to forgive me, too. I promise I won't lie again . . . leastwise, I promise to do my best to never lie again."

"Do you mean that, Marty?" Jake asked, rolling to his side.

Marty nearly jumped from the floor at the sound of his clear voice. Obviously, he hadn't been sleeping. "I do," she said, barely able to speak. Her heart pounded so hard she could hardly hear his voice. For several long moments Jake simply stared at her. When he did finally speak, it pierced Marty to the heart.

"You know, I couldn't believe you would do such a thing. I didn't see how you could say you loved me and yet lie like that. Josephine betrayed me like that. I loved her and thought she loved me, but she didn't. She was a liar and betrayed my trust. And then you went and did the same thing."

"I know. What I did was horrible, and I have no right to ask your forgiveness. I've spent a lifetime lying to get myself out of uncomfortable situations and never thinking of the cost. It was only my love for you that made me tell the truth." Marty knew he probably couldn't see the details of her face, but she hoped he could hear the sincerity in her voice. "I didn't want to tell you. I thought after . . . after . . . our night together, that maybe I didn't need to tell you. But my conscience wouldn't leave me be. I knew I had to tell you, but I also knew it was going to destroy any affection you had for me. All I ask is that you give me a chance to make it up—to prove my love."

Jake sat up and reached out to take hold of Marty's hands. He pulled her to her feet and had her sit on the side of the bed. "And there will be no more lies between us?"

"No more. I know it's in my nature, but I'm sick of my nature—and I want to be a good wife to you, Jake. Please forgive me. Please. I never meant to hurt you, but I know I did and for that I'm so very sorry."

"I love you, Marty, but your lie really tore me apart."

"I know. Please forgive me."

"I wanted nothing more than to return to Texas and own my own spread again. I wanted to be back in the saddle rather than in a bank office."

"I know. Please . . . forgive me."

Jake drew a deep breath and let it out slowly. "But mostly I want a wife I can trust. A wife I can plan a future with—have a family with."

Marty felt a pang of sorrow and drew in a deep breath. "I don't think I can have children, Jake. Thomas and I tried for ten years, and they all ended in miscarriages." Silence hung heavy between them, and Marty thought she might burst into tears anew.

"There's always your orphans."

Marty laughed and cried at the same time. She fell into his arms and sobbed again. "Please forgive me, Jake. I can't bear one more minute if you don't."

With a tenderness she had never known, Jake pulled her close and kissed her wet cheek. "Ah, Marty, God knows I've needed enough forgivin' in my life. I love you, and love sometimes comes in pain as well as joy. I forgive you, Marty. I forgive you."

★

Standing before the justice of the peace, Marty and Jake held hands as Mrs. Landry and Mr. Brighton exchanged their vows. Alice and Mrs. Standish had also come to witness the marriage, while Samson waited patiently at the back of the church. His smile clearly showed his approval, and Marty couldn't help but glance back at him from time to time.

"I now pronounce you man and wife," the justice declared. "Groom, you may kiss your bride."

Brighton's face turned several shades of red, but Mrs. Landry was not nearly so embarrassed. She took hold of the man's face and planted her lips on his. Marty couldn't help but giggle and ducked her head to try and disguise her glee.

Jake didn't bother. He laughed out loud at the scene and squeezed Marty's hand. "He said we could kiss."

She looked up in surprise. "He said that the groom could kiss his bride."

"Well, I'm a groom, and I want to kiss my bride." He leaned over and placed a very chaste kiss upon her lips. Marty didn't even have time to close her eyes, but rather met his blue-eyed gaze. They were the same color as a Texas summer sky.

Marty congratulated the new couple, and Alice and Mrs.

Standish did likewise. Brighton had arranged a private carriage for them and soon swept his new bride off for some mysterious honeymoon that he'd not shared the details of—not even with Jake.

Outside the day was perfect and bright, a bit warm but not unbearably so. Marty thought of humid summer days on the ranch and smiled. The dry Denver air was so very different.

"You seem very pleased with yourself, Mrs. Wythe," Jake whispered in her ear.

"I'm just happy that things could work out for Brighton and Mrs. Landry. I know they'll probably bicker and pick at each other the entire time they're away, but I'm also certain they'll forgive each other and go on."

"As am I," Jake said, heading toward the open carriage where Alice and Mrs. Standish were already waiting.

"It was a lovely ceremony," Mrs. Standish declared. "Made me think I might one day find another husband for myself."

"Why, Mrs. Standish," Marty said, "I didn't know you were of a mind to remarry."

The older woman shrugged. "Didn't know I was, either, but it doesn't seem like a half bad idea. Mrs. Landry certainly looked happy."

Jake nodded and gave Marty's hand a squeeze. "Indeed she did. Brighton looked rather pleased with himself, as well."

They shared a chuckle and gazed at the city as Samson drove them home. Marty thought Denver a wonderful mixture of elegant town, cowboy respite, and miner's playground. It intrigued her, but there was a small part of her that longed for the open spaces she'd left behind.

"Extra! Extra! Read all about it! Silver prices fall by half!" a newsboy called out. "Extra! Extra!"

Marty stiffened and looked at Jake. She could see the worry in his eyes and though Alice and Mrs. Standish chattered on as if nothing were amiss, Marty knew that somehow their world had just crumbled around them.

Jake patted her hand, then held it tight. "We're in for a bit of a Texas twister, I think."

Marty nodded. "I'm sure you're right."

Mrs. Standish heard the exchange and exclaimed, "Why, there's not a cloud in the sky! And besides, we don't get cyclones up here. The mountains don't allow for it."

Jake and Marty smiled and looked back to the older woman. "I'm sure you know the place better than I do," Jake replied.

★

"Do you suppose the bank will close right away?" Marty asked Jake later that evening. They had decided to take a stroll in City Park to enjoy the beautiful weather. Samson kept the horses and carriage at a distance, ever ready to pick them up when they tired of their walking adventure.

"I don't know. I don't know what's going to happen. Thousands are out of work and more businesses are folding by the day. The closing of banks is just a natural progression of this mess, and no one will feel it more than Colorado. I doubt there's a single silver mine still producing."

Marty tightened her hold on his arm. "I know we'll be all right no matter what. We have each other and for me . . . that's everything."

Jake stopped, and in the fading light he beheld his wife as if seeing her for the first time. Her delicate beauty never failed to stir his heart. "It's everything for me, as well. I have my Lone Star bride and nothin' else matters."

She laughed lightly and kissed his cheek. "And I have my Lone Star man—troublesome though he may be."

"Troublesome?" he questioned. "If you wanna know about troublesome, let me tell you a story. It starts with a little gal who shot at bandits on her way into Denver, then hoisted herself up to the driver's seat and took the reins of a team of half-crazed stage horses and brought the wounded driver and passengers to safety. You, Marty Wythe, are the very picture of trouble itself."

She laughed and put her arms around his neck. "I concur, Mr. Wythe, and don't you forget it."

"Mrs. Wythe . . . you forget who you are. You are making a spectacle of yourself. What will the Morgans and the Keystones say if they see us?"

Marty grinned. "I don't reckon I much care what they say."

Jake shook his head. "Neither do I, little gal. Neither do I."

Tracie Peterson is the award-winning author of one hundred novels, both historical and contemporary. Her avid research resonates in her stories, as seen in her bestselling HEIRS OF MONTANA and ALASKAN QUEST series. Tracie and her family make their home in Montana. Visit Tracie's website at www.traciepeterson.com and her blog at www.writespassage. blogspot.com.